UNCLE HENRY'S HACIENDA

CHARLES A. STEVENSON

First published in Australia by Aurora House
www.aurorahouse.com.au

This edition published 2024
Copyright © Charles Stevenson 2024

Typesetting and e-book design: Amit Dey (amitdey2528@gmail.com)
Cover design: Donika Mishineva (www.artofdonika.com)

The right of Charles Stevenson to be identified as Author of the Work has been asserted in accordance with the Copyright, Designs and Patents Act 1988.

ISBN number: 978-1-763572-60-7 (paperback)

All rights reserved. No part of this publication may be reproduced, stored in a retrieval system, or transmitted, in any form or by any means without the prior written permission of the publisher, nor be otherwise circulated in any form of binding or cover other than that in which it is published and without a similar condition being imposed on the subsequent purchaser.

 A catalogue record for this book is available from the National Library of Australia

Distributed by: Ingram Content: www.ingramcontent.com
Australia: phone +613 9765 4800 | email lsiaustralia@ingramcontent.com
Milton Keynes UK: phone +44 (0)845 121 4567 | email enquiries@ingramcontent.com
La Vergne, TN USA: phone +1 800 509 4156 | email inquiry@lightningsource.com

DEDICATION

This book is dedicated to my siblings and cousins with whom I share our Uncle Henry.

ACKNOWLEDGEMENTS

Many people have helped me to improve this novel and to correct various kinds of errors. My wife, Aideen, read the text in draft form and, as well as providing constant encouragement, offered many useful suggestions for improving the text. My sister, Kay Herndon, read and re-read drafts of this book and her comments were always incisive, clear and thoughtful. Our good friend, Val Kent, also read the text in draft and offered several ideas about improving the final version, as did Ted Ritter, an American author and correspondent of mine.

I owe a special debt of gratitude to Ryan Waters of Aurora House Publishing Company, who provided me with a comprehensive assessment of an early version of this novel. His thoughtful suggestions for improving the quality of my book have proved to be most valuable to someone writing fiction for the first time. Susan Prior, the editor of the published version of this book, deserves even more my thanks and praise. Her many hours of hard work and her cheerful, positive support have helped me to produce a far better book than I thought possible. I also wish to thank Anne Lawton, who applied her professional proofreading skills to my text, and Oliver Smuhar and the rest of the publishing staff at Aurora House, who guided my book through its final stages of publication. My final words of thanks go out to Linda Lycett, publisher at Aurora House, who accepted this project and organised the complex task of bringing a raw draft of Henry's story to fruition as a polished and handsome book.

I offer grateful thanks to all the people above, although I must emphasise that any flaws in the final version are entirely my own doing.

CONTENTS

Notes on the Family of Henry Rawson Anderson   xi
Notes on Henry Rawson Anderson   xiii
1. Henry Has a Problem   1
2. A Glance at Henry's Village   7
3. Preparations for the Trip   11
4. The Trip from Hell   15
5. The Hospital   23
6. Floresville, Texas, 1891–1902   27
7. Surprising New Directions   31
8. The World Is Henry's Oyster   39
9. The Good Life   43
10. Romance   45
11. Another New Direction   51
12. A New Life in Arizona   57
13. California, Here We Come!   63
14. The Lifestyles of the Rich and Famous   67
15. A Sad Event With a Silver Lining   71
16. A Hacienda Near Acapulco   75
17. The Good Life Rolls On   81

18. Henry Almost Loses Everything	85
19. Maddy	91
20. Worrying Signs	95
21. Disaster	99
22. The Mexican Pipe Dream	103
23. Henry's Positive Spin on Everything	107
24. Reality Bites	113
25. The Family Expands	117
26. The Family Disintegrates	121
27. Henry Heads for Home	125
28. A Trip to the Coast	129
29. Henry Begins to Claw Back His Life	135
30. Henry Returns to the Oil Business	139
31. Back to Arizona	143
32. Henry Joins the Black Market	147
33. Henry Plans a New Venture	151
34. A Promising Start	155
35. A Smuggler's Life	161
36. All Good Things Must Come to an End	163
37. A Prospector's Life Is Not an Easy One	169
38. Henry Reassesses His Options	175
39. Telegraph Operator, Mark II	177
40. Prospector, Mark II – or III or IV	181
41. A Few Teething Problems	187
42. Fortune Favors the Brave	193

43. Eureka!	197
44. Time for a Fiesta!	201
45. After the Music Stops	205
46. The Crows Come Home to Roost	207
47. A Boring Interlude for Henry	211
48. Back to the Beginning	215
49. Henry Encounters the Police	221
50. Henry Encounters a Revolution	225
51. When the Red Revolution Comes	233
52. Nothing Is Simple	237
53. And Now, the Consequences	241
54. And You Thought Hell Was Bad?	245
55. Henry Rises from the Dead	249
56. Henry Gets Some Help	253
57. It's All About Who You Know	257
58. Rest and Recovery	263
59. Henry Bides His Time	267
60. Shock, Sadness and Anger	271
61. From the Past to the Future	275
62. A Time for Deep Reflection	279
63. Once Again, the Prospector	283
64. The End of the Dream	287
65. An Ironic Conclusion	289
Author's Note	295
About the Author	299

NOTES ON THE FAMILY OF HENRY RAWSON ANDERSON

His father was Alfred Rawson Anderson. Alfred was a lawyer, and later county judge. He died young, in 1902. The family lived in Floresville, Texas.

His mother was Mary Katherine "Kate" Overton; she had been previously married to Reverend Rufus Field (it was his second marriage) with whom she had had two daughters, Lenora and Susie Lee.

Alfred and Kate, together, had three children: Henry and his twin sister, Emma, born in September 1891, and a younger brother, Rufus Alfred, in April 1894.

Willie Field, a son of Rev. Rufus Field from his first marriage, remained close to his stepmother Kate and his half-sisters, Lenora and Susie Lee. Willie was married, but when his first wife died his youngest child, two year old Charles Maxwell "Maxie" Field, went to live with the Anderson family.

Henry married Cora Clancy, from San Antonio, in 1913 and they had one child, a daughter named Madeleine Frances ("Maddy") Anderson born at the end of 1914. Maddy went on to become a world-famous Spanish dancer. She married her dance partner, Louis Lopez, and used the stage name "Laia Lopez".

Cora's parents were Fred and Eliza Clancy. After Fred and Eliza's marriage broke up, Eliza married Jonathon Brown and continued to live in San Antonio. Fred moved to Nogales, Arizona, where he was joined by Henry and Cora in 1919.

Henry's sister, Emma Anderson, married Clarence Cleaver and they had three children: James Alfred, Rawson, and Annie. The Cleavers lived on a farm near Sutherland Springs, Texas. Clarence died in the early 1950s and Emma died in 1959.

His brother, Rufus Alfred Anderson, married Lee Bolton. After they were married, they lived on a farm near La Vernia, Texas, before moving to Port Lavaca, Texas, where they bought and operated the Sea Shell Restaurant until the late 1940s. In 1949, Rufus and Lee bought the Grand Hotel in Kenedy, Texas, which they traded for a cattle farm near Crystal City, in 1956. They eventually sold that property and lived most of the rest of their lives on the old Cleaver farm. They had three children: Rufus Alfred Jr (called "Al"), who became a medical doctor; Katie Lee, who married a businessman and lived in West Texas; and Clarence, who became a lawyer and later a judge. Both Al and Clarence (and their families) lived most of their lives in Victoria, Texas.

Apart from Crystal City, all the places in Texas associated with the Anderson family are located in south-central Texas. Floresville, Kenedy, Sutherland Springs and La Vernia are all just south of San Antonio. Port Lavaca is located on the Texas coast and Victoria is about 30 miles inland from there and about 110 miles south of San Antonio. All placenames of cities and towns in Mexico and in the other U.S. states besides Texas are genuine placenames and can be found on maps; however, the Mexican villages that Henry visits are all fictitious creations and do not appear on any map of Mexico.

NOTES ON HENRY RAWSON ANDERSON

Henry was very much a man of his time and place. Born at the end of the nineteenth century in rural Texas, Henry grew up in a patriarchal society. His behavior towards women and his attitudes reflected the central contradiction at the heart of such a society, namely that a man's privileged social superiority over a woman also involves a duty to protect her and the assumption that he would always treat her with respect.

Despite living through a time when women began to reject patriarchy and to demand social and economic equality, Henry would never have realized that his paternalistic behavior towards his housekeeper–lovers contributed to the subjugation of women in general. He would have believed sincerely that never behaving with violence towards a woman, indeed, never even raising his voice in anger, and always treating his housekeepers with kindness and ensuring that he improved their economic situations demonstrated clearly that he loved women and treated them respectfully. Of course, hindsight reveals that he was wrong.

Henry had many admirable qualities, but his attitude towards women was not one of them.

1

HENRY HAS A PROBLEM

Henry woke up slowly. Something was wrong. He was boiling hot to the touch and his side of the bed was soaked in perspiration, but his body shook in shivering spasms and seemed cold.

Henry never got sick. He looked after his health obsessively, choosing his food carefully to avoid fats and unnecessary carbohydrates, and lifting weights every morning before breakfast. Pumping iron the young folks called it. He avoided tobacco altogether and limited his alcohol intake.

Yet, here he was, obviously suffering from some kind of virus or bacterial infection.

As his consciousness slowly returned, a stabbing pain pierced his forehead, just above the eye. Yes, something was definitely wrong.

Rosita, his latest housekeeper, slept soundly on her side of the bed, every now and then emitting a soft, whistling snore. Clearly, their lovemaking earlier in the evening had left her satisfied and contented. Henry smiled to himself, despite his pain and worry.

"Not bad for an old fellow who turns ninety in a few months," he thought. "Not bad at all."

Henry was vain, almost obsessively conscious of his appearance. Despite this flaw in his character, he had a positive approach to life, a generosity of spirit and a loyalty to his friends that prompted others to admire him and seek his company. He prided himself on his physical fitness, paid careful attention to his grooming and always wore freshly pressed khaki shirts and trousers, and polished boots. He was a tall man, standing 6 feet 2 inches. At just 170 pounds, he seemed almost slim, though his body was hardened muscle throughout, without an ounce of flab or fat. His piercing grey-blue eyes peered out from a deeply tanned, weather-beaten face. Once, he had been considered handsome. In a major concession to his vanity, he dyed his naturally white hair jet black. He knew he looked like a man of sixty-five or seventy, which he credited to a lifetime of taking care of himself.

Yet, here he was, in an isolated mountain village in northern Mexico, apparently — and for the first time in decades — quite seriously ill.

There was no local doctor in the village, only an old woman who provided herbal remedies for common mild complaints. Undoubtedly, a descendant of a tribal healer, she was well-versed in the old ways that long preceded her people's conversion to Christianity more than 400 years ago. Her knowledge had survived the pressures of this "new" religion.

But Henry felt that this problem was far too serious for her ministrations — which were, after all, mostly hocus-pocus, with a few effective herbal treatments thrown in. No, he needed to get to a serious doctor, someone trained in a modern medical school. Unfortunately, the closest medical clinic was more than 250 miles away, over rocky terrain and roads that were little more than dusty dirt tracks. The way he was feeling, he doubted he'd be able to drive that distance by himself. He'd need to convince one of the young men in the village to drive him. That doesn't sound like much of a problem, until you realize that the round-trip would probably take at least a week and that Henry's finances wouldn't provide much of a cash reward for the driver.

As he pondered his options, the bedroom gradually brightened. His little adobe house had only two rooms – the bedroom, with a blanket draped across the open doorway for privacy, and the main living area, with a couple of comfortable chairs and a dining table with two chairs in the far corner. The kitchen was a kind of lean-to shelter just outside the back door, but at least it had a relatively new wood-burning stove and a small, gas-fired refrigerator. There was enough room for a wooden cupboard with a large metal sink on top. The property boasted a reliable water well with a hand pump, just outside the kitchen. Henry used to joke, "I've got plenty of running water, as long as I do all the running!" Further down the backyard was the outhouse, a deep-drop toilet.

The only buildings in the village with electricity were the cantina, the little general store and the priest's house – all of which had their own generators, bought from profits or donations. Henry's little house had oil lamps and candles for lighting.

At last, a sharp beam of sunlight bore through the window above the bed, illuminating the opposite wall. That daily event, unless it was cloudy – and the crowing of at least a dozen roosters whether it was cloudy or not – announced the dawning of another new day, and time to rise.

As Rosita began to stir herself awake, Henry said softly, "Rosita, my little flower, I need your help."

Whether speaking English or Spanish, Henry's speech patterns were normally carefully controlled. His attention to correct pronunciation and enunciation made his speaking voice sound slightly artificial and rather like an actor in a stage play. He usually spoke with an air of confidence and authority, which contrasted pointedly with this rather weak plea for assistance.

Suddenly, Rosita was wide awake. He had never made such a request before, had never revealed that he was vulnerable in any way. He was always "The Boss", in control, telling her what to do, and, more often than not, how to do it.

Nevertheless, he had always been gentle and kind to her, and paid her parents every week for her housekeeping services. He always remembered to bring her small gifts and special sweet treats when he returned from his prospecting trips into the mountains – events that were becoming less frequent as he got older.

"Yes, señor Enrique, what can I do for you?"

"Rosita, please fetch Roberto for me right away. I am feeling unwell, and I need him to drive me to Chihuahua as soon as possible."

The girl immediately jumped from the bed and moved quickly to the chair, where her clothing was neatly folded from the night before. She began to dress hurriedly.

Even in the fog of his headache and the aching of his joints, Henry was still able to smile in appreciation at the naked Rosita's bouncing breasts and quivering bottom. Most nights, despite his eighty-nine years, she gave him great pleasure and – he proudly boasted – her cries of joy and shuddering climaxes were the direct result of his well-honed sexual expertise.

Yes, she was quite young, probably seventeen or, at most, eighteen. Normally, Henry's housekeepers were a bit older. He was certainly no paedophile and despised men who deprived children of their right to an innocent childhood. But, in this village, he had little choice. In any case, most young women were married by the age of sixteen in rural northern Mexico; Rosita had missed out on a husband only because of the scarcity of young eligible men in her village.

As was Henry's practice over many years of living in the mountain villages of Mexico, when he arrived in a new place he first negotiated the use of a suitable house. Then, he let it be known that the new gringo needed a live-in housekeeper.

As if by some magical, almost instantaneous, communication process, families would appear at his door to offer him the services of their daughters. Sometimes he was spoiled for choice, but in this small, poor place, he had interviewed just two applicants for the job. Rosita was clearly the only one qualified to clean his house, to cook for him and – as was clearly understood by all parties involved in the negotiations but left unstated – to keep him warm at night.

As Rosita hurried out the door, Henry felt an urgent need to visit the outhouse. He struggled out of bed and threw a poncho over his nakedness, then headed down the path to the outhouse. Having relieved himself, on his way back to the house he became quite dizzy and if the raised post of the water pump hadn't been so close he probably would have collapsed onto the dusty path. He finally made it back to his bed, but the morning's cool mountain air had left him shivering uncontrollably.

Yes, something was wrong.

2

A GLANCE AT HENRY'S VILLAGE

Henry saw clearly that most of the men in the little village of Santa Áurea had their community duties to perform. The most important man in the place was Alberto, the fellow who kept the village's precious petrol-powered water pump working. Their hard-won crops of corn and beans depended on the supply of irrigation water. The equation was simple: when the water pump worked, the crops flourished; if it failed, the crops quickly withered and died, and the villagers faced a long period of hunger until the pump could be repaired or replaced, and the next crop grown.

A fast-flowing mountain stream, which splashed over rocks and through narrow mini-gorges, was one source of water for the village, but it was difficult to collect. The main water supply was an apparently abundant underground artesian reservoir, not too deep and easily pumped to the surface. In a few places, several miles from the village and in an area considered too rough and dangerous to cross, the water rose to the surface naturally and formed a series of small lakes.

While these lakes were difficult to access, they attracted an abundance of birds and other wildlife, most notably herds of deer and a few mountain sheep and feral goats. Of course, predators were also attracted to such a source of food, so wild cats and mountain lions were often seen near the lakes. People from the village, too, supplemented their basic diet of corn and beans with the meat of rabbits, deer and feral goats, which they trapped or shot. Otherwise, their only meat came from their chicken flocks and the few pigs they bred.

Apart from the man who tended the pump, the men of the village took on tasks, such as tending their crops, weeding and keeping the fences in good repair to guard against rabbits and feral goats – animals that could strip a field bare in a few short days, if they weren't kept out. Others would hunt and set traps for wild animals, to obtain that valuable supplementary source of food, while serving to protect their crops at the same time.

A few men had more specialized skills. There were two car mechanics, Patricio and Juan, both of whom had worked on Henry's old Studebaker, and Pablito, a small, gnarled man, who had an uncanny ability for locating the perfect spots for water wells and then drilling and maintaining them. He was a local legend, both for his special talent and his uproarious sense of humor, which Henry enjoyed on more than one occasion. Then there was Carlos, who also played an essential role in village life. His large stone wheel ground the dried corn into *masa*, which the women used to make tortillas.

The cantina was, in many ways, the center of the village – though the local priest would dispute that. It was owned and operated by a large, jolly man named Ernesto and his equally large and jolly wife Guadalupe. They offered cold beer and shots of tequila – of varying qualities and prices – as well as food. Whatever the family was eating that day was available to the rest of the villagers for a small price. They had one of the few phonographs in the village; the patrons of the cantina would often dance in the evening air to the sound of *conjunto* or *ranchero* music played at the highest volume.

The second most important building in the village was the general store – though the local priest would dispute that, too. It was run by a rather dour man, a childless widower named Luis. He stocked an amazing array of essential goods, ranging from tinned food and sweet treats to all types of tobacco products, washing powder, tins of kerosene, soft drinks, ammunition for the local guns, cheap cutlery and glasses, and so on. A big truck supplied him twice a month with his standard stock, as well as with less common items for special orders.

Henry ate most of his evening meals in the cantina and, like the other inhabitants of the village, he depended on the general store for his basic supplies.

The village had a very old church, dating back to the Spanish conquest in the eighteenth century. Behind it was the priest's house. Because of the shortage of priests, Mass was only celebrated every second Sunday, although the important feasts like Christmas and Easter were always celebrated every year.

These three institutions provided important links between the village and the rest of the country. Among the denizens of this little spot hidden deep in the mountains, only Ernesto at the cantina, Luis in the general store, and the padres who ran the church owned satellite telephones with access to the outside world.

In a strange twist of history, the people of this little village – maybe 200 souls in all – celebrated, most fervently of all the Holy Days, the Feast of the Ascension of Jesus into Heaven, which traditionally occurs forty days after Easter Sunday.

Apparently, when the local population was converted to the Catholic faith by Spanish friars, the villagers insisted on keeping at least one of their pagan feast days. That feast, the most important day in their pagan calendar, feted the rise of the sun god into the sky. Every year, at the summer solstice, they would pray for good harvests and fertility. For years, the missionary priests tried unsuccessfully to stop this ceremony. In the end, they Christianized the celebration, allocating it to the Feast of the Ascension. After offering Mass in the church, the priest now presided over a procession from the center of the village to the nearest high hill, with the most prominent villagers — who had previously carried an idol of the sun god on a litter — now carrying a statue of Jesus. When they reached the summit, they prayed for a good harvest and then raised the statue into the air three times, to a chorus of loud cheers from the rest of the villagers. After returning to the village, everyone joined in for a night of feasting and drinking, as well as some other behavior definitely not approved of by the priests.

Initially, Henry had been attracted to the village of Santa Áurea because of its name — that of an obscure Spanish saint — which translates into English, more or less, as "Saint Golden". Henry decided that was a good omen for his prospecting. He also came to enjoy the isolation and the peaceful monotony of life there.

3

PREPARATIONS FOR THE TRIP

Henry had decided to ask Roberto to drive him to Chihuahua because he was a reliable young man who could drive a car, and because he had no pressing duties to perform during the between-harvests slack season. Most of the villagers rode horses or donkeys if they needed to go far. Only nine families were wealthy enough to own a car and most of them used them sparingly because of the high cost of fuel, repairs and spare parts. Given the poor state of the local roads, repairs were frequent and tires didn't last long.

Roberto's family owned a relatively new Volkswagen Beetle which, Henry had noticed, Roberto treated with respect when he got the chance to drive it. He was not like most of the other young men who roared through the village scattering chickens and children, driving like maniacs, whenever they got the chance to get behind a steering wheel.

He could rely on Roberto to get him to Chihuahua and back. In his mind, it was settled.

As he lay in bed recovering his composure after the frightful trip to the outhouse, Henry heard Rosita coming through the front door. He was still shaking and shivering uncontrollably when she walked into the bedroom.

"Roberto is coming. He will be here shortly. I've told him that you're not well and that you need him to drive you to Chihuahua. Now, señor Enrique, can I get anything for you?"

"Thank you, Rosita. I'd love a cup of hot, black tea, please. I'm hoping it will warm me and stop this shivering."

Henry decided to concentrate on the trip to the doctor. He had few possessions and tended to pack virtually all his clothes and documents whenever he left on prospecting trips into the mountains. He never knew how long the trip might be, so he planned for all contingencies.

This trip to Chihuahua would be different, of course. He'd have no need to pack his camping gear, though he'd still put his mining tools in the car in case the car got bogged or he needed to remove an obstruction from the road. But he'd still pack all his clothes and his other important possessions because he had no idea how long he would be away from Santa Áurea.

Rosita arrived with a mug of steaming tea just as Roberto announced his arrival with several loud knocks at the door.

"Come in, my friend, the door is open. I'm in the bedroom." Henry had to raise his voice slightly, but the distance was short, and he didn't have to strain.

Rather shyly, Roberto pushed aside the blanket and entered the bedroom. Even in his own family home, he had rarely entered his parents' bedroom, and then only in special circumstances. He was a bit uneasy walking into the bedroom of the gringo, señor Enrique, a man he did not know well.

"I've come as you asked, señor. Rosita tells me you're unwell and need a driver to take you to Chihuahua."

"Yes, Roberto, I'm not at all well and I need to see a doctor as soon as possible, but I'm afraid I can't drive that distance on my own like this. I don't know how long it will take, but I think we should plan on being gone about a week."

Roberto looked down at his sandals, clearly contemplating the pros and cons of such a journey. He was wondering about his young wife, Anita, and his unborn child.

"I know it's inconvenient, especially since your Anita is due next month, but I'll pay you for your time. Would you agree to drive me? We need to leave as soon as possible. I'll cover all your expenses during the trip and pay you twenty-five Yankee dollars. Who knows, we may find a nice crib or clothes for the new baby in the city."

Roberto thought for a moment and then replied:

"Thank you, señor, for asking me. I can use the money, for sure. As you say, it is not the best time for me, but I'll do it. Please give me an hour or so to tell my wife and my father and then we can leave."

It was settled then. Henry was pleased to be leaving so soon. He had prepared himself to wait until the next day, if necessary, but he was quite anxious about his illness. The sooner he could be seen by a doctor, the better.

He was shaky on his feet, but he managed to pack all his clothes into a battered old suitcase, along with his important documents and the hoard of U.S. dollars and Mexican pesos that he always kept safe near him.

Rosita prepared some food for the trip and filled several large bottles of water to put in the car. The road was long and dry – even water would be hard to find along the way.

Henry paid Rosita her parents' weekly money in advance and gave her a few pesos for herself. He made sure she understood that it was fine with him for her to stay in the house while he was away; although, if she felt more secure, she might want to stay with her parents until he returned. In any case, he told her to use up the perishable food, rather than waste it.

"And one last thing. Rosita, please be sure to fill the water bowl next to the pump each day and put out a few vegetables in the little dish on the ground next to the kitchen door – for my Jacquito."

Rosita smiled and said she certainly would do that. There were many things about señor Enrique that she didn't understand – and this was one of them. No one in her village would ever think of saving the life of an injured jack rabbit, much less nursing it back to health and then letting it go free again – even though he did put out food and water. No, if she found an injured jack rabbit, she'd do what anybody else would do: knock it on the head, skin it and add it to the next pot of chili she made – even though jack rabbit meat is tough and needs to be cooked for a long time.

Her señor Enrique was surely a puzzle at times. Still, he looked after her as well as she could expect him to, and – who knows – maybe, after this illness passed, he might decide to settle down in her village for the rest of his days, give up his prospecting in the mountains, and make her his official wife. She could do a lot worse than marry a man, admittedly an old man, who treated her with kindness and affection. And she was sure he would leave her a nice inheritance when he died.

It was a pleasant dream for Rosita.

4

THE TRIP FROM HELL

By the time Roberto returned with a knapsack over his shoulder containing his necessities for the trip, Henry's belongings were already packed in the car, along with the food and water. The tank was full of fuel, the oil pan was full, and the tires were all at the right pressure. Henry kept his car clean and ready to go at a moment's notice. He'd done so for years, since a turn in the weather once saw him stuck in the mountains for three weeks when he'd neglected to fill his fuel tank when he could.

Henry slowly and rather shakily walked out to the car and got in the passenger side, while Roberto threw his backpack on the back seat and climbed in behind the steering wheel. Even though the car was fairly old and an odd make and model, a Studebaker station wagon, it started immediately. With a wave to Rosita, they pulled out onto the road.

They had only gone a few miles when it deteriorated into a dirt track – old tire tracks through the stony, sandy ground. Drivers had to stay alert – one distraction and you could lose sight of the track and find yourself bogged in soft sand. When the land flattened out for a few miles, it was tempting to speed along the sandy track, but the risk was too great. You would not want to make contact with a protruding stone in any car, especially an old one like Henry's. You could blow a tire or even break an axle. Consequently, Roberto drove carefully and not too fast.

They'd been on the road more than two hours and were making good progress considering the conditions, when Henry began to feel his fever return. While his forehead was boiling hot, and his shirt soaked with perspiration, he felt cold and began to shiver and shake.

Roberto, concerned, asked, "Señor, are you alright?"

"No, Roberto. But there's nothing we can do about it. Just keep driving. Every hour is an hour closer to a doctor."

They drove on for another hour, before Henry asked Roberto to stop for a rest and some food. Roberto pulled the car off the track onto a safe-looking flat bit of sandy desert. He parked under the only small tree in sight, which offered a bit of shade on what was now a hot afternoon.

They nibbled at Rosita's food – some corn cakes and cold beans wrapped in tortillas, and especially enjoyed the fruit from a bag she packed – a couple of mangoes, a pineapple, some tart native plums and two oranges. They washed the food down with water from the large bottles Rosita had filled before packing the remainder away so they could resume their journey.

There was one pressing imperative. They had to make it to the paved highway that led to Chihuahua by sundown. Otherwise, they would have no choice but to bed down in the car for the night. It would be suicide trying to drive that track in the dark.

They climbed back into the car and Roberto turned the key. All they heard was a solitary, ominous "click".

"No battery, señor," said Roberto, in a worried tone.

"Maybe not," said Henry, who knew this car very well. He had had a similar experience once before, several years ago, and he, too, had thought it was a dead battery, but it turned out to be a loose cable connection to the starter motor.

Unfortunately, Roberto was no mechanic and sending him under the car to find the fault was probably pointless.

Henry climbed back out of the car. He walked around to the front and lifted the hood. Then he laid down on his back and wriggled under the car's engine until he could just see the starter motor. Sure enough, the cable had come loose. He could press the cable back into position, but it would, almost certainly, work itself loose again. That would not matter greatly if the car started, because once the engine caught it would not require the starter motor again, unless it stopped completely. They would have to hope that: a) the car would start; and b) they could make it to Chihuahua without having to turn the engine off.

Henry pressed the cable back into position on the starter motor, which required him to lift himself awkwardly and twist his hand into a very small space.

"Try starting it again."

There was no hesitation. When Roberto turned the key, the motor leapt to life immediately and began to idle as it should.

Henry wriggled back out from under the car, now covered in sand, decorated with a few drops of engine oil. But, despite his normally fastidious concern with his appearance, the state of his clothing didn't cross his mind. All he could think about was how dizzy he felt and how out of control. He slumped forwards and grabbed onto the front fender to keep from falling. After a few deep breaths, he managed to reach up, disengage the bar holding up the hood, and close it over the engine. A few more deep breaths and he was able to work his way down the side of the car and, finally, climb back into his seat.

He was exhausted, overcome by fever, but he managed a weak smile and said, in English, to the uncomprehending Roberto:

"Home, James, and don't spare the horses!"

They were back on the track again but had lost precious time. Roberto pressed on as fast as he dared, but their tight deadline was now becoming an impossible goal. The shadows stretched out as the sun slid behind the western mountains. There was no choice. With at least an hour to go before they would reach the highway, Henry and Roberto would have to pull off the road and stop for the night.

Such a move was fraught with danger. In the fading light they had to judge the state of the ground correctly or find themselves bogged in sand. But, at the same time, they had to get far enough off the road that they couldn't be spotted from the track. They were in the middle of nowhere, not a village or even a ranch house within 40 or 50 miles. And here, at night, *banditos* roamed, looking for easy prey. These men cared little for human life. They'd shoot someone for his watch, or even his cigarettes, or just because they took offense at the imagined way someone looked at them. A car stopped at the side of the road was a tempting target; all they needed was for a friend to report it to them, or to stumble across it for themselves as they roamed through the night looking for trouble.

Henry did have a pistol, an antique Colt 45 six-shooter that he kept, loaded, in a pocket beneath the driver's seat. But that kind of gun was really only useful for shooting snakes and other dangerous animals, and as a deterrent in a hostile confrontation with some amateur would-be robber. Against a well-armed band of *banditos*, Henry's pistol wouldn't have been much more use than a pea shooter.

Roberto managed to find a stand of scrubby bushes a couple of hundred yards off the track. He pulled the old wagon in behind the bushes so they couldn't be spotted – at least not easily – from the track. But they would have to turn off the engine. It obviously couldn't run all night – in the deathly quiet of the desert the engine noise would roar like a landing jet plane, and, in any case, they'd run out of fuel before morning.

Having screened the car from the road as best they could, Henry and Roberto ate a bit more of Rosita's food and drank the remainder of the water in one of the bottles. They had two left – enough to get them to Chihuahua the next day.

They struggled to find some sleep, with Henry stretched out on the back seat and Roberto in the front. Henry's fever and chills tormented him. He had a terrible night as he drifted in and out of a shallow, disturbed sleep. Twice he awoke with a fright, thinking he'd heard the sharp crack of a twig broken by the footstep of an unwanted visitor. Both times he heard nothing more and went back to his troubled wanderings, into and out of a surreal semi-conscious state.

At last, the sun's rays began to light up the eastern horizon. In the half-light they finished the food and drank most of the second bottle of water. Once the sun was up enough to see the track, they could leave.

Finally, Henry sensed that the time was right.

"See if she'll start. If all you get is a click, I'll have to go back under the engine and ground that damn cable again."

Henry rarely swore, but the way he felt, he wasn't sure he could manage to crawl back under the car and fix the problem. In which case they really would be stuck.

Roberto turned the key, and, with a most wonderfully loud roar, the engine kicked into life. They could get back on the road.

An hour and a half later, they met the paved highway to Chihuahua. The first sign they passed said "Chihuahua 190 km" – about two hours of normal highway driving.

It was still early enough in the morning for the road to be free of cars and trucks. Roberto took the Studebaker up to about 55 miles per hour – the limit for Henry's old car.

They drove without incident until about 30 miles outside Chihuahua, when they encountered another potential disaster. The radiator hose sprang a leak, sending clouds of steam pouring out from the edges of the hood. Roberto had the good sense to pull off the road immediately and stop the car.

Henry found a roll of adhesive tape in his first aid kit that he kept in the back of the car; once the engine had cooled down sufficiently, they wound that around the hose in a thick wad, tying it off with a piece of wire. Water could still seep out, but not at such a great rate. Still, they'd lost quite a bit of water and didn't dare to run the engine on an almost empty cooling system. It would probably have seized on them within ten to fifteen minutes.

The remaining bottle of water in the car almost topped up the radiator, giving them a chance to make it, if not into the town itself, at least to the outskirts of Chihuahua, where they would hopefully find a filling station with water and a replacement hose, as well as fuel. Almost miraculously, for the second time, the car started without a problem and they were back on the road.

A few miles out of Chihuahua, they pulled into the first filling station they could find with an attached garage. It took some imaginative "bush engineering" but the mechanic eventually managed to get a hose to fit. Waiting for a proper Studebaker part would probably have taken weeks. He also managed to secure the loose starter motor cable. Roberto topped up the radiator and filled the fuel tank. Now they were in Chihuahua all they had to do was find a doctor.

They were directed to the grandly named Hospital General de Chihuahua Dr Salvador Zubirán Anchondo, which had Chihuahua's only emergency room. Chihuahua was quite a big city with around half a million residents, but they had no trouble finding the hospital.

By the time Henry finally saw a doctor his fever and chills had returned with a vengeance. He could barely communicate his symptoms as he slipped into hallucinatory daydreams. The emergency room doctor looked worried. Possibly because they'd had to use that third water bottle for the Studebaker, Henry's condition – diagnosed as a severe case of influenza – was complicated by his rapid dehydration. The doctor immediately ordered the administration of intravenous antibiotics and a saline drip.

Henry had given Roberto enough money to cover the cost of food and a cheap hotel near the hospital. In a brief moment of rationality, he told Roberto to enjoy himself for the rest of the day and not to bother checking on him until the next afternoon. At that moment it was obvious to Henry that he would be in hospital for a few days, at least.

In fact, he would be in a hospital, first in Mexico and then in Texas, for almost three weeks, vacillating between hallucinations and episodes of clarity.

5

THE HOSPITAL

Henry woke up in confusion. The bright lights, the strange bed, the needle in his arm attached to a tube that led up to a plastic bag on a stand, the noises from the corridor, the beeps and whizzes of electronic equipment – it was all so confusing. At last, he remembered. He was in a hospital bed in Chihuahua. How long had he been here? When could he leave?

His body was still wracked with pain. His joints ached, he had a sharp pain in his head and his breathing was labored and painful in his chest, a pain exacerbated by frequent bouts of uncontrollable coughing. A face appeared above him, the pleasant face of a fairly young and not unattractive señorita – a nurse.

"Aha, señor Anderson, you are finally awake. I am here to take your blood pressure and temperature. Afterwards, if you think you can manage something small to eat, I will see to it for you. In the meantime, you must try to take in as much liquid as you can. There's fresh water in your pitcher and here's a curved straw for your glass. You are severely dehydrated. This saline drip will help re-hydrate your body."

She pointed to the bag on the stand above him.

"But you must also drink water orally."

Once again, he began to cough, shaking with the pain and the effort as she fitted the blood pressure cuff around his upper arm. As he came to a wheezing stop, she inserted a thermometer under his tongue. A minute or so later she removed the cuff from his arm and the thermometer from his mouth.

"Doctor Ybarra wants to see you. I'll let him know you're awake."

Yes, Henry was awake, but only just. He had barely finished processing the words uttered by the nurse, when a short, middle-aged man in a white hospital coat and a stethoscope around his neck appeared above him.

"Hello, señor Anderson, it is good to see you awake at last. I am Doctor Jesus Ybarra and I'm in charge of your case. You are a very sick man, señor. You have contracted a severe form of influenza that I am treating with antibiotics and a new anti-viral drug."

Henry opened his eyes briefly and nodded sleepily.

"You presented to us the other evening severely dehydrated and, unfortunately, you have also developed pneumonia. We are doing everything we can for you, señor. You are obviously very fit for your age, and this can only be a good factor in your condition, but I must warn you that you have a fight on your hands. Several of your organs have been affected. The next seventy-two hours or so will be critical."

Henry blinked. Too much information, not enough time to take it in. But one thing was clear, he was in big trouble.

"Do you think I am going to survive?" Henry asked in his most impeccable Spanish, albeit slightly slurred.

"You have a fighting chance, my friend, but it won't be easy. The young fellow who left you here three days ago gave us your basic details – name, age, residence in Mexico – and assured us that you had the means to pay for your treatment. But I need to have the name of a close relative whom I can contact about your condition."

"My closest living relatives are my two nephews in Victoria, Texas. Dr Rufus Anderson, Jr, a dermatologist, and Judge Clarence Anderson. Their addresses and telephone numbers will be with my things in my suitcase."

Henry managed this long sentence with difficulty. As soon as he finished, he was wracked again with a severe coughing fit.

"Try to relax, señor. I fear I have over-taxed you. I will ask the nurse to give you a mild sedative. Sleep is your friend – embrace him whenever possible, but when you are awake you must try to drink as much liquid as you can."

With that, the doctor turned and walked away.

Henry's mind was racing. He had always avoided thinking about death. To tell the truth, he was terrified of dying – yet, here he lay, in a Mexican hospital, with death trying to stare him down. He wouldn't give up without a fight. He still had much to live for even though his best years were behind him, and while he didn't have too many left, he did have some!

He would beat this threat and return to the village and his sweet Rosita. He had become very fond of the girl and their nights together – and he wouldn't give that up easily.

And then there was that promising valley he'd found on his last prospecting trip.

It was late on his final day when he panned a few grains of gold from the little stream. In fact, there were more than a few grains of alluvial gold in that water, which suggested to Henry that there would certainly be a useful deposit of ore somewhere up near the head of the valley. He would survive this setback and he would return to that valley and claim the vast riches he had dreamed about for years. He would, once again, be a wealthy man. He would build, or purchase, a magnificent hacienda and live the rest of his life in luxury. He might even decide to share his good fortune with the delectable Rosita.

Henry had spent his whole life chasing such dreams. His eighty-nine years had so far been a kind of crazy roller-coaster ride, with exhilarating high points of achievement and satisfaction and depressing low points of failure and self-doubt, but throughout the journey he had always overcome the setbacks and survived to follow his dreams of good fortune and success.

He would overcome this setback and resume his life as a prospector. He focused on this point and reinforced it by remembering his only other time in hospital, nearly fifteen years ago, when a badly broken leg had been repaired surgically. His nephews, Al and Clarence, had arranged for his treatment in a hospital in Victoria, Texas.

That time, he had to undergo a few months of rest and rehabilitation, the first weeks spent with his nephew, Rufus, Jr, who was always called Al, and his wife Betty, in their house in Victoria. Then he finished his recovery on his late twin sister's farm in Sutherland Springs, just south of San Antonio. After that, he had been as good as new, eventually able to return to his life in Mexico.

The arrival of the nurse broke into his musings. She gave him an injection and, almost immediately, Henry fell back into a deep, dream-filled sleep.

6

FLORESVILLE, TEXAS, 1891-1902

Alfred Rawson Anderson sat back in his rocking chair and took a long drag from his pipe. It hadn't been a bad day at all. His beloved Kate had finally delivered their babies, twins, a boy they would name Henry Rawson and a girl they would call Emma. Dr Hammond had pronounced the mother and both children to be in the best of health. He didn't often imbibe alcohol these days – it was more or less a condition of his marriage to Kate – but Alfred decided that this event deserved a little tipple from that bottle of Irish whiskey that old George Plant had given him, in lieu of payment, mind you, for sorting out his father's will.

His two stepdaughters, lovely, obedient and helpful girls, Lenora and Susie Lee, came out on the porch and each gave him a hug. Of course, they still missed their father, Kate's first husband, the late Reverend Rufus Field, who would never have let a drop of Irish whiskey pass his Baptist lips, but they had come to love and respect their stepfather as they grew up. They were now six and eight years old, respectively, and were becoming old enough to help their mother around the farm.

It wasn't really much of a farm, truth be told. A mere three acres on the edge of town, but still enough land for a decent vegetable garden, an orchard with peach and plum trees, as well as half a dozen pecan trees, and grass enough for a cow and calf. Kate looked after a promising flock of poultry, consisting of chickens, ducks and geese – the girls were old enough now to gather the eggs – and a hog and two sows that produced large litters of piglets every year.

It was early September; the fruit was ripe and some of the vegetables were ready to pick and preserve. And, among this bounteous harvest, Alfred observed sagely, were his own two new offspring.

His law practice was flourishing, and the local politicians were already starting to sound him out for a judgeship. In a few years' time he would be the county judge of Wilson County.

Time passed quickly and erratically, as it does in a dream. Suddenly, it was 1902. Young Henry, now eleven, and his twin sister, Emma, were looking after their young brother, Rufus, who was now eight. The three of them were playing with young Maxie Field, who, at the age of two, had come to live with them when his mama passed away. He giggled and laughed out loud as they pushed him in the swing their dad had tied to a big branch of the live oak tree.

Then, suddenly, the mood changed for them all. Lenora, their big half-sister and Max's half-aunt, was running towards them crying.

"Papa's dead! Papa's dead!" she wailed. Then she gathered them all together, taking little Maxie in her arms, and slowly led them back to the house.

Earlier that day, as he was in the middle of delivering a ten-year jail sentence for a conviction of attempted murder, Judge Alfred Rawson Anderson suddenly stopped talking, made a strange sound like a suppressed cough, slumped across the judge's bench and dropped dead. He was just forty-six years of age, with a wife and their three young children, as well as another three children they were raising as their own.

In a state of shock, Kate was facing widowhood for a second time in her life. This time, however, she was forty-four years old and unlikely to marry again. The future was suddenly very uncertain.

She and Alfred had been making plans for their future. He was a successful judge, popular in the community, and maybe a future representative in the state legislature. They would expand the farm and add badly needed rooms to the house. They might even consider buying one of those new-fangled "horseless carriages" – but only after the price came down a bit and they became a bit more reliable than they were now.

Now, all her dreams were dust. Kate had no idea how she would cope with her new vulnerability. In the short term, she was sure that her family, the Overtons, would help her, as would Willie Field as much as he could. His construction business was beginning to grow, and he might soon re-marry and take back little Maxie. Her big girls, Lenora and Susie Lee, would be a great help to her in the future, as they had been already these last few years. But they would soon want to spread their wings and get ready to leave her nest so they could build their own.

And what would happen to young Henry and Rufus? Her daughter, Emma, would soon be grown up enough to be a real help around the farm and in the house, but how would she ever manage to educate her boys now? Henry was doing well at school. In fact, he was excelling in most of his subjects. Miss Carmody, the local schoolmistress, had already suggested that they should send Henry to a boarding school in San Antonio next year. There he would be challenged and would have a chance to prepare properly for university admission. But that was now impossible. Even if she managed to sell the land and move into a smaller house in town, they would still not be able to afford expensive private school fees.

Rufus was only eight and followed in his big brother's footsteps whenever he could, but he'd shown no signs yet of potentially high academic achievement. He seemed inclined to enjoy life on the farm much more than he liked his schoolbooks, helping with the animals and working in the garden whenever he could. Maybe his future lay on the land. If she could manage to hold onto the farm for a few more years, perhaps Rufus could step in and take it over. It was a plausible plan, a dream with potential, if she could persuade her and Alfred's families to help them out for a few years.

And then this memory faded away, into a brief, but chaotic series of scenes: the preparations for his father's funeral, the interminable ranting of the preacher in the church, the final, empty feeling as the diggers began to shovel the dirt down onto the coffin, the long, poignant silences back at the house as visitors and relatives drank tea and fruit-bowl punch and ate sandwiches and slices of cake.

7

SURPRISING NEW DIRECTIONS

As his dream dissolved into abstract shapes and muted colors, Henry gradually became conscious of his hospital surroundings. The drip was still there. And the noises. He was still rather befuddled because of the sedative, but he slowly became aware that he was not alone. Just at the end of his bed, seated in a chair, young Roberto was studying him intensely.

"Señor Enrique, you are waking up, no?"

Henry found it hard to co-ordinate his thoughts and his speech, but at least he managed a response:

"Roberto ... how are you?" It was a weak response, but all that he could manage.

"Señor, I am fine. But I cannot remain in Chihuahua for very much longer. I need to get home to my Anita. Her time will come soon, and I must be there."

Again, Henry found it difficult to respond clearly. He spoke slowly, so that he could control his words more easily.

"Yes ... yes ... Roberto. I see. You must go."

His next words were even harder to produce, as the fog in his brain seemed to congeal into a kind of soporific blanket that settled over his consciousness.

"Yes ... Roberto. Go home ... take my car ... I don't need it just now." Even in his faltering speech, Henry could still manage a joke. "My suitcase ... Roberto, get my suitcase. In the top there is a ... a black wallet. Take one hundred Yankee dollars ... for your trip ... for fuel ... and fuel when you ... when you come back for me."

He was struggling to put his ideas into words, but he pushed on.

"Roberto ... I will get word to you ... through the padres ... or, maybe ... maybe Ernesto in the cantina ... to come for me again. Also, my friend ... Roberto ... take another fifty Yankee dollars ... for yourself and Anita."

As he sank back into sleep, exhausted from his efforts, he barely heard Roberto's words of thanks and promises.

★ ★ ★

The old Sutherland Springs community hall had seen better days. Nevertheless, Henry and his small, but enthusiastic, cast and stage crew had managed to transform the old building into "The Star Theater". He had organized a solid program, which included no less than five reels of motion pictures and four live vaudeville acts, as well as a farce – a one-act play – to end the evening's entertainment.

He could see the play bill as if it were yesterday – he'd ordered 300 copies and posted them on fences, trees and sheds throughout Sutherland Springs, La Vernia and Floresville. The top lines read:

Don't Miss This!

THE BIG SHOW OF THE SEASON!

Henry had come up with the name "Sutherland Amusement Co.", and styled himself as "H. Rawson Anderson, Manager".

It was August 1910 and Henry was almost nineteen. His love of literature and drama had been judged a frivolous waste of time by nearly everyone in his deeply religious and, by necessity, hard-working family. But Henry had a dream – he fancied himself as a famous actor–director, strutting the stage in New York and making motion pictures in California. In his mind, it was "Today – Sutherland Springs, Texas; tomorrow – the world".

His first foray into the world of theater attracted a total of eighty-three adults and seventeen children – at 25c per adult and 15c per child. His total take at the door amounted to the grand sum of $23.30. A new career was launched, sort of.

After the hire of the hall, the hire of the motion picture equipment and the printing of the play bills were paid for, Henry and his company cleared precisely $7.39.

Undaunted, Henry pressed on. A second program was performed on the day after Christmas that same year, 1910. Again, the play bills were printed and distributed. Again, the hall was hired, as was the motion picture equipment. And, once again, a program of vaudeville acts, silent movies and another farce was presented to the public of Sutherland Springs.

Despite the new acts and the new motion pictures, the second performance was a catastrophic failure. Only nineteen adults and three children appeared and bought tickets. Clearly, the day after Christmas was not a time when people were willing to pay for entertainment. Henry was left personally liable for the costs of the production – more than $12. He had exhausted his meagre savings and had to beg and borrow to cover his debt.

For the first time in his life, Henry was forced to face reality and admit that his dreams of success in the theater business were never likely to be realized. He had failed.

★ ★ ★

"At last, Mr Anderson, you honor us with your presence." It was Mr Wilkes, the owner of the commercial college and the teacher of typing and secretarial office skills.

I *am* late, thought Henry to himself. If only I hadn't stayed on for that one last beer and that one last cuddle.

"Sorry, Sir, I overslept. I must get a new alarm clock."

A pathetic excuse, but it would do. After all, this wasn't like a proper school – it was a commercial college, training secretaries and clerks, and the pupils paid for the privilege. Mr Wilkes could never risk losing a student for something as insignificant as disciplinary lapses. He needed their fees too much for that.

"Right, Anderson, get to your desk and complete the copying assignment you will find there. And don't let this happen again."

"Oh, no, sir. I won't."

On the desk was a black, upright Worthington typewriter. Beside it was a text for copy typing. On the other side were extra paper, an ink eraser and some carbon paper sheets.

Henry rolled the blank page into his machine and began to type. His fingers flew at a remarkable speed for someone who had only learned three months ago. He had a natural flair for typing – his fingers were supple and quick and, more importantly than most people realize, he never lost concentration – even for a second. When he was typing, his whole being was focused on the task at hand and he would not be distracted.

"Good, Anderson, very good. Your speed is exceptional, but your accuracy is even more impressive. You know, I think with a bit more practice you should seriously consider entering the next San Antonio area speed typing competition."

He already knew about these speed typing competitions, although he hadn't considered that he would ever be good enough to enter one. The prizes were certainly worth winning. Even the local San Antonio competition paid $100 to the grand champion

– more than a month's wages for a secretary – and the chance to move on to a regional competition and even to the national championship. Yes, he'd give it a go.

While his poor mother managed to pay his fees and give him enough of an allowance during the teaching terms to feed himself and, if he was careful during the week, indulge in a little entertainment at the weekends, he couldn't afford his own typewriter. And paying for one was out of the question. He'd have to ask Mr Wilkes for time to practice on the school typewriters in the evenings.

Henry was always a dreamer. His unfortunate experience in the theater business was only a temporary setback. He loved to imagine himself with lots of money and a beautiful house. Not a house in the city or even in a town, no, a proper big ranch house with thousands of acres for raising cattle. Maybe he would go to Mexico, where everything is cheaper and money goes further. There he would be a powerful and respected man. The gringo in the big hacienda.

But the reality for Henry was that his mother could only afford to send him to a commercial college to learn a useful trade. If you had a "useful trade" – like typing skills and office expertise – you'd never starve to death. But you'd never make enough money to own more than a modest house in a town. Forget about the grand Mexican hacienda.

When it was harvesting time, Henry was expected to return home and help out. He resented having to do the chores and the hard work in the garden, but he had no choice. He knew he was cut out for better opportunities than his siblings. Emma, his twin, to whom he remained close despite being away in San Antonio for much of the year, led a simple life and, as far as he could tell, had few ambitions. She worked hard and knew what was required of the wife of a farmer. She would make a good match and fall on her feet – eventually.

Young Rufus was also developing all the skills and attitudes that would eventually make him a successful farmer. He seemed content with that and could not understand why his older brother Henry was so attracted to life outside the farm. Henry's love of books and the cultural life of the city were a mystery to Rufus. Why couldn't he just help on the farm, find a nice wife, settle down and work towards getting his own place?

It was March 1911. Henry was hungry for some kind of success, some kind of pathway to a better life. He diligently applied himself to the improvement of his typing. He spent hours at the college after normal closing time, honing his skills, increasing his speed, maximizing his accuracy.

Mr Wilkes had entered Henry in the San Antonio area speed typing championship. There would be preliminary rounds in various parts of the city, through which, if he was good enough, he could progress to the area final.

Henry's first speed typing contest was held in the gymnasium of a high school. Rows of tables were evenly spaced, one behind the other, fifty places in all – each with an upright Worthington typewriter, and the name of each competitor written on a card lying on top of the typewriter keyboards. The Worthington Company sponsored the competition.

Names were arranged alphabetically, so Henry easily found his. He sat down and limbered up, stretching his fingers and arching his wrists. A practice text lay beside the typewriter, so he rolled in a clean sheet of paper and began to type. The exercise relaxed him, so he was ready when the moderator, at the end of the hall, announced that the test materials would now be distributed.

The contest texts were face down. At the sound of a bell, the competitors turned over their pages and began to type, with the adjudicators patrolling the floor to ensure that there was no cheating. After a set period of time, the bell rang again and the competitors stopped typing. This process was repeated for three five-minute tests and five one-minute tests, after which the adjudicators collected the typed pages.

Several competitors gave up, walking out of the hall before the full range of tests was completed, intimidated by the tense atmosphere. But Henry thrived on the electric charge of competition. Not only did he do well – he surpassed the rest of the competitors with room to spare. His times were excellent – upwards of 120 words a minute for the short texts and more than 110 words a minute for the longer ones. In speed typing contests, errors are counted against the final score, with each error in the finished copy-typed text reducing the final speed by five words a minute. But one of Henry's strong points was his accuracy. He rarely had even one error in a text.

He won his first competition with ease.

Now he faced the regional San Antonio area competition, which included the top five competitors from each of the five area contests. All told, there were twenty-five competitors seated at their typewriter desks in the hall of the civic auditorium.

The format of the competition was the same as before. Yet again, Henry did remarkably well. When the final results were announced, he had finished in second place, beaten by an average total of less than two words per minute.

His prize was $25 and a new Worthington typewriter.

8

THE WORLD IS HENRY'S OYSTER

Henry was now beginning to dream again – seriously. With his new typewriter, he could practice many more hours a week than he did now. He was aiming for success at the highest level. He knew he could improve his typing speed – the more hours of practice he put in, the better he would get. One day, who knows? He could be the state or even the national champion.

The weekend after his success in the San Antonio competition, Henry travelled back to his mother's farm in Floresville. He proudly told her of his good fortune and presented her with $20 from his winnings, excitedly announcing that he was aiming even higher in the world of speed typing. He would do them proud.

The Sunday dinner was very special that weekend. Kate, with Emma's help, produced a wonderful fried chicken meal, complete with mashed potatoes, cream gravy, and fresh snap peas from the garden. Emma baked a tray of biscuits. For dessert, there was a magnificent chocolate cake.

This is one of the happiest days of my life, Henry thought, on his journey back to San Antonio.

Again, the dream began to falter. He was sitting in his room, practicing non-stop for hours. Then he was in the college and

Mr Wilkes was standing over his desk, yet again praising his progress as a typist. Then he was competing once again, fingers flying over the keyboard at remarkable speed, until the bell signalled to stop.

★ ★ ★

The bell. A bell. A ringing bell woke Henry from his deep slumber. A machine near his bed was ringing loudly. He was barely aware of it when a nurse ran into his room and silenced the machine. He could sense a lot of activity around him as the nurse was joined by a doctor and another nurse. His eyes slowly opened, and he saw them all engaged in fast movements he couldn't follow. They replaced his drip bag, then they gave him an injection. He slowly slid back into the world of his dreams.

★ ★ ★

For a few seconds, Henry couldn't work out where he was. The room was a lavish ballroom, heavy curtains hanging from the windows. The dance floor was set up with tables and typewriters. Henry was sitting at his table in front of his machine, waiting for the bell to begin typing. It rang. He tore away at the fastest rate he had ever managed. He kept it up. Again, and again. The bell rang. Start typing. Find that rhythm, that wonderful rhythm that bound together the words he read on the page with his flying fingers. Stop typing. On it went. And then it was over.

The pages were collected from each table and brought to the front of the room to be checked and analysed. The wait was interminable. Finally, several distinguished-looking gentlemen in suits walked into the ballroom and up to the front table. Papers were shuffled and passed among the men. At last, the official who controlled the competition approached the podium.

"Ladies and gentlemen, welcome once again to the grand final of the Worthington speed typing championships for 1912. I will now call on Mr Oliver Stuart of the Worthington Typewriter Company to announce the winner."

A rather young-looking man in a suit walked up to the podium. He glanced down at the card in his hand.

"It is my pleasure to announce the winner of the Worthington Typewriter National Speed Typing Competition for 1912: Mr Henry R. Anderson of Texas. Please put your hands together in his honor."

Henry remembered the event as a kind of dream, within a dream, within a dream. The room was no longer still but began to sway and swirl. And then the applause stopped, and the form of the room reasserted itself.

"Not only has Mr Anderson won this competition by a clear margin, but he has also set a new national speed typing championship record, averaged over eight tasks, of one hundred and fifty-three words per minute."

For a moment, the audience sat in stunned silence, and then erupted in wild applause.

"Mr Anderson, please approach the podium and I will present you with the winner's check. Normally we award the winner of this competition the handsome prize of two thousand five hundred dollars, but in order to recognize your remarkable achievement, a new world record for speed typing, on one of our machines, the committee has decided to double your prize to the grand sum of five thousand dollars. And, of course, you have also won a year's contract to travel the country, promoting our wonderful Worthington typewriters, at the salary of two hundred and fifty dollars per week."

Henry couldn't believe what he was hearing. He now had more money to put in the bank than he had ever dreamed of, and he was on a marvellous salary for the next year, an income that compared favorably with the earnings of most high-ranking executives in large companies.

Henry got up and walked quickly to the front of the room. He shook Mr Stuart's hand and accepted the check, then he leaned over the table and signed the contract that was placed before him. A new life had begun for Henry Rawson Anderson.

9

THE GOOD LIFE

The next few months were a heady mix of train travel, hotel rooms in a new city nearly every day, and speed typing demonstrations in municipal halls and hotel ballrooms. Henry was expected to display his typing skills at every venue and then to mix with the spectators, chatting to them and singing the praises of his employer's product, the Worthington typewriter.

He had now achieved a kind of celebrity status. People stood in awe of him. He was a record-beating world champion. For the first time in his life Henry was financially secure. In fact, he felt quite rich. The $5,000 prize was safely deposited in high-interest bank certificates in San Antonio, and he was paid so well that he managed to add a substantial sum to his savings every month.

Henry thrived on all the adulation he received. Every day, he was the center of attention in yet another city. Everywhere he went he was approached by star-struck young women, anxious for his acknowledgment and a word or two.

Henry was living the high life. With a generous expense account, he slept in hotel rooms and ate in hotel restaurants. He even had a drink or two in hotel bars every now and then – although he was never a heavy drinker. Henry realized very early in his triumphant year as speed typing champion that he needed to pay attention to his health and fitness. Otherwise, he would put on excessive weight, become careless about his appearance, and lose his normally intense focus on whatever he was doing.

So, Henry bought a set of exercise weights, which he used each morning wherever he was to keep fit. This was a practice he never abandoned throughout the rest of his life. He also paid careful attention to what he ate, avoiding fattening foods and eating a sparse but balanced diet. He religiously avoided all excesses.

The same cannot be said of his romantic assignations. Henry rarely slept alone in his hotel bed. Young women, secretaries mostly, flocked to his demonstrations. Like many a rock star in later years, he faced the problem almost every evening of which young woman he would choose to accompany him to his room for the night. He always made it clear to his partners that he was not looking for a long-term relationship. It might not have been wrong to describe Henry as a bit of a cad, but he made a point of never promising more than a night of mutual pleasure, without commitment or consequences.

And then, one day late in 1912, Henry met a young woman in Sacramento, California, who would change his life.

10

ROMANCE

Henry's day had developed exactly as it had for the previous five months. He arrived in Sacramento and got a taxicab from the train station to his hotel – his taxi was one of those relatively new Model T Fords – very exciting for him. He had a meal in the hotel restaurant and a good night's sleep. The next morning he was met in the hotel lobby by the local Worthington representative and taken to the auditorium where he would give his demonstration of speed typing and sing the praises of the Worthington brand.

After his presentation – a "pretend" contest between him and half a dozen of the local speed typing champions, which he won easily – Henry acknowledged the applause and left the stage to mingle with the crowd. As usual, he was approached by a throng of starry-eyed young women, each eager for his attention. He did his best to be friendly and interested as he spoke to each of his admirers but, in truth, Henry was rather distracted. On the edge of the crowd, in a group of well-dressed and clearly important men, he'd spotted one of the most beautiful women he'd ever seen.

She was young, about his age, and quite petite, but she was mingling easily with the wealthiest and most powerful men in the place – not only the local Worthington executives, but others, probably state politicians and their supporters. Slowly, Henry managed to work his way through the crowd towards this attractive young woman. At last, he was able to address her without seeming overly enthusiastic.

"Hello, my name is Henry Anderson. Did you enjoy the presentation?" It was a pretty weak opening, but all he could come up with at the time.

She smiled at him in the most open and attractive way he could imagine.

"Oh, yes, indeed I did. But I must tell you, speed typing is not one of my primary interests. I'm only here because my boss at the *Sacramento Bee* sent me to cover the story."

Quick as a flash, Henry responded: "I'd be happy to give you an exclusive interview – just name the time and place."

"Now suits me," she replied. "To be honest, I'm bored to tears hanging around with these politicians and their buddies, hoping for a slip of the tongue or an unguarded comment. They're so predictable – and this bunch is not exactly in the top tier. There's only one state government politician – he's in charge of the civil service. He's obviously here looking for a nice, personal political contribution from Worthington so the government will buy their typewriters for the state's bureaucrats. Otherwise, there's no one of any importance that interests me."

Henry didn't need a repeat offer. "Now suits me perfectly. I'm expected to mingle and talk to as many people as possible, but I'm sure an interview with a local newspaper reporter takes precedence."

They wandered together to the hotel bar and sat in a booth at the end of the room. A waitress arrived to take their order.

"What'll you have?" Henry asked. "I'm on a good expense account, so I'll pay."

"In that case I'll have a gin and tonic."

For himself, Henry ordered a bourbon on ice with soda water.

"I'm afraid I don't know your name," Henry said.

"Cora, Cora Clancy," she replied.

"Where're you from?" asked Henry.

"Oh, I'm a long way from home. I was born and raised in San Antonio, Texas. I've only been here in California for the last couple of months. My family came here a few years ago and we lived in Los Angeles for about a year and a half. We went back home to San Antonio, but when I finished school I decided to try California again, this time on my own."

Henry couldn't believe it. "I'm from Texas, too. I was born in Floresville, but I was educated in San Antonio. My mom still lives in Floresville."

What started out as a formal "interview" became an increasingly personal conversation between them. They found things in common. He'd known a girl she went to school with. She had friends he knew from the commercial college he attended. As the afternoon progressed, and the drinks flowed, they became more and more animated and familiar with each other. In the end, they discussed their aims and their dreams for the future.

Henry revealed that he hoped to exploit his current celebrity to his advantage by allowing him to meet potential investors. With enough financial backing, he could buy a ranch in Mexico and export prime beef into the U.S. market. His costs would be relatively low, and his profits would be relatively high.

Although he had been born and raised on a farm, the repetitive life of a farmer did not appeal to him. However, for reasons he never quite understood, he always pictured himself as a great landowner in Mexico – owning a large tract of land, making money, and living in luxury. A wealthy local grandee. Maybe growing up influenced by the Hispanic culture of San Antonio had driven him towards his recurring romantic dream of ending up in a magnificent Mexican hacienda.

Cora revealed that she, too, had a romantic dream of living in Mexico in a beautiful hacienda in the country. Before their short sojourn in Los Angeles, her family had spent almost a year living in Hermosillo, in the state of Sonora in northern Mexico, where her father was managing a mining camp just outside the city. Although she had been quite young at the time, she never forgot the experience and always yearned to return someday to live in Mexico. Henry's dream matched hers, and together they spent the rest of the evening – including a meal in the dining room, and a night in Henry's bed – planning the rest of their lives.

In the morning Henry had to catch a train to San Francisco for his next appearance. He was distraught at the thought of leaving Cora behind. They had fallen madly in love – after only one day!

"Come with me, Cora," Henry begged as they finished their room service breakfast. "I'll look after you and we can work out a way to be happy together, as we go along. I've got plenty of money at the moment, and with my expense account we should be able to get by for a while, until we organize our plans for the future."

He was already assuming that they'd spend the rest of their lives together.

Luckily, Cora was as love-struck as Henry. Impetuously, she phoned the newspaper and resigned on the spot. They caught a cab to the train station and bought her a ticket to San Francisco. It was a crazy emotional whirlwind that enveloped them, but they were now together, both happier than they'd ever been before.

Cora was normally a cautious and thoughtful person who considered her decisions carefully before committing herself, but she was completely caught up in Henry's impulsive behavior.

She had never let herself go in this way before and, while she was quite aware that it might all end quickly and in tears, she embraced the unknown future with enthusiasm, determined to enjoy the experience whether it lasted a week or a lifetime. For the first time in her life, Cora Clancy was experiencing the madness of love.

11

ANOTHER NEW DIRECTION

A different consciousness intruded. Dr Ybarra was leaning over him.

"Ah, señor Anderson, you wake again, at last. I have contacted your family in Texas and your nephews are organizing a medical evacuation flight for you. They should be here tomorrow evening, or the next day, Wednesday, at the latest."

Henry managed a brief nod and a croaking "Si."

"They will take you back to Texas where you can be cared for very well and be much closer to your family. In the meantime, you must sleep as much as possible. Sleep is a great healer."

And, with that, the doctor retreated from the room.

A nurse soon arrived with water and a light sandwich of ham and cheese. She let him eat before she administered yet another injection and Henry's world drifted back into his dreamy memories.

★ ★ ★

Texas.

Yes, Henry realized, he was back in Texas. He and Cora were in San Antonio, in a taxi heading towards her family's house in

Alamo Heights, a pleasant neighborhood not far from the center of the city. He was both excited and a bit anxious about meeting Cora's family for the first time. Of course, she had written to them, explaining her new circumstances, and Henry had added a few lines to several of her letters. He had even spoken to them on the telephone when Cora had called to tell them they would soon be in San Antonio.

Henry's contract with Worthington had less than a month to go and he had already informed the company that he intended to leave their employment when it finished. The young couple planned to marry as soon as possible after that. It only remained for Henry to formally ask Cora's father for his permission to take her as his bride and, assuming that the answer was positive, he then would get to know the Clancy family and introduce Cora to his family in Floresville.

The welcome extended to Henry by Fred and Eliza Clancy could not have been warmer. They could see that their daughter was happier than she'd ever been before, and they were more than ready to welcome her "beau" into their family.

Fred and Henry hit it off immediately. In some ways, they were very similar – both were dreamers, but neither was afraid of hard work. Fred Clancy had spent much of his life chasing success in the mining industry and in oil exploration. He was convinced that anyone who worked hard and took reasonable risks would eventually make plenty of money in mining or oil. The fact that he had never made a major "killing" did not deter him. He was always sure that success lay just around the corner. While he had never made the big money, he had made enough to fund a comfortable lifestyle for Eliza and himself, and he'd paid for his daughter's college education, which had helped her start a life of her own.

Henry asked to speak to him privately. Fred invited him into his "office" – the room where he kept his financial records and his stock of good Irish whiskey. He offered Henry a glass of the good stuff and, sensibly, the young man did not refuse – but he was careful to add plenty of water. They had a few sips and Henry got to the point.

"Sir, I love your daughter with all my heart, and I am confident that she loves me, too. We would like to be married and I would be honored to receive your blessing."

Fred, too, did not beat around the bush.

"Young man, I like what I see. Obviously, my darling Cora has chosen you to be her partner and I trust her judgment. I can only ask that you look after her in the future as I have. Yes, you may have my blessing and I wish you both a long, fruitful and happy life."

With that they shook hands, and Fred poured another glass of whiskey.

That night, and on many subsequent nights, Fred Clancy and Henry Anderson established a deep relationship built on trust and respect. Fred was confident that Henry would lead a successful and prosperous life with his daughter – the young man, not yet twenty-five, had almost $10,000 in the bank and displayed the ambition to make even more. All Henry needed was good advice and the support of more experienced businessmen, which Fred was determined to provide for him. He would help him get a start in the oil industry and, perhaps later, help him expand into mining. He would offer to teach him the lessons he had learned in his life – how to minimize his risks and maximize his chances for profit – and he would introduce Henry to the right people to help him succeed.

★ ★ ★

Henry's dream began to pick up speed.

Images and sounds flashed through his brain. His final weeks with Worthington, the glorious week of his wedding festivities, the wonder and the joy of his honeymoon with Cora – two weeks of bliss in the Hotel Galvez in Galveston, the best hotel on the island – their return to San Antonio, and his immediate search for a suitable position in business and opportunities to invest and increase his capital.

The many meetings, Fred's introductions, and the long lunches culminated in Henry's eventual success – an executive position, albeit a junior one, with an oil company owned by one of Fred's close friends.

Nineteen-thirteen seemed to fly past at great speed. A kaleidoscope of images changed and blurred into one another, and then clarified into a scene where Henry was walking through the scrub south of San Antonio, somewhere between Three Rivers and Pleasanton.

He was accompanied by a petroleum engineer and geologist who specialized in spotting potential oil fields.

"Mr Anderson, I can assure you, this parcel of land is the most promising site I've seen yet in this area. Claims have already been lodged by people I know on two sides, with drilling set to start in the next year or two when they've lined up their financial backers. This block is still available for purchase. It's one hundred and seventy acres in size and the owner hasn't yet realized its potential value as an oil site. If I had the money, I'd jump in now. No point waiting."

Henry looked around. On the surface, this country was not very attractive – the mesquite and huisache scrub, dotted here and there with patches of prickly pear cactus, covered the sandy soil. It was useless for farming and not much good for grazing. Rainfall was unpredictable, with dry years more common than wet ones.

It was a fairly flat landscape of muted colors, beige and pale green, in harsh sunlight – but Henry wasn't interested in what was above the ground. The value of this place, potentially, was well beneath the surface.

The asking price for the 170 acres was $35 an acre, $5,950 in total. Henry wasted no time. He withdrew the money from his bank investments and bought the land. Strictly speaking, he was working for Mr George B. Webster, owner of Alamo Oil Enterprises, and any potential oil properties he found should have been reported to his boss. But Henry was willing to risk being sued – the potential profit was huge. He covered his tracks by quickly registering a one-dollar company, which he called 'Cora Investments', and then transferred ownership of the property to the new company.

His nest egg was not exhausted by this purchase. Henry still had more than $4,000 in the bank. He waited a few weeks and resigned from the Alamo Oil Co. Now he was on his own.

12

A NEW LIFE IN ARIZONA

Henry set out on his own, taking the biggest risk of his life at exactly the same time as his responsibilities increased. Just a year and a half after their wedding, at the end of 1914, Cora gave birth to a beautiful baby girl, Madeleine Frances, who they immediately began calling "Maddy".

At the same time as their own happiness was increasing immeasurably, Henry and Cora were saddened by the breakdown of her parents' marriage. Eliza had finally had enough of Fred's drinking and his financial risk-taking. Even though they were both besotted by their little granddaughter, the Clancys formally divorced in July, 1915. Eliza received the family home in San Antonio as her share of the settlement, and Fred left Texas early in 1916 and moved to the hot and dusty border town of Nogales, Arizona, where he still had a few old friends from his days in the mining industry.

Cora refused to take sides in the unhappy divorce. She could see clearly that her father had his faults. He was too fond of his store of Irish whiskey, and he had chased his dreams with money that otherwise could have been added to the family's assets. On the other hand, she felt he had always ensured that their interests were looked after first, by educating her and providing a fine house for her mother.

Cora was also aware that Eliza was never happy with the family's status in San Antonio. Eliza had always wanted Fred to play a more prominent role in the social life of the city, and she resented his risky investments in oil and mining. She would have preferred that he spent all his money acquiring a more impressive house to advance their social standing in the community.

Eventually, their differences had become too great and Eliza had sued for divorce.

Despite the acrimony, Cora, Henry and Maddy maintained contact with Fred and, because they lived close to the Clancy family home, visited Eliza regularly. However, Eliza expected Cora's unconditional support, so when she discovered Cora was refusing to abandon contact with her father, she became rather cool.

Henry corresponded regularly with Fred Clancy in his own right. Soon Fred was urging Henry to join him in Nogales. He assured Henry that new mines were being opened all the time and that many people had made fortunes.

The idea appealed to Henry, who enthusiastically embraced the idea of a new life in Arizona. He eagerly read everything he could get his hands on about this most recent U.S. state.[1] It was clear to him that Arizona was a "new frontier", a vast area of land in the far west that offered almost limitless possibilities for development – especially in the mineral-rich south of the state, where promising finds of gold, silver, as well as copper and some other useful minerals, were attracting large numbers of prospectors and miners who were willing to work hard for the chance of gaining instant wealth.

---

[1] Arizona had only been granted statehood in 1912, becoming the forty-eighth State in the United States of America.

Henry's infectious enthusiasm for the great promise of a new life in Arizona had its effect on Cora, who offered him her full support. Together, they poured over the history of the area and the recent accounts of successful mining operations there.

★ ★ ★

In 1854, the U.S. government had paid Mexico $10 million for a little less than 30,000 square miles of land in southern Arizona and south-western New Mexico, known as The Gadsden Purchase. This agreement was effectively the final outcome of the 1846–1848 war between the U.S. and Mexico. That southern part of Arizona, in the town of Nogales, is where Fred Clancy had settled, and it was there that Henry and Cora decided to make their new home.

The Mexican–American war erupted in 1846 after Texas was annexed as a new American state in 1845. Prior to this, the independent country of Texas, which existed from 1836 to 1845, claimed a vast tract of land as its own, outside its recognized state borders, including most of modern Oklahoma, New Mexico and Colorado. When the U.S. appropriated this land for itself, the Mexicans declared war. They were quickly overwhelmed by the U.S. Army under General Zachary Taylor and surrendered unconditionally when the U.S. forces occupied Mexico City. General Taylor, regarded as a war hero for his victory over the Mexicans, was elected U.S. president in 1848.

The victorious Americans not only secured their hold on all the lands claimed by Texas, but they also demanded and received the whole of "Upper California" as their spoils of war. That vast area included the modern states of California, Nevada, Utah and Arizona. The Gadsden Purchase was part of the post-war negotiations that finally fixed the border between the U.S. and Mexico. Lines were drawn on the map, and the new border was declared, transferring the future cities of Tucson and Yuma, in Arizona, from

Mexico to the U.S. In the process, the town of Nogales was split down the middle by the new border, which ran down the center of one of its wide streets.

That area, with Arizona to the north and the Mexican state of Sonora to the south, had been known for its gold and silver mines since the Spanish conquest. Between about 1895 and 1925, Mexican mining companies south of the border and American mining companies on both sides of the border opened up hundreds of gold, silver and copper mines. Some of them were ancient mines, first dug by the Spanish missionaries – or, more accurately, by their newly converted local Indians – and were now being re-opened, viable once more because of new technology. Other mines were new ventures in previously un-mined areas.

Investors in the new and re-opened mines often became millionaires within the first year of operation. But other investors lost everything when the mines turned out to have ore that was too low-grade to be profitable or when the mine shafts became too dangerous and unstable to work – usually through flooding.

★ ★ ★

It was in the middle of this mining boom that Fred Clancy had moved to Nogales. He lacked the necessary finances to take full advantage of the situation on his own, but he was sure that Henry, who still had money to invest, could make a lot more if he got involved. It didn't take long for Henry and Cora to follow Fred's advice and join him in Nogales.

In 1917, Henry travelled to Nogales to meet up with Fred, who introduced him to several of his friends. After discussing possible ventures, Henry returned to San Antonio with a clear plan in his mind.

Fred's friends were successful businessmen in Nogales. One, Bertram J. Thomson, was a banker and later the elected mayor;

Gordon F. Lister was an executive with the railway that ran through Nogales, and he, too, served as mayor for a while, as well as chairman of the county council; a third man, Josh J. Wagner, known as "J.J." to his friends, was described as "a successful farmer and businessman" and he also ran for the city council. Fred secured the job of town clerk, which, while not particularly well-paid, kept him in touch with the grandees who ran the town.

Throughout 1918, negotiations between Henry and the Nogales "big wigs" continued, moderated by Fred. Eventually, an agreement was reached. Henry would move to Nogales with his family. Upon their arrival he and Mr J.J. Wagner would buy the local stationery store – which they would re-name "The Anderson Stationery Company". Henry's contribution would be one thousand dollars, for a half-share in the business.

Shortly after Henry's arrival, the five men (Thomson, Lister, Wagner, Fred Clancy and Henry) would form a company called the 'Three Sisters Oil and Refining Company' – named after a local landmark, three mesas known as 'The Three Sisters'. This company would have an initial capitalisation of $100,000, split into 10,000 shares at $10 each. Henry negotiated a trade of his potential oil property in Texas for 2,000 of these shares. Fred managed to borrow enough to supplement what he already had and purchased his 2,000 shares. The other three partners in the company also each bought 2,000 shares.

This arrangement was not as speculative as it might seem. In 1918, Henry had received good advice that the properties neighboring his had already drilled viable wells. All he needed was the additional capital to develop his property. The Nogales investors supplied that money.

Meanwhile, Henry and his business partner, J.J. Wagner, modernized and re-opened The Anderson Stationery Company. It made a nice profit, selling not only pens, paper, ink and other stationery and office supplies, but also had a viable trade in cigars, other tobacco products, candy and snacks.

In April 1919, both the local Nogales newspapers reported that the town clerk, Fred Clancy, had returned from a week's visit to San Antonio accompanied by his daughter and son-in-law, Mr & Mrs R.H. Anderson, and their "baby daughter", who was by then four years old.

Within three weeks, the sale of the stationery business was completed. Another three weeks after that, The Three Sisters Oil and Refining Company was registered as a corporation in the state of Arizona.

In January 1920, the Nogales papers reported that there was "good news" for a local company. Land holdings by The Three Sisters Oil and Refining Company were surrounded by new, flowing oil wells that had just come in. It was only a matter of time before the local company would also bring in a well.

In February 1920, a well drilled by The Three Sisters company on its land in Texas had proved viable and three more wells followed quickly.

By June 1920, the four wells were pumping oil out of the Texas ground as fast as possible. The profits were high, and the financial rewards were staggering – each of the investors in The Three Sisters had, by then, received more than $200,000, making Henry and his father-in-law very rich.

13

CALIFORNIA, HERE WE COME!

It was a hot night in early June 1920 when Cora and Henry sat down after dinner and putting young Maddy to bed. It was time for them to make a decision that might well determine the direction of the rest of their lives.

Nogales had its good points, but basically it was a hot and dusty border town. True, there were some impressive stone buildings, including the court house and a fine, new school, but Nogales was very much a man's world, a world of dust and dreams and sweat; a world where quickly made decisions meant fabulous wealth or instant ruin; a world only slightly less lawless than many similar towns on the Mexican side of the border and a world where men vastly outnumbered women.

The wealthiest men built grand houses surrounded by high walls, which were defended by armed caretakers. Some of them were joined by their womenfolk – almost everyone of note in Nogales had moved there from their original homes in California or other parts of the U.S. – but, in many cases, the wives stayed where they were, while the men lived in Arizona.

The poorest men were laborers – many of them were from the local indigenous population, or had come from Mexico or the eastern U.S. – who were hoping to save enough cash to eventually buy a stake in a mining venture. Most of these men lived on their own in rough accommodation and relied on the numerous bars and bordellos for entertainment and female company.

The only parts of the population of Nogales who lived like "normal" middle-class families elsewhere in America, were the families of merchants, shopkeepers and some civil servants. Their children went to the local school and the wives entertained one another, joining together to pursue "worthy" causes while the men ran their businesses.

While Cora and Henry had to some extent joined that section of Nogales society, their new wealth gave them status that required them to build a grand house and join what life there was at the very top of the social pecking-order in Nogales. This proposition appealed to neither Cora nor Henry.

While Henry was anxious to move from their rented apartment, he did not like the idea of living in a fortress, albeit a very comfortable and prestigious one. He was sure that he and Cora would never be happy in such a house and did not consider it a good environment in which to raise their child.

"Henry, we've got to consider Maddy's education. She'll be starting school next year and I really don't want her going to school here in Nogales."

Henry nodded in agreement.

"The new school building may have all the most modern furnishings and equipment, but the teachers are still the same as those who staffed the old school. Frankly, I don't want them teaching our child. Equally, I can't bear to send her away to boarding school – at least not yet."

Cora also made it clear to Henry that she could not contemplate a long-term future living in Nogales.

"Cora, *mi amor*, I am well aware of the needs of our child – and of your needs. I have been considering our future seriously in the last month. Now that the wells in Texas are doing well I no longer see any need to remain here. Wagner is happy to purchase our share of the shop and there's really no need for me to be here to oversee Three Sisters. It's running well. I'll only have to show up a couple of times a year for directors' meetings from now on."

Cora's reaction was the beginning of a broad smile and a loving focus on Henry's bright blue eyes.

Henry continued:

"I have a proposition for you. Let's move to Los Angeles. We can certainly find a good school there for Cora. There'll be cultural attractions and many options for investing our money. You'll not feel so isolated, and I can easily travel back here to Nogales when required. I know it's a big new direction for us, and only a little over a year since our last move, but I'm enthusiastic about the possibilities in California and I think we'll be happier there. What do you think?"

Cora's reaction was clear and decisive; she threw her arms around Henry and gave him a mighty hug. "Let's go for it, my wonderful man!"

14

THE LIFESTYLES OF THE RICH AND FAMOUS

Once again, the focus of Henry's dream faded into shadow, and then re-focused, briefly, on several separate images: the goodbye handshakes and hugs with Fred at the Nogales Railway Station; their arrival in Los Angeles; their brief few weeks living in a grand suite in the new Beverley Hills Hotel – opened in 1912 and now being frequented by the newly arrived Hollywood "glitterati"; their search for a suitable house; and, finally, their choice of a Hollywood mansion named La Paloma as their new home. It was the former property of a moderately famous actress, Melissa Mulcaire, who had died quite young from a mystery illness – as it was reported in the press. It was actually a drug overdose.

Their mutual reaction to La Paloma – or The Dove, the name the actress had bestowed on her dream home – came back to Henry clearly in his dream.

★ ★ ★

"Oh, Henry, what a wonderful place! It's perfect."

"Ah, Cora, *mi amor*, our new life is in front of us, and this will be our starting point!"

La Paloma was a rather typical Hollywood mansion, if such a concept can be entertained. There were grander and more expensive residences there, but this one had all the necessary features: an imposing entrance gate, a semi-circular drive to and from the front entrance, lined with mature palm trees, and a grand front facade with four columns and twelve steps up from the drive to the entrance door.

The main building was constructed of pink stonework, with the window and door frames painted a light blue. The house had eight bedrooms on the second floor, each with an ensuite bathroom; on the ground floor, a large entrance hall led from the front door to the living room – a grand sitting room with massive over-stuffed couches and a huge fireplace – and to the dining room with its bespoke table that sat eighteen people comfortably for a meal. There was a library – with floor-to-ceiling bookshelves, filled mostly, Henry had noticed, with volumes whose bindings were much more interesting than their contents – and a grand ballroom, where a hundred people could easily mingle and dance.

At the back of the house, there was a huge, well-appointed, modern kitchen, a large larder, a cool room, a laundry, and other spaces for the use of the servants who maintained the house.

In an annex connected to the ballroom were a games room with a billiard table, and a private cinema, which seated sixteen. From the games room, French doors opened onto the back gardens, complete with a large swimming pool and a building that housed changing rooms and showers.

It was, in so many ways, the kind of home that Cora and Henry had dreamed about for years. Now, Henry's success in the oil business made that dream a reality. Nevertheless, he never abandoned his original plan for an equally grand house in Mexico, a hacienda surrounded by thousands of acres of cattle country. In his heart he regarded their current happy and prosperous life as a step on the path to his grand dream.

Their first few months in the new house were like a fairy tale. The magnificent furnishings were part of the sale contract, and the household staff were mostly the people who had worked there for the actress, so Cora and Henry spent some time acquainting themselves with their surroundings and their new employees. For weeks, each day brought a new discovery and the whole ongoing experience, while exhilarating, seemed quite surreal to the young family, so recently housed in a rented apartment in Nogales, Arizona.

Meanwhile, Henry was busy setting himself up in business. He rented an office in an area of Hollywood where many talent companies and managers for actors had their offices. He hired a secretary and had the door painted with "R.H. Anderson, Director and Company Secretary, Three Sisters Oil and Refining Company". Underneath, he added, "Investment Advisor, Specializing in Oil and Mineral Opportunities". Furthermore, he announced his presence in impressive advertising blocks in the local newspapers.

Henry was naturally gregarious, and it didn't take him long to meet people with power and influence in Hollywood: people who had money to invest and their friends, also with money to invest. Henry's own success was evident – he dressed the part of a wealthy financial advisor, wearing the best suits, with shoes and ties to match. He frequented the "watering holes" of his potential customers, made numerous useful acquaintances, was invited to join exclusive country clubs and began to mix with the top tier of Hollywood society, often with the petite and beautiful Cora at his side.

They began to entertain their new friends and business associates at home. Each month or so, they would have a dinner party with twelve or fourteen guests, and, once they had established themselves as part of the Hollywood social set, they held an annual charity ball at their house, with a dance band in the ballroom and a grand canvas gazebo in the back gardens. Their guest list included not only the Hollywood "money men" – the owners and producers of the movie industry – but also the star actors and actresses of the day. At their summer soiree of 1924, no less than Douglas Fairbanks, John Barrymore, Gloria Swanson and Mary Pickford were in attendance.

15

A SAD EVENT WITH A SILVER LINING

On the night of that first grand soiree – in fact, in the early hours of the next morning, just after the last of their guests had left – the doorbell rang.

A housekeeper answered the door and immediately went to find Henry.

"Mr Anderson, there is a man at the door with a telegram for you. He says it is a matter of urgency. He will not deliver it to anyone but you."

Henry was a bit disgruntled. He and Cora were relaxing with glasses of champagne while chatting about their successful party. They were just about ready for bed. Nevertheless, Henry got up and went to the front door.

"Are you Mr R.H. Anderson?"

"I am."

"I'm afraid I have some bad news for you, sir. If you want, I can read the telegram to you. Otherwise, you can sign for it and I'll hand it over for you to read."

"Thank you, I'll take the telegram and read it myself," said Henry, not knowing what he was about to receive.

The telegram was from his old business partner in Nogales, J.J. Wagner, who was still one of the Directors of The Three Sisters Oil Company – in fact, the Treasurer. It read:

To Henry and Cora Anderson. Stop. Unavoidable bad news. Stop. Fred Clancy passed away last night. Stop. Cerebral haemorrhage. Stop. Nothing could be done for him. Stop. If I can help in any way, let me know. Stop. So sorry. Stop. J.J. Wagner.

Henry went straight to Cora with the terrible news. She was, of course, distraught. She had always been close to her father and, in the years since her parents had divorced, she and Henry had become even closer to him. Fred had been devastated when they left Nogales, but he understood that it was the best move for them to make. Nevertheless, he greatly missed his daughter and son-in-law and, especially, his granddaughter.

He had come for visits to California to see them several times since they moved, and Henry had gone back to Nogales twice a year for meetings of the oil company board, staying with him when he did. They also had discussed the possibility of Fred moving to Los Angeles, but he was still looking for mining investments in Arizona and Sonora, and preferred to remain close to the action.

Now, it was too late.

Henry and Cora took several weeks off to travel to Texas for Fred's funeral. He was buried in San Antonio. Afterwards they took the opportunity to visit family. Cora's mother had re-married in 1923 to Mr Jonathan Brown, a wealthy man and a pillar of San Antonio society. Henry and Cora spent some time with them and also spent a few days on the farm in Sutherland Springs with Clarence Cleaver and his wife, Emma, Henry's twin sister. They contacted his younger brother, Rufus, and arranged to meet him and his wife, Lee, at their farm near La Vernia for a day. Then they returned to California.

Fred's death was a shock, but for them there was also a positive side to it: he left everything to Cora in his will. Her inheritance included Fred's 2,000 shares in The Three Sisters Oil Company along with their monthly dividends, which in 1924 amounted to a monthly payment of between $10,000 and $20,000, depending on the oil price and the amount produced by the four wells. His other assets included a respectable house in Nogales, some shares in various mining ventures – which all proved, basically, worthless - and a few thousand dollars in cash. Now, Henry and Cora owned 40 per cent of The Three Sisters Oil Company between them and received 40 per cent of the monthly dividends. If they were rich before, now they were, to all intents and purposes, twice as rich.

16

A HACIENDA NEAR ACAPULCO

Once again, Henry's dreams became blurred as he slowly regained consciousness. He was aware of movement around his bed, and he gradually realized that his nephew, Clarence, was there.

"Uncle Hank."

Only Clarence and, sometimes, Henry's late brother, Rufus, had called him by that nickname.

"Al and I have come to take you back to Texas. As soon as the local doctors here have handed you over to the medivac staff, we will go to the airport and fly you back to Victoria."

Henry murmured his thanks and closed his eyes again.

"Mr Anderson, my name is Joe Bundrick. I am an emergency medical evacuation doctor. I will oversee your care from now until we hand you over to the staff at County Memorial in Victoria. I am now going to administer a very strong sedative, which should help you to sleep soundly until we get back to Texas."

Henry nodded his understanding and then felt the pinprick of the injection. He was back in a deep sleep within seconds.

★ ★ ★

Henry felt the warm pressure of Cora's body leaning into him. They were on a sofa in La Paloma. He recalled that her father had died not long ago. She took his hand in hers and began to speak:

"Henry, I know you've been very busy at the office, catching up since Daddy's funeral. But, as soon as you can manage it, I'd love to go away for a while on a proper holiday."

Henry looked into her beautiful eyes and felt the warm glow of contented love in his heart.

"We've been in Los Angeles for over two years now and, apart from the couple of weeks we were in Texas for Daddy's funeral, we have never had any time away. We need some time to relax and to share some happy times together. What do you think?"

"Cora, *mi amor*, I think that's a great idea. We could both use a break in our routine – as lovely as it is, our wonderful life here can be very stressful. Sometimes I feel like we're playing acting roles in our own motion picture, saying the lines we have to say, making all the right gestures to the right people."

Cora nodded in agreement.

"Who would have thought that a life like we have now – able to buy whatever we like – could be anything but perfect. You are absolutely right! You pick a place, and we will go for as long as you like."

Three weeks later, a brief article in a gossip column "Hollywood Whispers" in the *Los Angeles Tribune* announced:

> *Mr and Mrs R.H. Anderson, new darlings of the Hollywood social set, have announced that they and their young daughter, Madeleine, will be on holiday in Acapulco, Mexico, for the next three months.*

Acapulco! Even in his deep dream, Henry's sub-conscious memories came sparking back to life at the mention of the word. Acapulco!

In 1924, the place was a small town on the Pacific Coast of Central Mexico with fewer than 10,000 people. Its wide and deep natural bay attracted cruise liners to stop for one-day visits and re-provisioning as they sailed between California and South and Central America.

In the popular gossip magazines of the time, which Cora read obsessively, she had come across a mention of Acapulco. In 1920, the British Prince of Wales, later King Edward VIII, had stopped at the little port on a cruise to Panama. He was taken with the natural beauty of the place and expressed the opinion that, one day, it would be a grand tourist destination. So, it was no less an authority than the British royal family that prompted Cora to choose Acapulco for the Anderson family holiday.

The future king was eventually proven correct. Acapulco became the favored playground of the Hollywood movie set during the 1950s and '60s, when high, multi-storey hotels rose to dominate the shoreline of the bay, and numerous nightclubs, bars and restaurants provided them with ample scope for their high-speed, non-stop, party life.

However, when Henry, Cora and Maddy arrived at the port of Acapulco by ship – having booked the trip on a cruise liner bound for Valparaíso – they found a quiet little Mexican coastal town. It's true that the scenery was spectacular and that the daily spectacle of local boys diving into the sea from the high cliffs at La Quebrada was a thrilling experience, but, in truth, there was not a lot to do in the little town – not that Henry and Cora found that a drawback. They were there to relax for a while and the slow and simple lifestyle of sleepy little Acapulco suited them well.

There were no grand hotels in Acapulco. Cora had booked them into a small but comfortable boarding house for their whole ten-week holiday. Formerly the townhouse of a wealthy landowner, it was situated on the Parque Papagayo. The meals were excellent. The owners of the place had two daughters, one just older and the other just younger than Maddy. She immediately formed a close bond with the girls, and they entertained each other, mostly going for swims at the beautiful beaches or treks along the cliffs. The town was a quiet, peaceful place and perfectly safe for children.

After a week or so of pure relaxation, Henry and Cora hired a local man with a motor car – a Model T Ford – to drive them around the countryside near Acapulco. The roads were in poor condition, so it wasn't possible to drive very far before the tracks became too dangerous to continue. Nevertheless, they were able to explore some of the area and visit many of the nearby villages and *rancheros*.

Just a few miles east of Acapulco, one particular *ranchero* attracted their attention. It was a relatively small cattle property, with a beautifully maintained and landscaped hacienda, more than a hundred years old. It was owned by an elderly, childless couple named Ramirez, who offered Henry and Cora every hospitality when they drove up unannounced. They were genuinely friendly people and they immediately warmed to their gringo visitors, as the gringos did to them.

Henry and Cora were both immediately taken with this lovely place. The location was perfect, and the hacienda was beautiful. It lacked the size and potential income of their ultimate dream home in Mexico, but as a temporary place to spend their holidays, it was ideal.

They arranged a second visit, when Henry made Tito and Maria Ramirez a proposition. He and Cora would buy the property, including the livestock, but would only live in the hacienda for part of the year, usually around Christmas. The original owners would continue to live in the house and manage the property. All the workers on the property would continue to be employed, paid by the new owners. When the Anderson family was there, Tito and Maria would move into a separate, smaller house, which was built for their only child, a son who had died before he could marry and start his own family.

By American standards, the *ranchero* was quite inexpensive. The lovely hacienda, almost 2,500 acres of land and 450 head of cattle, cost about as much as a modest house in Beverley Hills. Eventually, when Maddy was educated and after they decided that they'd had enough of the rat race in Hollywood, they intended to find a larger, grander property in Mexico and move there for good.

The legal arrangements were finalized, the contract was signed, and the money transferred – no small matter in rural Mexico in the 1920s – just two days before Henry, Cora and Maddy returned to Los Angeles, this time as passengers on a ship sailing from Panama to California.

17

THE GOOD LIFE ROLLS ON

For the rest of the 1920s, Cora and Henry continued to live as popular, well-known members of Hollywood high society. Henry's natural flair for drama led him to associate with the actors in the film industry. He also counted as his clients and friends several producers, directors and owners from the film studios in Hollywood.

By the late 1920s the oil exploration industry in the U.S. had expanded greatly. The demand for oil was constantly rising as the motor car became the standard means of transport. New oil fields were being discovered all the time and anyone with the foresight or luck to own land where new wells were viable made a fortune. On the other hand, plenty of people bought land speculatively, often paying far more than the land was worth, and too often their exploratory wells produced nothing but costs from the drillers and the other necessary employees. As many speculators lost a fortune as those who made spectacular profits.

Henry relied on his contacts with oil insiders in Texas to find likely properties for investment. He put quite a lot of his own money and the money of his client-investors into speculative ventures in West Texas, the most recent area for new oil exploration.

But his investments there proved far less lucrative than his earlier ventures. In the end, Henry just about broke even – he would have made more money by putting it into bank deposits.

Henry worked hard for his clients and often travelled to inspect potential investment properties in Texas and elsewhere. He reasoned that his personal presence at such sites, and his ability to question their owners, were important aspects of his service to his customers, as well as providing him with a sound basis for his own investments. Of course, the downside of his travels was that he was not at home with Cora and Maddy as much as he would have liked.

He also began to devise schemes for investment in new oil fields in Venezuela and Mexico, which were potentially worth a fortune, but with a higher level of risk, partly because of the instability of the governments in those countries and partly because of the higher costs of development. A number of existing fields were located in coastal salt marshes, but much larger oil reserves were to be found offshore, under the seabed, and it would require new, expensive technology to exploit those reserves; the increased cost of transport to refineries in the U.S. also had to be considered. Unfortunately for Henry, none of his schemes in Latin American oil fields ever made a profit. He and his clients lost quite a lot of money on them.

Nevertheless, throughout the 1920s, Henry's original source of income, The Three Sisters property in Texas, continued to pay out enormous sums each month. He could afford to speculate in other areas because he could rely on his oil royalties for more than enough money to cover any losses.

He and Cora continued to host regular parties at La Paloma, attended by the leading stars and studio owners of the film industry. They also began to invite select groups of movie people to accompany them to Acapulco each year. Their hacienda had enough rooms to accommodate at least six couples, and any other guests could find rooms in the little town. It's thought that it was Henry and Cora who established the idea of Acapulco as a fashionable place to holiday among people in the Californian entertainment industry. And, indeed, other entrepreneurs from the 1940s through to the 1960s ensured that idea became a reality and sleepy little Acapulco developed into a playground for Hollywood movie stars.

18

HENRY ALMOST LOSES EVERYTHING

In 1923, Henry and Cora celebrated their tenth wedding anniversary. It was a memorable occasion for them both. Their life together was as happy as either of them could hope for: they had a beautiful, loving young daughter; they mixed socially with the rich and famous; and they had just about everything they wanted that money could buy. Most importantly, they still loved each other deeply; their affection for one another was frequently noted and commented upon by their friends in the often-superficial world of "Tinseltown".

Privately, Henry often thought to himself what a wondrous change Cora had made in him. When he met her, he had been living a hedonistic existence, sleeping with a different woman almost every night and following in the footsteps of Don Juan and other famous seducers and pleasure-seekers from history and literature. However, from the very moment he had first seen Cora, he had never wanted or needed any other lover. His previous focus on himself and his fleeting moments of pleasure had matured into a stable and ongoing happiness as a husband and a father.

For a decade of contented marriage, Henry had been totally faithful to Cora and never considered any kind of extra-marital affair. Unfortunately for the happiness of the Anderson family that began to change in the mid-1920s. Looking back on that time Henry could not really put a finger on the precise moment when he began to be tempted by other women. From the time of their arrival in California Henry's lifestyle involved almost daily working lunches with his clients and potential customers. Most of these people were connected in some way to the Hollywood film industry and, as often as not, Henry found himself eating and drinking with his customers' ambitious young female companions, as well as with the men themselves.

Almost all Henry's clients were men, a fact that simply reflected the social reality of the 1920s. While women were increasingly becoming more independent and more in control of every aspect of their lives, very few of them were prepared to oversee serious financial matters for themselves. Even the richest, most famous Hollywood film actresses, with a few exceptions, were willing to leave their financial affairs in the hands of managers and husbands. In fact, those who didn't marry other movie stars often married their managers.

Henry could count his independent female clients on one hand: a couple of actresses, one widow of a film producer, and the ex-wife of a film studio executive. Otherwise, his clientele was entirely male. While he enjoyed the company of actors and cultivated their friendship, Henry found early on in his time in Hollywood that most of the money there was under the control of the producers and the owners of the major studios. Consequently, he spent much of his time socializing with the "big money" men, for the obvious reason that they were the ones with the funds to invest.

Many of these investors in movies – producers and studio owners – exercised the power that came with their wealth and took advantage of young female actors trying to break into the industry. Such abuse was not universal but it was widespread. Henry encountered it almost every day as he wined and dined his clients. He was still a handsome man and wealthy enough in his own right to attract the attention of unattached young women. He often felt flattered by their advances but relied on his position as a happily married man to deflect such approaches.

Henry often met clients for dinner in country clubs and fine restaurants, with Cora frequently accompanying him. She was popular in her own right among Henry's business clients and their spouses and partners, and contributed to her husband's success. However, she participated less frequently in Henry's luncheon meetings or in his after-work drinking sessions.

Finally, it happened. After a particularly strenuous sales pitch at a long and very boozy lunch in a Hollywood hotel, Henry realized he'd had one glass of champagne too many. He booked a room to sleep it off for a few hours before heading for home. How he ended up with a beautiful young blonde actress on his arm as he entered the elevator is still not clear to him – but she was there and went with him to his room and into his bed. Several hours later, Henry woke up and realized what he'd done. His shame was deep and intense and he vowed to himself never to let it happen again.

But six months later, it did happen again. This time Henry was quite conscious of what he was doing. Having fallen once it was easy to fall again. What began as an accident, of sorts, became a pattern of behavior. He never had ongoing affairs, but when the opportunity arose for a quick tryst, he seized it.

Like many men, Henry tried to justify his selfish and thoughtless behavior as insignificant and "just some fun". After all, he rationalized, he still loved Cora and as long as she didn't know about his dalliances, no harm was done. Of course, he was deluding himself. She eventually found out.

Cora noticed slight changes in Henry's behavior. Sometimes, he came home later than he used to; sometimes, he seemed distracted and anxious to shower immediately after he arrived; and, sometimes, she thought she could detect the scent of a strange female perfume on Henry's clothing. Finally, she overheard two of her friends furtively whispering about Henry in the ladies' room of a restaurant. When they noticed her, they stopped talking immediately, appeared embarrassed, and quickly left.

Initially she was incandescent with anger, but that gradually subsided into a deep sadness. She resolved to confront her husband and then, depending on his response, decide on a course of action.

It was a weekday in early December 1927 and Henry had been invited by one of his clients for a Christmas drink after work. He arrived home shortly after 8.30 in the evening. Maddy had already gone to bed and, as usual, the kitchen staff had prepared a late supper for him and Cora in the dining room. When he walked in Cora met him with a strange look on her face, one he'd never seen before.

"Henry Anderson, I know you are up to something. Something that's not good for us and our marriage. I want you to tell me everything and then I'll decide what to do. You have hurt me deeply and this won't just go away."

Henry was flabbergasted. He could see that the situation was serious, and he decided to be as open and honest as he could. Denial was not an option.

He grovelled, he pleaded, and he begged, until eventually he revealed to Cora exactly what he'd been doing. He emphasized that as far as he was concerned none of it was serious. He was not having an affair. He was being selfish and indulgent, seeking quick and insignificant pleasure with women who didn't matter to him. He stressed again and again that he never wanted to hurt her; his love for her had never lessened; he would never again be unfaithful to her; and he would never again give her even the slightest reason to doubt his commitment to her and to their marriage, if only she would just give him the chance to prove his love for her again.

Cora had almost always been careful to take her time before making major decisions in her life. The one exception had been her crazy and impetuous agreement to give up her life as a journalist and go off with Henry Anderson. Until now, she hadn't regretted that choice. But now she wasn't so sure. She decided to think carefully about everything Henry had said. She was sure that he had told her the truth and that there wasn't another woman in his life. On the other hand, he had abused her trust in him and that was a serious matter.

Cora made it clear to Henry that she would sleep on her decision, which could only be one of two possibilities: immediate divorce, or she would seek from him a commitment to make the marriage work.

Neither of them slept much that night. After Maddy left for school, Cora once again confronted Henry.

"Henry Anderson, I can't begin to describe how much this has hurt me. I've decided you and I are worth a second chance, although it is going to be really hard for you to regain my full trust and confidence."

Henry reacted with a sigh of relief, mixed with regret.

"I don't expect you to do anything more than remain faithful to me. Always. Show me that you are fully committed to our marriage and I'll willingly forgive you. But I'll never forget what you've done to me and the risk you've taken with the happiness of our family."

Henry mumbled a contrite, "I'm so sorry."

"I heard everything you said last night, both the good and the bad. I don't want any more apologies or promises. I just want you to love me unconditionally and totally for the rest of our lives. I will do my best to get over my hurt and take you back as we were before, but if you're ever unfaithful to me again, our marriage will be over."

All Henry said was, "Cora, *mi amor*, I will never again give you the slightest reason to doubt my love for you."

With that they embraced and clung together for what seemed like many minutes.

Henry was determined to remain faithful to Cora after that and he once again returned to the straight and narrow path he had followed before.

Slowly, and almost imperceptibly, their life together returned to happiness and contentment.

19

MADDY

As soon as Henry and Cora had moved to Los Angeles and bought La Paloma, they found a good primary school nearby and enrolled Maddy.

Maddy was a bright girl, who as a young child had loved playing with her cousins on the Anderson family farm in Texas. At the age of four she was taken to the town of Nogales, Arizona, a place where she made few friends and was often forced to entertain herself. Because she spent most of her time with adults, her language skills and her social awareness were very advanced for a pre-school-aged child.

When the family settled in Los Angeles, Maddy started her formal schooling in a local private primary school run by a lady named Mrs Frieda Johansson. The classes were kept small, and the tuition fees correspondingly large, but the academic preparation offered by Mrs Johansson was second to none and many families in Hollywood sent their daughters there.

Maddy was never an outstanding student. She did well in the subjects she liked – art, drama, music and reading – but was not interested in history, arithmetic, spelling and geography, which was reflected in her rather low grades in those areas. She was reported to be an outgoing, friendly girl, who got on with her classmates well and posed no disciplinary problems for her teachers.

By the end of her time in Mrs Johansson's school, Maddy had developed a love for drama, music and dance. After the family returned from their first visit to Acapulco, early in 1925, Maddy, then ten years old, was enrolled in an extra-curricular dance program at the California International Academy of Dance. She flourished there.

In the autumn of 1927, Maddy was accepted as a student in the exclusive all-girls school, the Bishop Montgomery High School. Founded in 1883 near Hollywood, it was frequented by the children of the film industry elite.

Maddy found the strict and demanding academic standards at Montgomery very difficult. She was not naturally gifted with academic skills, and she struggled to keep up with the pace of learning.

On a warm Sunday morning in July 1929, the Anderson family were enjoying breakfast, as they usually did on a Sunday. Suddenly, in the midst of their normal chit-chat, Maddy dropped a bombshell.

"Mom, Dad, I need to talk to you, seriously. I appreciate all you've done for me, and I want to make you proud, but I don't like Montgomery. I'm not happy there. I don't want to go back in September. Most of the teachers are lovely and I've made a lot of friends, but I know in my heart of hearts it's not the place for me. I've worked hard, but most of my grades haven't been very good and I'm sure I have disappointed you. Next year, I'll have to begin the subjects I need for university and they're much harder."

Henry and Cora looked at each other quizzically, then focused again on their brave, beloved daughter.

"My love is dancing; you both know that and I want to make it my career. I don't need an education at Montgomery. If I could go into a full-time course at the Academy, I know I would do well – and that would make me the happiest girl in the world."

As she finished her obviously well-prepared speech, Maddy's lips began to quiver and she burst into tears.

Henry and Cora were both taken aback by Maddy's request. Cora immediately rose from her chair and put her arms around her sobbing daughter. It was she who had chosen Maddy's school, and she who discussed her schoolwork with her, so inevitably it would fall to her to make a decision about Maddy's request. If the truth be told, Henry, while always being an indulgent, loving father to Maddy, had been quite happy to abdicate responsibility for her upbringing. His time spent traveling to inspect potential investments, and the evenings he spent with clients, left him little time for any meaningful interaction with his daughter. He and Cora had, of course, always discussed important issues, like the choice of school, but overall, Cora made the decisions about Maddy's life.

"Maddy, my darling child, this news is very sudden. I feel we need some time to think about it and discuss it carefully. Your father and I have only ever wanted the best for you – and the very best is your happiness. I can see that you have been thinking about this long and hard and I want you to know that we'll always do our best to help you to succeed, wherever life takes you."

The sobbing girl laid her head on Cora's shoulder and embraced her mother in a tight hug.

"We chose Montgomery for you because we thought it offered the best opportunity to get a good start to your life. The academic education there is second to none. You've met many girls who could be wonderful life-long friends. Still, I, and I'm sure your father, would never force you to return there if it is only going to make you miserable. I promise you, darling, that whatever we decide will be what we think is best for you."

With that, Henry added his support.

"'Teenie,'" he said, using his pet name for Maddy, "I agree with everything Mom has said. You must know that we love you more than anything in the world and we want you to be happy."

Later that day, Henry and Cora reached their decision. They would allow Maddy to leave Montgomery and enrol full-time at the Dance Academy. It seemed clear to them that their daughter was not just acting on a whim but had given her life, and her future, careful consideration. They genuinely wanted her to be happy and, while the life of a dancer might not be as attractive to them as a more conventional choice, they felt they had to support her on her chosen path.

Secretly, Henry was rather proud of his daughter and sympathetic to her proposal. Her attraction to the world of dramatic arts and entertainment was very like his own – but his life had taken him down a road that didn't allow him the chance to pursue such a dream. Cora, who always represented the more practical side to their partnership, had reservations about their decision, but she wanted the best for Maddy. She knew that any other choice would probably be counterproductive.

20

WORRYING SIGNS

Henry, Cora and Maddy spent a week at a beach house owned by one of Henry's Hollywood customers, finishing on the Labor Day weekend of 1929. Monday, 2 September was the official Labor Day holiday, so Henry returned to his office on the Tuesday morning. Young Maddy began her new, full-time course at the California International Academy of Dance the same day.

That day, and for the rest of the week, Henry became aware of worrying developments on the New York Stock Market. The press and the radio were full of reports about the wild gyrations in prices of stocks, especially blue-chip stocks. It appeared likely that the boom in stock prices, which had pushed the Dow Jones average to an all-time high, was stalling and possibly entering a correction phase when prices would begin to fall.

Henry's oil and mineral investments were mostly not listed on the Stock Exchange. He had a small block of shares in Standard Oil that had climbed steadily in price since he bought them, but otherwise he was not personally involved in the stock market.

The same, however, was not true for most of his investors. If the stock market did go into a prolonged decline, many of his clients would be financially badly damaged and that would negatively affect Henry's earnings as an advisor. Still, he was not particularly worried. His main source of income, his 40 per cent ownership in The Three Sisters Oil Company, was not directly affected by fluctuations in the Dow Jones average, although it was true that any long-term decline in the price of oil would drag down his monthly dividends. In any case, he was sure that any market "correction" would not last long and, while his income might suffer for a few months, in the long term the outlook was still rosy.

Six weeks later, things didn't look so positive.

Between the 24th and the 29th of October, the market plunged and rallied in a dizzying cycle. Finally, on Tuesday (known afterwards as "Black Tuesday") the 29th of October, the market crashed. The huge volume of stocks being traded overwhelmed the New York Stock Exchange, and almost every trade substantially reduced the value of the shares. People panicked and raced to dump their stocks. Fortunes were lost in minutes. There were reports of Wall Street investors jumping to their deaths from their high-rise office buildings.

Henry's clients rang him in panic.

"Sell it all – get what you can."

"Get me out of this mess, sell off everything."

"Save me something, Henry – I'm facing ruin."

But there wasn't much Henry could do. He realized the maximum value he could secure for his clients, but in many cases this was a tiny proportion of what they had invested. Henry's own stocks in Standard Oil, which had peaked in value only eight weeks earlier, lost more than 20 per cent of their value in one day and that value was 40 per cent less than their peak price.

The pessimism and the panic were infectious. People with perfectly sound investments, at least at that time, insisted on getting out no matter what they lost. Henry was shaken by the mass flight from stocks. He still felt that he could survive and do reasonably well in the long term because his investments were not so exposed to the wild gyrations of the stock market, but he could see that the future would not be as rosy, nor as reassuring, as it had seemed to be just a few months ago.

As the weeks went by after the great crash, the whole economy began to contract. Money available for lending dried up and banks failed in their hundreds. Unemployment skyrocketed and prices began to drop across the board for all commodities. Ultimately, everyone was affected in some way. Primary producers were badly hit. Farmers went bankrupt in large numbers – they had planted and invested in their farms when prices were high, but now they could hardly find a buyer for their produce, and the prices they did get were far too low to make a profit. The economic depression also badly affected minerals production.

21

DISASTER

As the demand for raw materials dropped and their prices fell, many mining companies were no longer viable and shut down. The great American love affair with the motor car, which had driven the steady rise in oil prices, cooled considerably. The production of automobiles in 1930 was less than in any year since 1926. Correspondingly, the demand for fuel declined and the price of oil dropped.

Henry's income halved and then quartered. By the end of 1932, he was earning little more than 10 per cent of what he had earned in the 1920s. He and Cora were forced to cut back on their lifestyle. The first thing that went was their *ranchero* in Acapulco. They could no longer afford to travel there every year and the running costs, while not great, were more than they could afford. They were lucky to find a buyer at all, and they lost heavily on the sale.

Shortly before the end of 1933, Henry received the kind of news that haunts investors in the oil industry. The four oil wells in Texas owned by The Three Sisters Oil Company, which had continued to produce viable quantities of oil for more than ten years, were losing volume. Even though oil had dropped dramatically in price, those wells still brought in enough oil for some kind of income for Henry and Cora. Now, the wells were drying up. The vast pool of underground oil had been sucked dry and the wells would have to be shut down.

While The Three Sisters still had some minor holdings in other Texas oil fields, and a few speculative land purchases that had never been tested or developed, the company's major financial resource was now gone. Apart from his shares in The Three Sisters, Henry also owned a few properties that were rented for housing by several Arizona mining companies.

The company directors of The Three Sisters Oil Company met in Nogales and decided to wind up the company. Each of the investors walked away with their proportion of the company's investment properties.

This was a disaster for Henry. He now had no secure source of income. He and Cora had led such an extravagant lifestyle that they had spent most of what they earned, as it came in. They put La Paloma on the market. While the movie industry had done better than most during the grim early days of the Great Depression — perhaps the population was still willing to spend its last few dollars on the dreams offered by the silver screen as an antidote to their hard reality — there was no demand for Hollywood mansions in 1934. After the property had been on the market for more than six months, they finally found a buyer. The payment they received from the sale covered the debts which had accumulated during that six-month period. In the end, they were left with a little over $100,000 in the bank — still a sizeable sum, but they had to buy somewhere to live, and they had no obvious major source of future income.

Meanwhile, Maddy's situation was becoming a financial problem for Henry and Cora. The tuition charges at the Academy were high and, with no foreseeable source of income, they could no longer afford to pay them. At the same time, Maddy, now nineteen years old, was well-established as one of the most accomplished dancers there. She was offered a full scholarship to attend a masterclass in Spanish classical dance, folk dance and flamenco in Madrid. The class began in March 1934 and ran for six months. The drawback was that Henry and Cora had to pay for her travel costs and some of her living expenses. The scholarship included only partial board in an apartment.

Despite their strained circumstances, Henry and Cora decided immediately that they would fund Maddy's new opportunity, even if they had to sacrifice elsewhere in their budget. In February 1934, Maddy set out on the trip of her life, traveling by train from Los Angeles to San Antonio, and then on to Mexico City. From there she went by train to Veracruz, where she boarded a ship bound for Spain. Her life had taken a dramatic turn and, from that point on, Madeleine Anderson's future was determined. She would return from Spain an accomplished proponent and practitioner of Spanish dance, and the rest of her life would be a story of travel and performance.

One of Henry's oldest friends and clients in Los Angeles, Hector Saldinas, who had wisely shifted most of his investments from stocks to real estate at the first signs of market instability in 1929, offered Henry and Cora a lease on a modest bungalow in McCollum Street, Silver Lake, just a few blocks off Sunset Boulevard. They moved into their new house in July 1934.

The Saldinas family had good connections in Hermosillo, the capital of the Mexican state of Sonora. Hector's eldest son, Oscar, had spent almost half his life there, living with relatives and working in the mining industry. Guided by Oscar Saldinas, Henry decided to try his luck there.

He and Cora agreed that, for the time Henry would be in Mexico, she should travel to San Antonio to visit their families.

That way, she would not be left on her own in Los Angeles in a new and unfamiliar house. Cora would have been isolated from their previous social contacts, in a house a fraction of the size of their beloved La Paloma.

They both set out on their respective journeys in September 1934.

22

THE MEXICAN PIPE DREAM

Henry had always been an optimist, a dreamer. Despite the heavy blows he had suffered, he was still convinced that he would be able to find another pot of gold – black or yellow – somewhere. He'd convinced himself that all he had to do was to find the right opportunity to set himself up again financially. With nothing likely in Texas in the near future, nor in Arizona, the only other possibility, he believed, was a mine in Mexico.

Most of the old gold and silver mines in Mexico had opened during the early stages of Spanish conquest – but some dated even further back to the rule of the Aztecs. Many of these mines were re-opened between about 1885 and 1925 and proved to be valuable investments, with the advances in mining technology making them viable once again.

Still, technical problems – often associated with flooding – and low prices due to the depression eventually led to the re-opened mines closing again in the late 1920s, but only after they had provided their owners with a good profit.

Henry was certain that he would be able to procure even more modern technology to solve the flooding problems and rejuvenate several profitable mines. He no longer had the cash reserves himself, so he needed capital investment to finance the operations.

For several months before he set out for Mexico, Henry did all he could to secure the financial backing he needed. He had a brochure printed that extolled the potential of the mining industry in Sonora. It quoted historical figures that laid out the staggering amount of money that was once made there and, Henry argued, could still be made there with prudent management and technological expertise.

Henry worked out that he needed a base capital of about $50,000. With that, he could hire a reliable mining engineer and survey a large number of potential mine sites. In addition, he would need at least another $50,000 to rejuvenate several of the most promising mines and bring them up to the point where they were producing a profit. After that, Henry reasoned, the scheme would be able to fund itself; the profits could be used to pay dividends to his investors and to open up new mines.

Most of his former clients who were still wealthy enough to consider such investments were in the motion picture industry. Owners, producers, star actors. Henry approached them all with his proposition. Eventually, he managed to assemble a consortium of investors who might be willing to risk that kind of money. The group agreed that, as soon as he could provide them with firm evidence that the proposal was viable – namely, fully costed plans for each mine, supported by a formal mining engineer's report – then they would provide the first tranche of $50,000. Once Henry could demonstrate that at least one mine was operational and functioning as planned, they would supply him with the second tranche of $50,000.

Henry had hoped to secure more funds up front. His own financial resources were dwindling fast, with his only income provided by a few shares in the Texas oil fields that were still producing, and his holdings provided only a small proportion of the dividends from each well. He probably had just enough money to cover his and Cora's daily living expenses, but certainly not enough for him to bring his scheme to the point where his investors' money would be released.

Desperate for quick money, and convinced that his scheme would eventually bring him enormous profits and restore their previous lifestyle in the Hollywood social whirl, Henry borrowed $25,000 from his friend Hector Saldinas. It was a deal made on a handshake between good friends, but Henry had to put up something as collateral. All he had was his small holding of oil shares and his third of the Anderson family farm in Texas – which he had inherited from his mother when she died in 1915. It was collectively worth far less than the money borrowed, but it was all Henry had. Hector accepted it as cover for the loan.

Henry knew he was taking a grave risk. Failure would mean bankruptcy. Nevertheless, in his natural optimism, he discounted that possibility. He would succeed. He and Cora would return to living in a Hollywood mansion and, eventually, own a grand hacienda in Mexico. For the first time since their marriage, Henry made a serious financial decision without discussing it with Cora. On the one hand, he didn't want to worry her, and, on the other, he was afraid that she would not agree to him risking everything they had on his Mexican mining scheme.

23

HENRY'S POSITIVE SPIN ON EVERYTHING

Henry tossed and turned in his stretcher bed on the medivac plane. The long, distressing dreams were disturbing his sleep. As he approached consciousness, he cried out and began to mumble incoherently, moaning and twitching.

A nurse immediately administered an injection of sedatives, and, within a few minutes, Henry was, once again, calm and breathing steadily. The jet flew on towards Texas.

★ ★ ★

Oscar. Yes, his friend, Oscar Saldinas. A lovely young man. Bright and cheerful, they always got on brilliantly. He and Oscar worked well together. As soon as Henry explained his plans, Oscar enthusiastically joined in.

Oscar introduced Henry to an American mining engineer and geologist, Carl Goedhardt, who had recently arrived in Hermosillo from San Francisco. Henry explained his situation to Carl, who agreed to join the scheme, in return for a share of the potential profits. This, of course, suited Henry, who wouldn't have to pay an engineer's salary out of his own pocket.

For many weeks, Henry, Oscar and Carl travelled around the mining areas near Hermosillo. They found several promising sites in the old La Colorada and San Javier mining areas. These sites were regarded as no longer viable, so Henry was able to negotiate the right to re-open them at very little cost. They also found mines in the old Zubiate and Ahogade areas that were flooded. Nevertheless, Henry was sure they could be drained by large, modern pumps and re-opened. The mining engineer refused to commit himself to that proposal, so Henry kept it in mind as a personal proposition, something he might pursue later when he had enough money.

In the end, Henry felt that he had enough of the required evidence to convince the Hollywood bunch, as he called them, to release the first $50,000. Carl wrote his technical reports and Henry expanded on them with projected profit figures and full costings for the proposed developments.

It was January 1935, and Henry had just sent off the reports to the Hollywood bunch. He decided to write Cora a long letter that would bring her up to speed on his proposed investments. He had done his best to write to her every day when he was in Hermosillo, but when he was in mining country, it was impossible to post letters with any certainty that they would be delivered.

What follows is the full text of Henry's letter, which was discovered in a box of documents in 2019:

HOTEL RAMOS

Hermosillo, Son. January 6, 1935.

Dearest Cora,

Just returned from a trip with a mining engineer from San Francisco who is down here sampling some of the old mines in this district, and which explains why you have not heard from me. We spent a couple of days at La Colorada, but it is almost a ghost town at present, with very few inhabitants and most of the buildings unoccupied. There is probably not one sixth as many people in the town as there were when you were there, thirty years ago. We also visited the old mines at Zubiate. I was away altogether for six days, and Oscar was waiting for me when I got back. He is here ready to open up a couple of rich mines in the San Javier district; that is, as soon as that Hollywood bunch puts up the necessary money, which they are supposed to do within the next ten days. I am also waiting on additional funds for the old Ahogade mine, since it will be necessary to purchase and install a large pump to take care of the water. These delays are aggravating, but cannot be helped, and meanwhile I am keeping busy examining different mines and prospects and lining up everything so as to be ready to start operations immediately when the necessary dinero is in the bank. You have no idea how many wonderful propositions there are in this country; principally because Americans have not been coming in here to any great extent for the past twenty years, being afraid of revolutions, bandits, Yaqui Indians, etc. But Oscar and I are not afraid, and therefore we are bound to make some money down here, and big money at that.

Recently we made the acquaintance of a Mexican here in Hermosillo (of very good family and standing) who owns a rich placer[2] mine in the Yaqui Indian country and who attempted to work this mine last month, with the help of four Mexican peon miners, but after being on the ground only a few days he and the others were run out by the Yaquis. As you know, these

---

[2] A placer mine involves the mining of gold deposits with a sluice.

Yaquis are bad hombres and they hate the Mexicans because the Mexicans took away from them all their rich valley farming lands, the same as the Americans robbed the American Indians of their lands. For this reason, it is really dangerous to mine in Yaqui territory unless there is a fairly large group of men in camp, with plenty of rifles and ammunition. Therefore, our friend, with only four peons in camp and two rifles, was forced to make a hasty departure, but before he was run out, he worked the mine, with only one small placer machine, for two days and took out over four hundred dollars in gold. I personally talked with the man to whom he sold this gold, and I know he is telling the truth. Well, to make a long story short, this man wants me and Oscar to accompany him on a return trip to the mine; this time taking along six good men, each one armed with rifle, revolver and fifty rounds of ammunition, so we can hold our own in case the Yaquis attack us. We have wired for Bill Barker, the aviator, and if he will fly down here in his plane and go along with us, I think we will take on the proposition, especially since we are merely marking time here now waiting for action on the part of the Hollywood bunch. This looks like quick money, and that is what we are after. Señor Rodriguez, our friend who owns the mine, has a letter from the Mexican general in charge of troops in that district, granting him permission to enter Yaqui territory, and if necessary, we can no doubt get the general to furnish us with a small troop of soldiers in the event the Yaquis are on the war-path when we arrive at the mine. If nothing happens to prevent, we will leave Hermosillo within four or five days; but if you should write to Mrs Saldinas or Oscar's Nana, do not say anything about this contemplated trip, because Mr Saldinas does not want Oscar to go into the Yaqui country. I thought I had better write you, though, so you will know where I am in the event you do not hear from me for two or three weeks. Cora, mi amor, this is a real chance to come back with some quick money, so do not write back that it is too dangerous or anything of the sort. I am determined to go, and so is Oscar, and we will bring back the dinero too.

I also will be glad to get back to L.A. with you and Teenie, but I am going to stay down here until I get one good proposition on a dividend basis; then I can return and enjoy life. Meanwhile, if you and Teenie will stay there for a month or two and just enjoy yourselves visiting all the home-folks, I am sure I will be ready to send you tickets to return to Los Angeles and I will join you there; but as stated above, I want to remain here until I meet with some measure of success, even if it takes a couple of months longer. I am especially anxious to do this, because we received word about two weeks ago that the Miami Copper Company was going to close down on the 1st of January, which means losing that casa and the revenue therefrom. However, their shutdown will be only temporary and I will get back the business as soon as they start up production again.

Phillips sent you a check about three weeks ago, but mailed it to McCollum Street; therefore, if you have not received same, please write Mrs Saldinas and ask her to forward it to you.

I know you are enjoying your visit with Mr Brown, Eleanor and Jim Bob. Give them all my best regards and tell Jim Bob he should be here to accompany us on the trip to the Yaqui Indian country. Will write you again before I leave. Hope Teenie is with you by this time and, if so, tell her to answer my last letter. And don't forget to give my love to each and every one of the family when you see them. If I have any luck here, I may decide *to join you in San Antonio and we can all three return to L.A. together. How is that, Cora Darling?*

Todo mi amor para ti y Teenie.

Como siempre,

H.

Am also sending a few Kodak pictures. These are the same that I sent to Emma recently.

24

REALITY BITES

Henry was still in a deep sleep. But in his dreams he remembered his letter clearly. When he had written it, he was still quite certain that he would have the money from his Hollywood investors very soon. However, he also remembered his desperation for some short-term quick cash for his proposal to enter hostile territory to re-open the mine while risking a Yaqui Indian attack.

As it happened, their aviator friend signed a contract with a major motion picture company to ferry staff and cast members from Los Angeles to a remote location in Arizona, so he was unavailable for several months. Henry and Oscar decided that a long overland trip was too risky. They would have to travel for several days through Yaqui country before they got to the mine site, and they would be vulnerable to attacks and ambushes the whole way. In the end, even the lure of quick money was not worth the dangers they would face. And so, the plan to help señor Rodriguez work his mine in Yaqui country came to nothing.

Nevertheless, in his drugged sleep the fitful dreams descended into fearful images of attacks by marauding Yaqui warriors, with Oscar and him desperately trying to defend themselves.

Eventually that passed, and his dream-memories became more stable again. He recalled the long, boring wait for a reply from his potential Hollywood investors, and another trip to visit mines that might be viable and available to the northeast of Hermosillo.

This boredom also led him down another, less honorable, and very risky path.

He had never forgotten his shock and distress when Cora caught him cheating on her, back in 1927. He remembered, clearly, every word that had been spoken that night. In particular, he recalled all too well the empty, sinking feeling in the pit of his stomach when he realized that his selfish dalliances might have destroyed the true happiness of his marriage.

Nevertheless, after another three years of total fidelity to Cora, Henry once more began pursuing the fleeting pleasures of sexual encounters with other women. He tried to convince himself that he needed the relief and the boost to his ego that casual sex could provide. It countered the stresses and worries he faced as his income, and with it his social standing, continued to decline.

Henry had always been impetuous, and tended to avoid serious introspection, especially when he understood it might lead to guilt and regret. He preferred to escape his problems through a superficial and temporary solution in the arms of a woman who was not his wife. Nevertheless, whenever he was once again alone after one of his brief sexual encounters, he could not escape the uncomfortable pangs of guilt.

He had learned the hard way to be extra-carefully discreet and, while Cora sensed that he might be falling into his old habits again, she had no proof. When she questioned him, Henry flatly denied her suspicions and feigned hurt and distress at being so falsely accused.

Now, on his own in Mexico, far away from Cora, Henry enthusiastically resumed his constant pursuit of bed-time pleasures. For a while, at least, he could immerse himself in the escapism of sexual seduction and conquest, postponing the pressure to confront the bitter reality of his financial position.

Unfortunately for Henry, his would-be investors in Hollywood were not convinced by his reports and evidence and decided to withdraw from their deal unconditionally. He was left holding the rights to develop a few mines that were worthless without a large injection of capital that he did not have.

In desperation, Henry wrote dozens of letters, begging his would-be investors to reconsider their decision. Again, unfortunately for Henry, in 1935 most people were very wary of risking any amount of money – and he could find no one willing to part with the amount he required.

Henry had failed, miserably. He had lost everything. He owed his friend Hector Saldinas far more than he could repay. Bankruptcy looked like his only option.

25

THE FAMILY EXPANDS

Henry's use of "Teenie", his pet name for Maddy, in his long letter to Cora, also recalled for him an aching desire to see her again after her trip to Spain. He loved her dearly and was bursting with pride at her dancing achievements – but he hadn't seen her for almost a year, and longed to once again give her a hug and a warm, fatherly greeting.

Poor Henry. At that time, he could not know that he would never see Cora again. And he would only talk to Maddy very briefly and see her once more, many years later and from a distance. From those brief encounters, he learned everything he was to know about the circumstances of his wife and daughter in 1935 and thereafter.

His feverish imagination now reconstructed an account from the sources his memory could access. He could not be certain about every detail, but he was sure that things must have gone something like the account that follows.

★ ★ ★

Shortly after she received Henry's letter, Cora received a telephone call from her daughter. Maddy excitedly announced that she would be arriving in San Antonio on the train from Mexico City the following day. She couldn't wait to see her mother again and tell her all her news.

That next afternoon, Cora answered the door and was immediately enveloped in the most forceful and joyous hug she had ever received from Maddy. For what seemed like several minutes, they simply clung to each other, sobbing with happiness. Then Cora became aware that Maddy was not alone. Behind her on the front porch, stood a most handsome, slim, dark-haired man.

"Mom, I have so much to tell you, but, first, you need to meet my new husband, Luis. I'm sorry I didn't tell you before, but we wanted it to be a surprise. I didn't want a big family wedding, so we simply pledged our vows in the City Hall in Mexico City and now we are man and wife and have been for ten whole days! Mom, this is my husband, Luis Lopez."

Luis proved to be a delightful young man, born in Mexico City but raised and educated in San Antonio. He had met Maddy in Madrid, where she was learning about Spanish classical dance. He was a talented musician, competent on the piano and on several stringed instruments: guitar, mandolin, and several similar instruments used in Spanish folk music. Before he met Maddy, he had already begun to learn Spanish and Latin American dance forms and, together, they forged a pairing that was quickly recognized as a most formidable exponent of Spanish dance – classical, folk and flamenco. They had already played to sold-out audiences in the *Teatro Real* in Madrid, and they had just come from a triumphant season with the *Ballet Folklórico de México* in the National Theater of Mexico in Mexico City.

Cora was overwhelmed by all the new information. The young daughter she had sent off to Spain almost a year ago had returned, not only a married woman but an internationally acclaimed dancer, who, with her new husband and dance partner, had already signed up for a tour of Mexico and Central America, to be followed by a grand tour of the United States.

Cora, Maddy and Luis spent the rest of the afternoon and most of the evening talking excitedly, getting to know one another and discussing the future plans of the young couple. Cora introduced them to her stepfather – her mother had died two years earlier – and her stepsister and her son. They would stay with Mr Brown and his daughter, Eleanor, for the next two weeks or so, during which they would also visit Henry's family in Sutherland Springs and La Vernia.

It is easy to imagine, in such a situation, that the girl's mother might regard her new and unexpected son-in-law with some reserve. But Cora immediately warmed to Luis, and he to her. It soon felt as if this new and previously unannounced marriage was as familiar and comfortable as a tried and tested relationship of many years.

After their visit to San Antonio, Maddy and Luis were booked to embark on a lengthy tour of Mexico and Central America. They would return to the U.S. later in the year to begin a new tour which would take them to thirty-two of the forty-eight states in eight months. They planned to arrive in Southern California at the end of 1935 to plan and rehearse their full program for the grand U.S. tour. Their first performance on that tour would be in San Diego, California, on 8 January, 1936.

And then, this happy and optimistic family scene was shattered by a knock at the door.

"Telegram for Mrs Anderson."

Cora signed the form and took the telegram from the delivery boy. It was from Henry.

Cora, mi amor, I have bad news. Stop. Hollywood bunch backed out. Stop. Please try to get money from Mr Brown and my family. Stop. I need twenty-five thousand by next week. Stop. The alternative is bankruptcy. Stop. Without urgent cash, I am ruined. Stop. Please, please do what you can. Stop. Love, Henry

26

THE FAMILY DISINTEGRATES

Cora pondered the starkly worded telegram. She had always known that Henry's schemes and dreams were risky, but she had trusted him to put enough money aside to protect them from total ruin. She now realized that her trust had been misplaced.

With a sudden clarity, Cora now saw that Henry would never change. He would forever chase dreams and propositions that had little chance of success. She could no longer ride on Henry's financial roller coaster, especially now that it had come hurtling down from its high point and, despite twists and turns, was unlikely ever to rise again. He was as careless and reckless with their money as he had been with their wedding vows. She knew that the best option for her was to leave Henry to chase rainbows on his own.

Cora's tears began to slide down her cheeks, landing on the telegram. She had loved Henry Anderson unconditionally and their life together had been a marvellous adventure. They had climbed to the highest levels of social standing and mixed with the rich and famous. The marriage had produced a beautiful, loving daughter and they had been able to help her become the internationally acclaimed dancer she now was. But that was all in the past. For her, their marriage had no future hope. She would have to move on with her life, somehow. For the time being, she knew she was welcome to stay with her stepfather and stepsister. Her longer-term future was impossible to predict. Perhaps, she would go back to a job in journalism.

"Mom, what's wrong?"

Cora realized that, in her sorrow and self-absorption, she had forgotten about her child standing next to her.

"I'm sorry, my darling. I've let my emotions overcome me. I've never experienced a day like today – and I'm sure I never will again. First, the wonderful news about you and Luis – your marriage and your career together; and now, news from your father that he has finally wasted our last dollar on his mad Mexican schemes and now wants me to find the money to bail him out of debt. When the money was pouring in, we were so happy, and life was a wondrous adventure. Now that we have nothing left, I'm afraid that I can't see any kind of future together for me and your father. I can never trust him again and the only solution, I'm afraid, is divorce."

With that, Maddy's tears began to fall. She had always loved her mother and father dearly, but she realized that her father's irresponsible risk-taking had ruined her mother's life. Her affection for her father evaporated in an instant. She could never forgive him for his thoughtless and selfish conduct, and she quickly decided never to see or communicate with him again. Ironically, in her impetuous behavior, Maddy was much more like her father than her mother.

"Oh, Mom, I love you more than words can say. Luis and I will be here for you from now on. We will look after you forever, won't we, Luis, my love?"

"Of course, *mi amor*. Your mother will always have a place with us."

The young man was not completely aware of all that was happening around him in his new family. He and Maddy had, of course, talked about her family – her mother, who had raised her and who was her rock, and her father, who had always been kind and generous to her, even though he had spent much of his time away from the family, pursuing business deals and investment opportunities. He could understand his young wife's protective embrace of her mother, which he was happy to share.

The rest of the evening was a strange mixture of smiles and tears, as they recalled happy times in the past and began to discuss the future. By the end of the night, it was agreed that Cora would accompany Maddy and Luis on their upcoming tours. They needed a manager and someone to offer them guidance and an objective opinion when required. And someone to look after their travel arrangements, accommodation and financial affairs, which neither of them was interested in doing. Cora agreed to try this plan on a trial basis. After their Central American tour, they could all decide whether to continue with the arrangement.

The next morning, Cora wrote Henry a long letter. She explained that his behavior was no longer acceptable to her and that his selfish wasting of their money was the last straw. She would be lodging divorce papers soon.

She let him know that Maddy was back from Spain and that they had decided to go off together for a while. She did not tell him about Maddy's marriage, nor about her successful dancing partnership with Luis, nor about their arrangement with her to manage their career. But she did warn Henry not to try to find them. If, and when, they wanted to see him again, they would contact him. Finally, she suggested that he write to his brother, Rufus, who was willing and able to send Henry enough money for a trip back home to Texas. Then she closed the letter with a postscript thanking him for all the good times they had and wishing him well in the future.

When they had begun to perform as a dance team, Maddy adopted the stage name "Laia". Her favorite teacher in Madrid had the name Laia and Maddy thought it had a wonderful, melodious sound. The young dancers embarked on their career as "Laia and Luis". After Cora left Henry and joined them as their manager, Maddy stopped referring to herself by her birth name. From then on, she was known as Laia M. Lopez. Perhaps this gesture signalled that she had severed all ties with her father.

The tour of Mexico and Central America was a resounding success for the young dance team. Once again at the National Theater in Mexico City, *Laia y Luis* received the adulation of the audience, gave multiple encores and received bouquets of flowers from their fans. They danced their way around the cities of Mexico, receiving rave reviews and standing ovations wherever they performed. The same was true in Guatemala, Honduras, El Salvador, Nicaragua, Costa Rica and Panama.

After their last performance in Panama City, they boarded a cruise ship for a leisurely voyage back to the U.S.

Cora and Maddy spent a nostalgic day in Acapulco, reviving happy memories and noting how the little town was beginning to show signs of tourist development along the shore of the bay. They arrived in San Diego on 12 December 1935, and soon after that began a most successful tour of the U.S. and Canada. Laia and Luis were now launched on a career that included nationwide tours, appearances in Hollywood movies, and parts in Broadway stage productions. Cora was at their side for much of it, managing their finances and looking after bookings, accommodation and the countless other requirements of traveling performers.

27

HENRY HEADS FOR HOME

Henry would never forget his overwhelming sadness and self-loathing when he read Cora's letter. Deep in his heart, Henry's pangs of guilt were accompanied by feelings of sympathy for Cora's unhappy situation, which, he could not deny, was his fault. But Henry was also a proud, vain man. Part of him was disappointed with Cora for not helping him to find some money.

Even in the face of his utter failure and disgrace, Henry still harbored a belief that, somehow, he could turn his fortunes around. All he needed was good luck with one Mexican gold mine, and he'd be back on track realizing his previous life as a rich, successful businessman and investor. He also harbored the unrealistic belief that, when Lady Luck once again smiled at him and he regained his former fortune and social status, he would also manage to repair the rift with Cora and return to a happy family life with her and Maddy.

Henry looked at himself in his bathroom mirror in the Ramos Hotel in Hermosillo. He saw the undisputed lines of age, despite his relative youth. It was December 1935 and he was forty-four.

He was down to his last $1,000 in cash, and he owed Hector Saldinas $25,000. Henry packed his bag, checked out of the hotel, and went to the train station. There he bought a one-way ticket to San Antonio.

His first priority was to find a job, any job, as long as it was half-way well-paid. That way, he could start paying off his debt to Hector, while keeping his eyes open for possible investment opportunities in the oil or minerals sector. Basically, he had no capital to invest; he was sure, though, that if the right proposition came along, he'd find the money somewhere, somehow. Unfortunately, this was not a very realistic plan in the mid-1930s.

When he arrived in San Antonio, Henry's first place to visit was the house belonging to Mr Jonathon Brown, Cora's stepfather. He was met at the door by Cora's stepsister, Eleanor, who was cool to the point of rudeness. Obviously, he was looking for Cora and Maddy, but Eleanor had been sworn to secrecy and only divulged that while they had been there, they had left months ago. She had no contact address for them.

Henry then made his way by bus to Sutherland Springs, getting a lift from the bus stop to the Cleaver farm, where his twin sister, Emma, lived. Sweaty and covered in dust, Henry climbed the wooden steps to the front porch and knocked at the screen door. When Emma saw who was there, she dropped the tea towel and the tray of cookies she'd just taken out of the oven onto the kitchen table and ran to embrace him.

Taking his hand, she led him to the spare bedroom so he could freshen up and put on clean clothes. By the time Henry emerged, Emma's three children, James Alfred, Rawson, and little Annie, were waiting to give him their excited welcomes, all talking at once, tugging on his sleeves and his trouser legs, looking for his attention. They all sat down in chairs on the screen porch, with glasses of freshly made lemonade and those warm cookies.

Emma explained that the farm was struggling to make ends meet because of the low prices for farm produce. They grew corn and watermelons, which thrived in the sandy soil, but they were lucky to make even a few dollars from them. They had six milk cows, and they grew grass for hay in the fallow field each year. Emma also had a small flock of almost three dozen chickens. She made a bit of extra money selling milk, butter and eggs at the local market.

Clarence had left three weeks previously for a six-month job working in the Venezuelan oil fields. It was hard and dangerous, but it paid better than most jobs. He'd spent some time there two years earlier, so when his former boss contacted him with the offer of a new six-month contract, he immediately accepted. It was hard on both Emma and Clarence to be separated, and the children missed their father when he was away, but his oil field income was keeping them afloat.

Henry briefly considered getting a job like Clarence's, but he had never had a job that required hard, physical labor and he wasn't sure he would be able to do it.

Emma told him that their younger brother, Rufus, and his wife Lee had sold their farm in La Vernia and bought a restaurant in the coastal town of Port Lavaca. There were several small oil fields in that area that were in the early stages of development, and this interested Henry. He was also fascinated to hear that some geologists were predicting that huge deposits of oil lay under the seabed of the Gulf of Mexico. The water was not particularly deep there, but, unlike the similar offshore oil fields in Venezuela and Mexico, which were quite close to the shoreline, the most likely sites near Texas and Louisiana were miles offshore and the oil industry had not yet developed the technology to exploit such potential sources for oil and natural gas.

Henry decided to travel to Port Lavaca, both to see his brother and sister-in-law and to check out the possibilities for work and investment in the area.

28

A TRIP TO THE COAST

After several relaxing days spent with Emma and her children, Henry caught the San Antonio-to-Victoria bus, which stopped at Sutherland Springs and every other little town along the way.

In his deepest of dreams, Henry recalled trying to amuse himself and deal with his boredom on that slow journey all those years ago, by dredging up memories and stories about each little town where they stopped.

La Vernia, the stop before he boarded the bus, was a small crossroads settlement, near which several of Henry's relatives had owned land at one time or another – including the old farm belonging to his brother Rufus.

Stockdale had a major livestock saleyard with cattle sales held every Tuesday. It also boasted a popular, live-music dance hall that attracted young people from rural properties for miles around to its weekly Saturday night dance. Henry had met plenty of lovely farm girls there in his youth.

Nixon was the largest of the little towns before Cuero, because it had a rail siding with facilities for loading livestock onto the trains and a large grain elevator for storing the harvested grain before shipping it out by rail.

Then there was Smiley. No one knew why it was called Smiley, unless it had been founded way-back by some old man named Smiley. It was known only for its poultry sheds and their attendant odor. Farms with poultry sheds for chickens and turkeys spread out along the highway for a couple of miles on each side of Smiley, where the only building of any consequence was the poultry processing plant. Once you'd been there, you'd never forget the smell.

Henry was amazed that the bus even stopped at Westhoff, a tiny settlement with one store, which also had a gasoline pump out front, and a dance hall used regularly by German and Czech polka bands. He remembered the old joke:

"Why do they call it Westhoff?"

"Cause the longer you stay there, the werst-off you get."

Cuero, on the other hand, was the largest town between San Antonio and Victoria. Like Smiley, it was also famous for its poultry production – especially turkeys. Every year, Cuero had a turkey festival that culminated in a crazy parade known as the Cuero Turkey Trot, when farmers and their families valiantly tried to drive their unruly flocks of turkeys through the streets.

Henry's brother, Rufus, had tried raising turkeys for a while, but he soon gave up. In his opinion, the turkeys were all hiding when God gave out the brains. He reckoned they were so stupid that until they were about twenty weeks old, if a shower of rain blew up, they would all run out of their sheds and stick their open beaks in the air, and in a moderate thunderstorm, a farmer could lose his whole flock by drowning!

Yes, that Cuero Turkey Trot had been some experience. Large flocks of turkeys, one after the other, were herded down Main Street – but, unfortunately, they didn't really take to being herded.

Every now and then, one would bolt and make a dash into an open door, any door. Shops, residences, even the police station, were all the same to a turkey. Usually, a young child would be dispatched to drive the escapee back out, when it might, or might not, rejoin the rest of its flock.

And then there was the problem of the turkey poo. Turkeys are never too fussy about where they deposit their faeces. This was very evident after the Turkey Trot, when the whole of Main Street, along with front lawns, porches and even hallways were splashed with turkey poo. One year, a particularly brazen turkey bolted straight into the police station foyer, where, frightened by the shouts of the desk sergeant, it proceeded to fly up to the main desk where it left an amazingly large deposit. In subsequent years, the police station kept its screen door shut.

Yes, Henry smiled, he remembered that Turkey Trot, not so much for the chaotic parade itself, but for the wonderful dance that evening in Cuero Hall and his introduction to the joys of sex later that night with Jennie Waterford, a distant cousin who took a shine to him.

The bus finally stopped in the large market town of Victoria, the county seat of Victoria County, with a lovely central park or plaza, and an imposing granite building that housed the law courts and the county offices.

Henry just had time for a quick sandwich and a cool drink before he boarded another bus for the short 30-mile trip to Port Lavaca.

He had never been to Port Lavaca before, so he wasn't sure what to expect. It was a small coastal town with several good harbors dredged out of Lavaca Bay. In fact, the local dredging company, Barker, Smith and Sons, was beginning to make a name for itself as a major operator throughout the Texas Gulf Coast region and beyond. There were plenty of shrimp boats, some in large fleets and a few owned by individual operators, as well as several other commercial fishing boats. The town boasted a fish and shrimp processing plant, with its own ice-making capability.

The small town center included a cinema, a drug store with a soda fountain, several clothing shops for men and women, some small cafés, and a Woolworths "five-and-ten-cent" store. Port Lavaca was also the terminus for a railway that connected it to Victoria, used exclusively for freight transport in those days. In addition to hosting a healthy seafood industry, Port Lavaca was surrounded by acres of cotton fields in all directions and was served by no less than three cotton gins, all of which worked flat out at cotton-picking time. Iced-down seafood and bales of cotton were sent north on the rail line.

The Sea Shell Restaurant was the best establishment of its kind in Port Lavaca, and it was this restaurant that Rufus and his wife, Lee, now owned and operated. The bus station was next door to the Sea Shell, so Henry only had to claim his case and walk the short distance to the front door.

It was late afternoon, and the cooks and wait staff were preparing for the evening meal rush. Rufus spotted Henry as soon as he stepped through the door and rushed over to him from behind the long lunch counter. They hadn't seen each other for more than three years. The brothers sat down at an empty table; Rufus brought them each a coffee, which was refilled several times before he rose and drove Henry to the house he and Lee had bought. It was a grand old two-storey wooden-framed house, with a peaked roof and an imposing entrance porch with four large columns under its roof. Lee embraced Henry and showed him to a spare room on the second floor.

The Anderson house was big, and it had to be. In addition to Rufus and Lee, there were three children – Rufus Jr, usually called

Al, fourteen; Katie Lee, nine; and the baby, Clarence, not yet two. Also living with them was an elderly aunt, Evie, a sister of Rufus's and Henry's mother, and one of Rufus's and Henry's half-sisters, Susie Lee Morgan, whose husband had died in 1931. And now Henry also became a member of the household.

29

HENRY BEGINS TO CLAW BACK HIS LIFE

Initially, Henry's intention was to stay with Rufus and Lee for a few months until he got back on his feet. In the end, however, he stayed with them for almost seven years.

The blows to Henry's ego and his self-esteem caused him deeper and longer-lasting wounds than he'd first realized. It was not easy for such a proud man to accept that he had failed miserably as a businessman and as a husband, and it took him years, rather than weeks or months, to regain his self-confidence.

Henry was very lucky to have a loving, warm family environment for his rehabilitation. Initially, he spent time fishing, often with his eldest nephew Rufus, Jr. He took long walks and concentrated on restoring his physical strength and health, lifting weights again each morning and restricting his diet to natural, healthy food.

Rufus and Lee never asked him to pay any rent. He was their guest for as long as he liked to stay. Aware of their kind generosity, Henry began to relieve Rufus in the restaurant when it was quiet and to provide an extra pair of hands when it was busy. He knew nothing about the food industry, but he was willing and able to man the checkout counter.

One day, a regular customer of the restaurant, Mr Harold Cook, who was the manager of the local railway station, asked if Rufus knew anyone who could type reasonably well and was willing to take on a full-time job as the Western Union telegraph operator in Port Lavaca. The previous occupant of the position had resigned and was moving to California, "to find more interesting and better-paid employment".

Henry didn't have to think twice. He took the job, effective immediately. Now he had a source of income and a chance to save and pay his debts and, eventually, pursue more lucrative employment and investments down the line. Rufus assured him that he could remain with his family as long as he needed. He made it clear that he would still expect no rent money from Henry. It cost them very little to support Henry, and he would still be helping out in the restaurant now and then.

The Western Union office was a comfortable, self-contained room in the railway station that had been built when passenger trains still ran between Port Lavaca and Victoria. The rise in motor car ownership and inexpensive bus services eventually made the railway passenger service unprofitable. Now the railway from Port Lavaca just transported freight. Nevertheless, the nicely appointed offices in the old passenger station didn't go to waste and Henry's new office was one example of that.

In those days, the telegraph system was an essential means of communication. Apart from personal messages that needed to be delivered quickly, the telegraph was used to transmit information around the country, like the prices on the New York Stock Exchange, or the various national market prices for livestock and primary produce. In addition, the local saleyard used the telegraph to inform people in the area about the current livestock prices. The local grain, fruit and vegetable markets did the same.

For that reason, Henry's hours of work in the Western Union Office were longer than in most comparable places of employment. He was expected to be at his telegraph machine by 7 a.m. and he did not close the office until 7 p.m. on weekdays, with an hour-long lunch break from 12 to 1 p.m. On Saturdays, the office was open from 7 a.m. until twelve noon. Normally, the office was closed on Sundays and public holidays, but it was understood that in times of national or local emergencies Henry would operate the telegraph machine as required. In effect, that could be any time of the day or night and any day of the week. He was permanently on call. For this commitment and for the long hours he worked, Henry was paid a good salary – certainly better than he could have earned in any other similar clerical job. And that meant that he could save more money, more quickly.

Henry's busiest time at work was when the national markets closed. Then he would receive long strands of teletype tape that had to be cut up and stuck to the yellow Western Union message forms. For many operators this was a tedious task that took hours, but for Henry, who had lost little of his hand speed and dexterity, the task was managed in a matter of minutes, rather than hours.

Henry quickly fell into a daily routine, centered around the telegraph office. His busy times each day could be frantic, but there were also long periods of time when he had nothing to do. During these slack periods, Henry read voraciously. He read the daily papers from Victoria, San Antonio, Houston and Corpus Christi every day. He also read anything he could get his hands on about the oil and mineral industries, and he kept a record of the fluctuating prices for oil, gold, and silver. Henry was sure that one day he would return to his old life and make money by investing in wells and mines.

On Sundays and public holidays, Henry was happy to help out in the restaurant. He knew that it was the least he could do to repay his brother and sister-in-law's generosity; but he also became aware of the value of having a family in times of need, whether that need was physical, psychological or financial. He came to deeply value the love and support offered to him by his brother and his sister-in-law, which to some extent caused him even more regret for losing the love of his own family.

Once he had settled into his new routine, Henry hardly noticed the time flying by. Years passed surprisingly quickly. Before he knew it, it was 1940. A new decade. There were ominous reports from war-torn Europe – of the fascist states of Germany and Italy against the European democracies of Great Britain, France, and their Allies in the west, and Communist Russia in the east. Despite its best efforts, and once the war began to affect American interests on a large scale, the U.S. was bound to be drawn into the conflict eventually.

The 1940 census documents list the same household members in the Rufus Anderson house as had been there when Henry arrived in 1936. Rufus, Jr – now usually called Al – was still listed as part of the household, even though he had started his medical studies at the University of Texas in Austin. Katie Lee and Clarence were still at school, old Aunt Evie was still there and so was Susie Lee Morgan. On the census form, Henry's relationship to the householder was described as "brother"; in answer to the question of where he was living five years before, in 1935, he replied "Los Angeles, McCollum Street", and he had described his occupation as "business executive". Clearly Henry regarded his daily work as a Western Union operator as a mere bridging period between times when he was, and would be again, wealthy and socially important.

30

HENRY RETURNS TO THE OIL BUSINESS

It was 1942. The whole nation was on a war footing – the young men were overseas, fighting the Nazis and the Japanese Imperial army. Older men and women of all ages were working in the manufacturing and service industry jobs left vacant by departing soldiers. Henry's job at the Western Union Office in Port Lavaca had changed little, though one noticeable difference was the plethora of reports on the progress of the war, which he duly posted each day on the office bulletin board. More distressingly for Henry, he also found himself having to deliver official telegrams to the families of soldiers who had died in combat.

And then, one day out of the blue, Henry received a personal telegram. It would restart his career in the oil industry.

> *To Mr H.R. Anderson, Port Lavaca Texas. Stop. Finally tracked you down. Stop. Dig up your old Three Sisters documents. Stop. Contact Lone Star Oil Company Houston Texas. Stop. Two wells now profitable again with war requirements. Stop. Nothing like before, but you will get some royalties. Stop. Your old friend J.J. Wagner.*

Henry had not realized that his old business partner in the stationery shop in Nogales was still alive – but he was certainly glad that he was and that he had made contact. The word *royalties* leapt off the page at him. Even if it wasn't *big* money, it was *some* money.

Henry immediately sent off a telegram to the oil company in Houston. They replied the next day. Basically, they had discovered during a routine review and testing of capped wells that two of the four wells that formerly belonged to The Three Sisters Oil Company in the Pleasanton oil field area were now considered viable again. Apparently, it sometimes happens that an exhausted oil reserve partly refills over time. It also happens when a well is capped prematurely. It is rare for such a well to reach its previous capacity, but it is often worthwhile opening the well again to recover the new or overlooked oil reserves.

With the American war machine on full throttle and American manufacturing industries working flat out to produce the weapons and machines of war, there was an insatiable demand for oil throughout the country. While wartime restrictions limited the scope for massive profiteering, it was still worth the effort to pump oil out of any source where it could be found.

Many years ago, when the Three Sisters Oil and Refining Company was wound up, all the land previously owned by the company was divided proportionally among the four surviving shareholders. The other two directors of The Three Sisters eventually sold their rights over the Pleasanton wells to the Lone Star Oil Company, which made it a practice to buy up depleted oil holdings very cheaply. They were willing to take the risk that at least some of the depleted wells would eventually become viable again. In that case, they would make a tidy profit. However, Mr Wagner and Henry declined to sell their land rights to Lone Star at the offered price; therefore, in the case of the old Three Sisters wells, The Lone Star Oil Company only owned 40 per cent of the rights to the Pleasanton wells. Mr Wagner still had his 20 per cent and Henry had his and Cora's 40 per cent.

Even though they only held a minority of the wells' rights, Lone Star Oil still held the upper hand in any negotiations with Wagner and Henry. If the two shareholders agreed to the redevelopment of their wells, they would have to cede to Lone Star Oil one half of their holdings to help pay for the costs of reopening those wells. In other words, Mr Wagner would then own only 10 per cent of the oil produced by the wells and Henry would own 20 per cent.

Such practices were not uncommon in the oil industry at that time. The decision was easy for Henry – and for Mr Wagner. Their shares were effectively worthless unless and until the wells were redeveloped. Once the oil field was operating again, they would at least get something – and that something was a lot more than the nothing they owned now – and which they would continue to own even if they vetoed the wells' redevelopment.

There were, of course, no guarantees. Re-opening old wells came with a risk – and, assuming that the re-opening process succeeded, there was no telling how long the wells might last. Their productive lives would certainly be shorter than their lives as new wells. With any luck, the company might be able to recover oil for the next four or five years, with Henry and Mr Wagner sharing any profits with it. If they weren't lucky, the wells might go dry again after only a few months of production.

Henry's first check arrived two months later. It was for $1,809.23. Given that the first month's production would probably be less than later months', because they had to reopen the wells gradually, Henry was very pleased.

The average royalty check over the next six months was just over $2,500.

This put Henry in a position to re-start his life. He still owed Mr Saldinas about $15,000, but his bank account now held almost $20,000 after his new oil payments were added to the savings he had so carefully built up over the previous seven years, while still paying down his loan.

Henry was far from being rich, even though he now had an extremely good income, but it could peter out to nothing at any time. Still, he decided to seize the moment. He resigned from Western Union and left Port Lavaca to return to Arizona and Mexico where he figured his best chances to make money could still be found.

Henry had learned several lessons during his years in Port Lavaca. He had become less willing to take wild risks and had learned the value of a financial safety net. On the other hand, his self-confidence had returned in spades and, once again, he began the search for that elusive dream of financial success and its associated lifestyle.

He also realized how important his family was to him. If it wasn't for Rufus and Lee's generosity and kindness, he could never have pulled himself out of the deep hole he had dug. He would never forget that again. His gratitude and love for his brother also caused him to ponder with deep regret the way he had treated his own family. He had never received divorce papers from Cora, so he believed that they were still legally married. However, he had no hope of finding her or Maddy. His only hope was that, one day in the future, they would contact him.

31

BACK TO ARIZONA

It was the very end of 1942 when Henry arrived back in Nogales. In fact, just two days after he arrived, the night-time sky was lit up with fireworks from both sides of the border to celebrate the brand-new year of 1943.

Henry immediately re-established contact with his old partner J.J. Wagner. J.J. had aged considerably since Henry last saw him eight or nine years ago and wasn't in the best of health. They had a long and enjoyable session catching up on what had happened to each of them in the meantime. J.J., whose wife had finally left him some years ago, invited Henry to stay in his large house until he had settled back into life in Nogales.

Henry had paid off half his remaining debt to señor Saldinas in a lump sum and promised regular repayments until he had the funds to finally settle with him.

He soon learned that the various mining areas near Hermosillo, which he had planned to develop almost ten years ago, had all been tried and tested by a large American mining consortium. They had declared that none of those mines was now viable and was ever likely to produce a profit again.

He explored various possible options with J.J. It now seemed very unlikely that any old mine in either Sonora or Arizona could ever be profitably re-opened. The only way to make a quick fortune in mining was to find a previously unnoticed source of gold or silver, stake a claim on the area, and, eventually, dig a new, viable mine. There were plenty of mountainous areas in northern Mexico that had never been properly surveyed and tested for mineral resources, with good reason. The most likely areas could only be accessed on foot, possibly with a pack animal, and the work was hard, isolated and dangerous.

Nevertheless, Henry resolved to try his hand at genuine prospecting, in the old-fashioned sense of the term. He would buy the necessary equipment and a burro, and he would adopt the life of a prospector. Despite this decision, Henry was still not sure that he'd be able to succeed in such a venture. Until now, his successes had all been due to his skills as a manager and a salesman – supplemented by a large dose of luck. From now on he would have to work physically hard in often hostile environments. He was fully prepared to give it his all, but it remained to be seen whether this would be enough.

One afternoon, Henry and J.J. were sitting in Consuela's Cantina in Nogales, pouring over a large map of northern Sonora and Chihuahua while discussing the most likely places for Henry to begin his search.

A large, well-dressed Mexican man entered the cantina, looked around, saw Henry and J.J., and immediately strode over to their table.

"*Hola*, Meester Hosh!" J.J.'s first name was "Josh", which a Spanish speaker would render as something like "Hosh".

"Hello, señor Gonzales. What can I do for you? Oh, excuse me, this is my old friend and one-time business partner, Henry Anderson."

Henry and señor Gonzales shook hands.

"I am looking for a man, preferably a gringo, who can drive a few cars for me, my friend. A capable and discreet man. I will pay well for a satisfactory person. Do you know anyone like that, sir?"

Henry looked over at J.J., whose eyes were cast down to the floor. It was immediately obvious to Henry that what was being proposed was almost certainly illegal. "I might be interested, señor Gonzales, if the pay is good enough."

Gonzales looked him up and down.

"If you do the job well enough, Meester Anderson, you will be paid well enough."

"What do you want me to do?"

"I need a good man to deliver several automobiles to Hermosillo over the next few weeks. You will drive the cars to Hermosillo, deliver them to the specified addresses, collect payment for the cars, and then return to Nogales by train. Each time, you will hand over the car payments to me and I will pay you a fair amount. Normally, I'm prepared to give the right man forty per cent of my profit on each car. I buy them here in Arizona cheaply and sell them in Hermosillo at a very fair price in Mexico. Normally my profit is at least three times more than I paid for the car. Are you interested?"

Henry had never considered a career in smuggling before. He knew that the Mexican government levied extremely high tax charges on the sale and importation of motor cars. Obviously, señor Gonzales was making his profit by avoiding the Mexican taxes. Equally obviously, he was providing false papers for his cars. How great was the risk of getting caught? That was Henry's only concern.

"Señor, I can believe that your business is a profitable one. To make profits, one must take risks, not so? How great is the risk I will be taking to deliver your cars for you and return with your profits?"

Gonzales smiled. This gringo was not a stupid one. But could he be trusted?

"You are so right, Meester Anderson. We must all take risks to make a profit, no? If I hire you, I will take a risk, no? You might take my profits in Hermosillo and disappear, no? That is my risk. Your risk is much smaller. You must be careful to cross the border in the right place at the right time. You must avoid being stopped by the Mexican Federales for any kind of minor traffic offense. You must ensure that the payment is in full and correct before you release the car. Finally, you must find a way to carry the payment, so that it is not noticed. If you call attention to yourself and arouse the suspicion of the Federales, and, if they discover the payment, you will spend a long time in a Mexican jail, no? And you will still owe me the profit I am due, no? Is that clear, sir?"

"*Si,* perfectly clear. When do you wish me to start?"

32

HENRY JOINS THE BLACK MARKET

Up to this point in his life, Henry had been a law-abiding citizen. Sure, he had maximized his tax deductions each year – but everybody did that. Perhaps, now and then, he had cut a few legal corners, but never to an extent that he worried about getting caught. This was an entirely different proposition. It required him to brazenly break the law. On the other hand, Henry relished the opportunity to make some quick dollars and he was quite confident, as usual, that he could talk his way out of any sticky situation with the Mexican Federales. No matter what happened, and even in the worst position he could imagine, he decided he would have enough cash to bribe his way out of trouble.

He was also quietly relieved that he could postpone his proposed difficult new role as a prospector for as long as possible.

Three days later, señor Gonzales contacted Henry. The first car was ready for delivery.

Henry had still not bought himself a car, so he walked the few blocks to señor Gonzales's warehouse, just off the Main Street in Nogales. There he met Gonzales and one of his employees, a rough-looking Mexican named Fernando, whose facial scars, and rather wild-looking eyes, suggested that he was one of señor Gonzales's enforcers.

The car Henry had to drive to Hermosillo was a beautiful Packard Clipper, a most luxurious automobile, with a straight eight-cylinder engine for power and an imposing, classical body. The interior design was the epitome of an American luxury car – leather seats, spacious leg room, various specialty features like cigar lighters and dome lights, and an early version of car air conditioning.

The license plates were from New Mexico. Señor Gonzales had purchased the car at an auction of repossessed vehicles in Santa Fe. His new employer presented Henry with the keys and $50 cash for his fuel expenses. He also gave him a delivery address in Hermosillo and provided him with the documents he needed to hand over with the car to its new Mexican owner when he collected the payment.

After that, Henry was on his own.

He had lived in Nogales long enough to know plenty of places where he could cross the border into Mexico without being detected. There were dozens, if not hundreds, of small roads that illegally crossed the line on the map that was the border between the two countries. Henry knew where he was least likely to be caught by the Mexican Federales.

He crossed the border that night without incident and eventually joined the main paved road to Hermosillo. The Packard was a dream to drive, and he was able to cruise on the highway at an average speed of just less than 60 miles an hour. The sun was just above the horizon as he drove into the outskirts of Hermosillo four and a half hours later.

Henry found the address quickly and delivered the car to its new owner. He was handed an envelope containing $3,000 in U.S. $100 notes, which he counted and verified as the correct amount.

He handed over a set of Sonora State license plates, removed the New Mexico plates, which he took away with him, and left.

On his way to the train station in Hermosillo, Henry passed several rubbish bins. He bent the American license plates in half and deposited them, wrapped in a bag of food scraps, in one of the bins.

He reached the train station just in time to catch the 10 a.m. train to Nogales.

When he arrived back in Nogales, on the Mexican side of the border, Henry nonchalantly walked through a customs and immigration check point and headed for señor Gonzales's warehouse.

His new boss was pleased to see him and quickly took the payment envelope, counted it, and handed over Henry's share. The total profit to him had been $2,200, so Henry was paid $880. It was certainly the easiest money he had made for years.

Over the next six weeks, Henry made another twelve car deliveries to Hermosillo. Of course, most were not as lucrative as the first luxury Packard car, but they were all good cars with low mileage and the profits were large.

By this stage, Henry had added $7,350 to his bank account. He was still receiving at least $2,000 a month from his oil well dividends, and he had finally paid off Mr. Saldinas. Fortunately, Saldinas had always trusted him, and they had remained friends despite the delays in Henry's repayment of the loan. Saldinas was quite satisfied when Henry's final payment, with a reasonable amount of interest, arrived in his bank account in Los Angeles. Now, rather than go prospecting, Henry could consider doing something less physically challenging. But what would he do?

He had seen the massive profits made by señor Gonzales, so he decided that he would now buy his own cars in the U.S. to sell in Mexico. All he had to do was find out how to arrange the false Mexican license plates and establish a clientele in Hermosillo.

Señor Gonzales was not going to welcome a competitor, so Henry needed to deal with him and, at least, ensure that he would not be hostile.

Unfortunately for Henry, things didn't work like that in the world of cross-border smuggling. Gonzales unequivocally let him know that he regarded any attempt by Henry to break into his lucrative car smuggling business as a hostile act. Moreover, he would send in his goons to teach Henry a lesson.

Gonzales immediately terminated their relationship. If Henry dared to drive a smuggled car into Mexico again, he would be handed over to the Mexican authorities, whom Gonzales had in his pocket, or, worse, beaten or even murdered by Gonzales's goons.

Henry's naïveté had almost got him killed. The people he was now dealing with were gangsters, *banditos,* bad *hombres,* and he was powerless against them. If he had not been scrupulously honest with señor Gonzales, he would probably be dead already.

So, what was he to do?

He considered grovelling at Gonzales's feet and apologizing, but he realized that would be viewed as a weakness, and he would lose all credibility. Instead, he sent a letter to señor Gonzales, acknowledging that he was powerless and apologizing for letting señor Gonzales think that he now considered himself a competitor. It was all a misunderstanding, he said. From now on, he was going to have to behave in a way that, clearly, was no threat to señor Gonzales's business. However, he did assert his right to engage in cross-border trade. But he promised that trade would not involve any motor cars.

33

HENRY PLANS A NEW VENTURE

Henry decided he would lie low for a while and take his time to assess carefully the items he might smuggle into Mexico most easily and for the greatest profit.

In 1943, the Mexican government committed to supporting the American war effort. Initially, the Mexicans had tried to remain neutral, but in 1942, when a German submarine sank two Mexican ships in the Gulf of Mexico that were carrying oil to the U.S., they threw their whole-hearted support behind the Allies. Their main contribution was to increase the supply of various raw materials destined for use by the American manufacturing industry.

They also signed the Bracero Treaty with the U.S., which allowed thousands of Mexican farm workers and other semi-skilled laborers to accept jobs in the U.S. in areas experiencing labor shortages because of the war. A *bracero* is a farm worker. This agreement benefitted both sides; Mexico could export unemployed workers and benefit from the money that they sent home to their families, while the U.S. could harvest its crops and ensure that its factories were operating at full capacity during the wartime emergency.

American farmers, especially those in the south and the west of the country, came to depend on cheap Mexican labor – to the extent that the treaty remained in place for almost twenty years after the end of the war.

To protect its economy, the Mexican government adopted a program supporting the establishment and growth of its own manufacturing industry. In the 1920s and '30s, Mexico went through a period of widespread social reform, including land redistribution. In the 1940s, when the importation of manufactured goods was severely restricted by the war, the Mexicans embarked on a period of industrialisation to become more self-sufficient.

The social reforms of the 1920s and '30s in Mexico arose out of the chaos of more than a decade of attacks on the federal government by factionalized revolutionary groups, and out of their violence towards each other. During this upheaval, the elite, large landowners – those who had controlled Mexico since the time of the Spanish conquest – lost some of their land and, therefore, some of their political and social power.

Now, in the 1940s, government policy shifted from revolutionary social reform to a more capitalist approach, supporting those who were willing and able to invest in and manage the growth of a Mexican manufacturing industry.

Henry pondered all this as he worked out how to benefit from the underground economy. It was obvious that the best chance of maximizing any financial gains lay in supplying those luxury goods that were in short supply or even non-existent in Mexico because of the wartime disruption of world trade.

Cars, of course, were the most sought-after of luxury goods, but Henry didn't dare risk offending señor Gonzales. Instead, he set his sights on supplying fine wines and spirits, electrical equipment like radios, and even perishable items like cheeses and other gourmet foods normally imported from Europe. Such goods were relatively small and easy to transport without drawing undue attention from the authorities. The quick and easy journey from Nogales to Hermosillo meant that he would have no problem carrying even perishables among the smuggled goods.

Henry was also aware of a large demand for bigger items like refrigerators, but their transport required a truck, and the Federales were always suspicious of trucks, especially those driven by gringos. So, Henry, quite wisely, decided against moving into that part of the smuggling market, lucrative though it might have been.

It now only remained for Henry to work out the logistics of how to obtain the goods he needed and to establish a reliable and discreet customer base. He applied for and received a legal license to buy and sell wines and spirits – a process that was made much easier by an enthusiastic letter of recommendation from the mayor of Nogales, who was an old friend of J.J. Wagner. He also contacted former friends in Los Angeles who had supplied him with fine wines and gourmet foods when he and Cora were living the high life in Hollywood. They agreed to ship him the items he required, subject to availability.

Henry also called on the support of several wholesale merchants he knew in San Antonio, who also agreed to supply him with the goods he needed whenever they could.

Henry just had to find the right kind of vehicle for his new venture. Not a truck – too risky. A sedan would be unlikely to attract unwanted interest from the Federales, but it would limit the amount he could carry. He decided to look for a reliable, used station wagon. One with some miles on the odometer would be less likely to be noticed than a new car.

He scoured the newspapers for the rest of the week looking for the right one. Finally, he spotted an advertisement in a Phoenix newspaper for a 1940 Ford "Woodie" deluxe station wagon. It had 60,000 miles on the odometer and the price was right.

The owner was selling the car privately, so Henry immediately contacted the man by telephone and made him an offer, slightly above the published asking price, which he accepted immediately.

Henry took the train to Phoenix the next day, handed over his payment in cash, and drove back to Nogales in his new wagon. It suited his needs perfectly. Mechanically, the car was sound. The interior showed signs of heavy use and the exterior boasted the wear and tear one would expect in a four-year old automobile with 60,000 miles of Arizona roads behind it. It was a reliable car with plenty of storage space, but it looked ordinary and was unlikely to attract the attention of the authorities.

Now it remained for Henry to find a trustworthy and reliable customer base in Hermosillo and the small towns and *rancheros* nearby. His old friend, Oscar Saldinas, was still living there. Henry arranged to pay him a visit and drove down to Hermosillo in his new car three days later.

34

A PROMISING START

Oscar met Henry at the door of his imposing house in Hermosillo. They greeted each other warmly, like the old friends they were. Oscar introduced Henry to his beautiful wife, Estella, and their son, three year old Eduardo. Estella was much younger than Oscar.

Thank God, thought Henry, because Oscar was well past the time to be raising a small child.

Their house was a compound, with buildings and walls surrounding a completely enclosed and beautifully landscaped garden. Henry and his old friend sat down on comfortable chairs that looked inwards to the native tropical foliage in the garden. A servant brought them glasses of margaritas, a pitcher of iced water, and some hot, spicy nibbles. Henry began the conversation:

"My friend, I have come to you for your sage advice and, I hope not too presumptuously, for your assistance. I have decided to open my own business. I'll be exporting luxury goods, wines and spirits, gourmet foodstuffs, et cetera, from the U.S. I'll personally oversee their transportation from Nogales to Hermosillo and will deliver them myself to my customers. I'm hoping you can introduce me to potential clients, who must, of course, be reliable and discreet."

Oscar knew immediately that Henry's proposal was illegal. In wartime Mexico, you chose your friends carefully, so Henry was wise to seek his advice. He was willing to help him get started, but he was not interested in any long-term involvement in Henry's scheme. Having said that, he would definitely buy from Henry because he loved French wines and Scotch whiskies, not to mention fine French and Spanish cheeses. But deciding who else to recommend to Henry would take some careful thought. Oscar could think of quite a few people who would love to buy from Henry, but not all of them could be trusted. He knew that several did not like gringos at all and would probably denounce Henry to the authorities – but only after they had taken possession of a large order of fine wine and imported whisky, and before they had paid for it.

"Enrique, *mi amigo*, I suggest you move very carefully at first. I can think of three or four potential customers whom I would trust completely. You can begin with them and then we can decide later who else you might add to your customer list."

"*Gracias*, Oscar. I have a suggestion. Why don't you organize a small gathering of your trusted friends, invite them here for an intimate wine-tasting and cheese-sampling session. I'll supply the wine and cheese and we can also sample several nice whiskies as well. I don't want to impose on you or presume too much, but, if you agree, that should get me started. After that, I can make my own way, though I may ask your opinion from time to time, if that's OK. What do you think?"

"That sounds like a good plan, my friend. I'll consult with Estella, but I am sure we can find a day sometime next month."

Henry agreed immediately. He needed several weeks to get in his first lot of stock; after that he would be ready to begin his new career.

The next few weeks passed quickly. Henry found a suitable shop in Nogales and leased it for a year. He bought a small walk-in cool room from a restaurant that had shut its doors and had it installed in his new premises. He built a wall of shelves and got a locksmith to provide strong locks and metal grills for all his doors and windows. Finally, he contacted his sources in Los Angeles and San Antonio and placed his first large orders.

He was in business.

Within the week, Henry was busy stacking his shelves with cases of wine and spirits, carefully storing his cheeses, a few fancy meats – salami and prosciutto from Italy – or, more likely, from Italian migrant manufacturers in New York; jambon ham from Spain; and other small goods in the cool room. From his contacts in San Antonio he even obtained a dozen of the latest table-top radios and eight phonographs. Finally, he was fully stocked and could make up an order form, which listed the available foodstuffs, wines and spirits. He had 500 copies printed.

His last task was to hire a sign painter to embellish the front window of his shop with the words: "H.R. Anderson, Fancy Goods Imported & Exported."

The initial soiree in Oscar Saldinas's house was successful beyond Henry's expectations. Six couples attended the event, where they sampled Henry's offerings and chatted among themselves. There was no hard sell; that would have been totally inappropriate. Instead, Henry circulated among his potential customers and discussed with them their preferences, asking if he might get them anything else that was not on his order form. At the end of the day, he had taken enough orders to almost exhaust his storeroom in Nogales.

Henry's business plan was quite simple. He worked on a normal mark-up of 200 per cent on his cost for all food and beverages, including transportation. While this might seem high – and it would have been if he tried to sell at those prices in the U.S. – the Mexican taxes on imported fine foods, wines and spirits often exceeded 400 per cent. To his rich Mexican customers, Henry's prices were, in fact, ridiculously cheap. Of course, they all understood that this was only possible because they were evading Mexican taxes, but their own risk of being caught and charged was minimal. It was Henry who was taking all the risks.

After his first few runs from Nogales to Hermosillo to deliver orders to his customers, Henry realized that he was taking a bigger risk than he needed to. He had to load up his station wagon as fully as possible and, despite the precaution of covering the crates of wine and the ice chests of cheese and meat with a blanket so they couldn't be seen easily, he knew that if he were ever stopped by the Federales his load would look very suspicious. A cursory inspection of his car would quickly reveal his cargo, and he could not risk that.

He also became conscious that his car, while not likely to attract attention for its normal appearance, would, in all likelihood, eventually be spotted and noted by the authorities for its frequent visits to Hermosillo.

With the profits he made on his very first deliveries, Henry got a mechanic he knew well to modify the spaces beneath the seats throughout the car. Apart from a minimum amount of metal framing, the space beneath each seat was filled with a built-in, insulated ice chest with a drain mounted in the bottom to release any melt water onto the road when it was safe to do so.

He also installed large, lockable metal chests in the rear compartment of the station wagon to hold crates of wine and spirits. He could cover these chests with a few suitcases of clothing and a few open crates of used mining equipment and camping gear. Then, if he were stopped, an initial inspection of his car would reveal nothing more than what was expected of a gringo prospector who made frequent trips between Hermosillo and the north.

Of course, any inquisitive Federale investigating his car in any thorough way would discover Henry's modifications, which would raise questions even if they contained no contraband goods.

35

A SMUGGLER'S LIFE

For several months, Henry's new career as a professional smuggler went from strength to strength. He cautiously added a few new clients to his list, but he soon realised that supplying a small number of wealthy Mexican families on a regular basis was about as much business as he could easily manage. He also tried to vary his routine, delivering to different locations around Hermosillo, changing the days of the week he travelled, and so on.

While Henry's primary worry was getting caught by the Mexican authorities, he also found that it was often difficult to source the goods he needed in sufficient quantities to satisfy his clients. As the war dragged on, certain luxury items became almost impossible to obtain, meaning he was not always able to fill his orders.

Despite these difficulties, the business proved profitable, and Henry was able to build up sizeable balances in a series of bank accounts. He was well on the way to his goal of having sufficient funds to resume his life as a major investor in oil and minerals. On top of his profitable export business, he still received monthly dividends from his share of the Texas oil wells.

Overall, Henry's life was simple. He lived in a modest house in Nogales, which he rented at a very favorable cost from his old friend, J.J. He did not entertain or spend a lot of money on his lifestyle. Being Henry, he did go out on the town at least several nights a week to meet women; however, almost all his liaisons were short in duration. In truth, while Henry craved and needed the company of women, he had no desire at all to establish another long-term relationship. Apart from anything else, the unpredictable nature of his smuggling business made it hard to manage anything more than a series of casual encounters.

Henry's life settled into a routine. Apart from the "nuts and bolts" of running his business – placing his orders regularly; ensuring that he had enough stock, but not too much; maintaining his car – he would make two or three runs a week from Nogales to Hermosillo to deliver his goods. By now he had successfully completed more than one hundred such trips, but he still felt the adrenalin flow, the edgy excitement, and the anxiety about being caught, before every trip he made. There were aspects to his life as a smuggler that, Henry decided, were not always easy to cope with.

36

ALL GOOD THINGS MUST COME TO AN END

1943 came and went. Before he knew it, Henry was once again standing in Main Street, Nogales, watching the New Year's firework displays. What Henry didn't realize was that 1944 would bring him little joy.

The Christmas–New Year period was predictably busy for Henry. All his customers wanted wine, whisky and fine foods for the festive season. It was particularly hectic for Henry, because the wartime disruption to world trade made the kind of stock he required increasingly hard to procure. He had placed his orders months earlier, but he still did not get all he needed, leaving some customers with less than they had ordered.

One of his oldest customers, señor Esquival, was particularly unhappy, although Henry was sure that the main complainant was his wife, señora Esquival. He tried to placate them by offering substitute items for the goods they had requested and a special discount, but they were still not satisfied. Henry decided that he could do no more for them, nor could he supply them with his contraband goods in future.

Unfortunately for Henry, a business dealing in illegally smuggled goods is different from a legitimate business. If you anger one of your customers, the outcome may not just be the loss of their custom; you could well find yourself under investigation by the authorities and you might even end up in a Mexican jail.

Perhaps señora Esquival complained about Henry to one of her lady friends, who just happened to be the wife of a local magistrate. Who knows? But whatever the reason, on the way back from Henry's very next trip to Hermosillo, the Federales stopped and questioned him. He had already delivered the contraband goods to his customers when he was pulled over at a roadblock on the outskirts of Hermosillo.

The Federales searched his car thoroughly and, while they found no illegal goods, they pressured him to explain the modifications to his car. Henry managed to keep his cool during his interrogation, insisting that he was just a prospector and that he needed secure storage spaces for any valuable ore that he might find, and he needed the ice chests to preserve his food on journeys into the mountains that might last a week or more.

He was hauled before a magistrate, who informed him that he was being charged with illegally modifying an automobile under some obscure law. He was fined the equivalent of US$2,000, an enormous sum and clearly much more than the claimed offense should cost. But worse, by far, for Henry was that the judge informed him his car was being seized as the key component of a suspected illegal smuggling operation.

In one sense, Henry was lucky because he had more than $2,000 in cash with him – he always carried at least $1,000 in a secure compartment under the dashboard of his car – plus he had the profits from his most recent deal, which amounted to another $1,300. The magistrate was clearly surprised and not very pleased that Henry could pay the fine on the spot. He had obviously hoped to throw Henry into jail for several days, from where it would be difficult for him to make any arrangements for a money transfer to pay the fine. He quite enjoyed seeing gringos suffer the privations and indignities of a few days in the holding pen of a Mexican jail.

Nevertheless, the Mexican authorities allowed Henry to go free once he paid the fine. With no car, he had to walk to the train station and buy a ticket back to Nogales.

Henry had plenty of time to ponder his future on the train trip back to Arizona. It was clear to him that he could no longer pursue his lucrative smuggling business in Hermosillo. He was clearly a target for the authorities, and he was sure that the police would harass him if he showed up there again. He had no real option other than to wind up the business and send apologies to his customers.

He would have to think long and hard about his future. Despite the handsome profits to be made, Henry was not really cut out for the constant stress and the mental and physical strain of an illegal smuggling venture. Fortunately, he had an extremely healthy bank balance – more than $35,000 in three separate accounts. If his oil dividends continued to roll in, he would be able to live quite comfortably and still have the wherewithal to seize an investment opportunity, if the right one came along.

It was time to return to his original plan and become a solitary prospector for gold and silver. It would be arduous and he would be alone in isolated, hard-to-reach locations, but, he pondered, perhaps that was what he needed for a while. He could live cheaply and cover his expenses by drawing on his oil money each month.

If he did eventually discover an economically realistic source of gold or silver ore, he could then sit back and let others do the hard work while he enjoyed the lifestyle of a wealthy man. Life at the top of the social ladder in an American city appealed less and less as he grew older, so his ideal outcome, the romantic dream that drove him, was to own a beautiful, large hacienda somewhere in Mexico where he could live out the rest of his life in comfort.

As the train rattled its way through a particularly rough stretch of rails on the final approach to Nogales, Henry was bounced from side to side. The shaking of the train carriage caused him to leave his dreams behind and regain a foggy consciousness.

★ ★ ★

Henry became aware of a different location. He was, in fact, bouncing around as his medivac plane descended through a layer of turbulence on its way to land at the airport in Victoria, Texas. The plane touched down gently and rolled to a stop outside a large hangar. A customs and immigration official met the pilot and stamped all the occupants' passports. Henry was wheeled down a ramp at the back of the plane, and his stretcher bed lifted into a waiting ambulance.

The medivac doctor and nurse rode with him on the short trip from the airport to the hospital, with Henry's two nephews driving their own cars behind the ambulance. When they reached the hospital, Henry was lifted out of the ambulance, still strapped down for the flight, and rolled into the patient reception area.

All this time, Henry was vaguely aware of what was going on around him. The brightness hurt his eyes, so he kept them closed, but he could hear what was happening. He heard the conversation between his medivac doctor and the reception doctor at the hospital, although he could not clearly make out all the words. He sensed that forms were being signed. He opened his eyes slightly as he was transferred to a larger bed before being rolled down a long corridor, into a large elevator, up several floors, then down a hall and into a large room filled with medical equipment and sensors.

A pleasant, and rather pretty, nurse took his blood pressure and temperature and then attached several electrodes to his chest and placed a clip on the end of a finger. She then removed the needle that had been inserted into Henry's left arm in Chihuahua, and which the medivac crew had used on the flight, and inserted a new needle in his other arm, which she connected to a tube coming from a bag of saline solution.

"Hello Mr Anderson, I am Doctor Garcia." A tall young doctor of Mexican descent introduced himself. "I will be looking after you here. You are in the intensive care section, and we need to stabilize you as rapidly as possible. After that we can do the tests we need so we know how to care for you. In a moment we are going to administer something to help you sleep. You'll remain heavily sedated for at least the next seventy-two hours." He added, "We'll get you back on your feet very soon."

Henry nodded groggily.

"For now, though," he emphasized, "we want you to sleep. If you wake, from time to time, we'll offer you some fluids but, otherwise, you'll receive everything you need intravenously. I'll leave you in the capable hands of Lucy. She's one of our most experienced intensive care nurses. Try sipping some water now before we get you back to sleep."

Henry tried to respond, but the "thank you" refused to come out of his terribly dry mouth as anything other than a slight grunting noise. The doctor left and the nurse put a tube in his mouth, through which he could suck a little water. Then she injected him with a sedative and Henry, once again, sank back into a confused world of wildly gyrating shapes and flashing rainbow colors.

Gradually, he returned to his deep dreams.

37

A PROSPECTOR'S LIFE IS NOT AN EASY ONE

It was 1948. Henry was leading his little burro, "Monsita", up a steep and dusty mountain track in the northern region of the Mexican state of Chihuahua. For the last four years, Henry had led a mostly solitary life, trekking through mountains looking for potential deposits of gold.

He did have a base, a small house in a mountain village several days' trek away. From there, he would decide where to explore next. Then he would travel to the nearest small village in his chosen area, rent a house, hire a housekeeper, and settle in for a few weeks as he assembled the provisions he needed – all the while attempting to discreetly pick the brains of the locals about likely sites to explore. It had become a tried and tested pattern for his life.

He could carry all his heavy, bulky camping and mining gear, as well as his little burro, in an old, high-sided Ford pick-up truck that he had acquired. He had become quite fond of the animal, whom he named after a milk cow called Monsita that his brother Rufus once owned. That cow was small but produced more milk than most of the larger cows, and reliably bore a calf every year for as long as Henry could remember. Like Monsita the cow, his burro was also small and dependable.

He had only managed one visit to his brother and sister-in-law in Texas since the end of the war, when he travelled back to Texas to sort out a legal issue with his oil property. The oil wells in Pleasanton, which he part-owned, had run dry again in the middle of 1945. Consequently, his royalty checks also ran dry. However, he had heard from an old friend that the oil company controlling the wells might not be telling him the whole truth. The rumor was that while they may have capped the old wells, they had also drilled a new well on the same property, adjacent to the old ones. Furthermore, they were making a fine profit on the new well, which they kept for themselves.

So, in early 1946, Henry travelled to Texas to see for himself what was going on with his oil property. He got to Pleasanton, made some enquiries, then drove out to the property. Sure enough, there was a new well, obviously pumping and producing copious barrels of oil each day.

He drove straight to San Antonio and consulted a lawyer who specialized in oil and minerals issues. He looked up the registration of the new well, which was held 100 per cent in the name of the Lone Star Oil Company. He then examined Henry's documents. Henry was sure that he still owned 20 per cent of the property on which the well had been drilled and he had never given his agreement for the oil company to drill a new one. Therefore, he concluded, he should be entitled to 20 per cent of the oil from the new well.

Unfortunately for Henry, the lawyer confirmed that, indeed, Henry was still the owner of 20 per cent of the land. However, when he agreed to the re-opening of the original wells, the fine print in the contract made it clear that he was handing over to the oil company not only half his ownership of the oil produced by those two wells, but he was also waiving his right to any further exploitation of the mineral rights on that plot of land. The new well was "further exploitation of the mineral rights", and Henry had no claim on a percentage of that oil.

He did have a reasonable chance of legal success if he wanted to sue the oil company for placing drilling rigs and other permanent fixtures on the surface of the land without seeking his permission. But if he pursued that course of action, it was unlikely to result in a substantial award for damages. In fact, the lawyer doubted that he would get much more out of such a case than the cost of his legal bill. Speaking of which, when Henry rose to leave, the lawyer presented him with a bill for $50 for an hour of his time.

Henry was understandably furious that he had been so careless when he signed the agreement with Lone Star Oil. There was nothing he could do that would make him any money, so he decided to walk away from the issue.

Since he was in Texas, he visited his sister Emma and her husband, Clarence, in Sutherland Springs for a few days and then travelled down to Port Lavaca, where Rufus and Lee still owned the Sea Shell Restaurant. He stayed for two weeks, during which he met his nephew Al's wife, Betty, and their newborn son, Charles. Al was now a qualified doctor in the army and was serving overseas in the Southern Ryukyu Islands, a chain of Japanese islands stretching from Okinawa towards Formosa, or Taiwan, as it was later called.

After his break away, Henry returned via El Paso and Ciudad Juárez to his village in Chihuahua, where he remained for several years. It was called Agua Dulce, meaning "Sweet Water", because of a permanently flowing spring of potable water. It was surrounded by numerous rugged canyons and steep-sided gorges, some of which had flowing streams of their own. Henry resolved to investigate as many of these places as he could. Any alluvial gold he came across in those streams would indicate that there might well be a large vein of gold-bearing rock somewhere upstream.

The only way to get into the canyons and gorges was on foot. There were no roads and only a few trails.

When preparing for a trip Henry would clean and pack his equipment carefully, being sure to take only what he needed, but not more than Monsita could carry. Rafaela, his housekeeper – a lovely twenty-three year old peasant woman, who had been widowed the year before Henry arrived – prepared food sufficient for a couple of weeks for the journey. Rafaela was a sweet girl with a placid disposition. She kept a spotless house for Henry and cooked him lovely meals whenever he was "at home". She lived with Henry in his house and shared his bed; consequently, the villagers chose to regard them as a married couple.

Not infrequently, Henry found alluvial gold in the mountain streams around Agua Dulce, sometimes as much as two or three ounces, but he was yet to discover a mother lode – a proper vein of gold or silver.

Henry's treks into the mountains were taxing – there was rarely a path to follow, and he had to find a way to get himself and Monsita up and over large fields of boulders and through narrow gorges. It was not easy to find suitable campsites, and finding enough grass nearby for Monsita was also a problem. There were few people in those remote areas, but Henry was wary of any stranger. Potentially they could be one of the lawless *banditos* who roamed the countryside, although, in reality, such sparsely populated country was probably not much use to a serious *bandito* searching for victims to rob.

For his protection Henry always carried a loaded .45-calibre revolver and a box of ammunition. Henry had been attacked in his campsite once. Alerted by the braying of Monsita, he woke up and grabbed his gun. He caught the intruder trying to untie Monsita's halter, but one shot in the air from his revolver sent the would-be burro rustler scrambling into the night.

There was more danger posed by animals than humans. Rattlesnakes, some of them as thick as a man's arm, infested the mountains. Normally, they were not aggressive, but it was easy to stumble into a rattlesnake's territory and provoke it to strike. Henry had a few close calls over the years; he had learned to examine carefully where he was going to put his feet, and was especially wary when stepping over large boulders or fallen tree trunks.

Henry was also wary when he set up his campsite, orienting his tent so a mountain lion could not attack it easily. More than once, he heard the scream of a mountain lion in the middle of the night, and not that far away. He would tether the poor, nervously shaking Monsita just outside his tent and make sure he had a good fire. Big cats tended to avoid a roaring blaze. And he slept with his pistol by his side.

So far, Henry had managed to avoid severe injury or snakebite, either of which could have proved fatal in such remote territory.

38

HENRY REASSESSES HIS OPTIONS

In the autumn of 1949, Henry decided to move on with his life. He had lived as a prospector for about five years and, having made no major discoveries of gold or silver, he was living on his savings. Since his oil royalties ceased, he had survived by drawing down on his money in the bank. The amounts of gold that he had found were negligible, and he knew that if he kept up his current lifestyle, he would exhaust his money in two or three years. Something had to change.

In a Christmas letter from his brother Rufus, Henry saw a feasible way to proceed. Rufus and Lee had sold the Sea Shell Restaurant in Port Lavaca and purchased the Grand Hotel in the small town of Kenedy, Texas, south-west of San Antonio. The Grand was an old, stone-faced building with sixty-two rooms, twenty-eight of which had ensuite baths and toilets. It also boasted a restaurant and three meeting rooms. Located in the front office of the hotel was the local Western Union telegraph business, and Rufus needed to find an operator for it. Rufus had said in his letter that Henry could have the job if he was interested.

Henry thought long and hard about his options. He could stay in Mexico, prospecting for gold and silver while continuing to bleed his bank accounts until they ran dry. Then what would he do?

If he accepted Rufus's offer and returned to Texas to resume the fairly boring life of a telegraph operator, he would at least receive a reasonable salary from Western Union. In addition, Rufus had offered him free room and board in the hotel, so he could save the bulk of his income. Once again, he might be able to build up enough savings to re-enter the investment market. And, besides that, Henry would become eligible for U.S. Social Security benefits at the age of sixty-five – in 1956, just six years down the track.

With a rock-solid American Social Security income, Henry could, once again, resume the life of a prospector and live well in Mexico. He was still a dreamer, and he was quite sure that, one day, he would make the big discovery he needed so badly. One day he would live in that big hacienda in luxury and comfort – ideally, reunited with Cora and Maddie.

He immediately replied to Rufus accepting his offer.

There was no point in holding onto his mining gear. He found another gringo prospector who was just starting out and sold him all his camping and mining equipment for a bargain price. He paid the rent on his house in Agua Dulce for a full twelve months, leaving it and his beloved Monsita to Rafaela, along with a gift of $100. He reckoned that would give her a chance to start a new life for herself.

And then Henry drove to Texas.

39

TELEGRAPH OPERATOR, MARK II

The Grand Hotel had seen better days. Its large lobby was furnished with what would have originally been expensive, over-stuffed couches and armchairs. Now threadbare and sagging in places, they were marked with cigarette burns. The carpet, too, was worn and frayed, and the coffee tables and magazine racks sported multiple scratches and dents.

Over time Rufus and Lee planned to refurbish the old hotel. They would start by lifting all the carpets in the lobby, polishing the floorboards, and breaking up the space with rugs of diverse colors and shapes. Then they would make or buy covers for the sofas and chairs and restore the coffee tables. As long as the hotel continued to bring in a reasonable profit, they would be able to undertake the improvements in stages.

Inside the main entrance to the hotel, one corner of the lobby was screened off by several glass-fronted display cabinets stocked with cigars, cigarettes and confectionery. There were two cabinets along one side and a third set at right angles. A small corner unit with the cash register on top filled the space where the cases met.

The display-cabinet counters were wooden, and on top were small display boxes of postcards, matches, pencils, pens, hotel notepaper and stacks of newspapers – the local weekly and the two main San Antonio dailies. The space behind the wall of glass showcases was entered by raising a hinged section of the countertop. Just near that gap was the entrance to the dining room.

The Western Union telegraph machine and shelves holding the telegram forms, other papers, and rolls of teletype tape were arranged along the back wall of this open office area. There was one large, high-set window above the machine and shelving, admitting rather dim light, mainly because it was too hard to clean.

The whole lobby was cooled by a set of fans hanging from the ceiling at the ends of long conduit pipes. One of them hung down over the open office space in the corner of the lobby, but in the hot South Texan summers the addition of an oscillating table fan was needed to make conditions more bearable.

Henry sat on a comfortable office chair with wheels in front of the teletype keyboard. When a Western Union customer appeared, he would rise and assist the person across the countertop. He used his own till for the takings.

As with his previous time with Western Union, Henry's main task was to receive information and post prices from the New York Stock Exchange on a bulletin board outside the hotel door, as well as the latest prices from the local livestock saleyard and produce markets. When the markets closed and the information piled in on the telegraph tape he was quite busy, but most of the time Henry amused himself by reading books and newspapers.

In the mornings, Henry shared the office space with Rufus or Lee, who perched on a high stool while looking after the main cash register and handling guests' arrivals and departures, as well as taking payments from the restaurant customers. After the lunchtime rush, they normally took turns going back to their room for a rest, leaving Henry to deal with anyone who might wander in for tobacco or chocolates during the afternoon.

While Kenedy was a small town with a population of only about 3,000, it had been founded by a man who owned most of the county and wanted the town to be suitably impressive. Consequently, Kenedy had some grand stone- or brick-built architecture – buildings such as a bank, an emporium and the Grand Hotel, for example – and more than you might expect for such a small place.

The town was at the intersection of two major highways, so it became a prime trading center for livestock and farm produce. The "city fathers" of Kenedy adopted the motto "The junction where good friends meet"; although, in the early years of the twentieth century, Kenedy was more famous for several major gunfights that had occurred between desperados and law enforcement officers. Obviously, not all meetings were good or friendly.

During the war years, a major detention center was built just outside Kenedy for "enemy aliens" – Germans, Italians and Japanese – many of whom were actually long-term residents or U.S. citizens. In the latter years of the war it was converted into a prisoner-of-war camp for German and Japanese prisoners. The camp closed shortly after the war ended, but locals still talked about it years later. There was not much else to talk about in Kenedy.

In the early 1950s, the small town wasn't exactly a lively place for night-time entertainment either. Because the population was about 60 per cent Hispanic and, therefore, nominally Roman Catholic – as opposed to the Anglo-Irish white population, who were mostly Baptists – it was legal to purchase alcoholic drinks. To cater for this, there were a few beer joints, but apart from a small and exclusive "country club" there wasn't a nice restaurant where patrons could have a meal with a beer or a glass of wine.

There was also a local cinema, which was directly across the road from the Grand Hotel, but aside from a Little League Baseball program in the summer for the boys and Miss Nellie Pearson's Dancing School for girls, there was not much for children or adolescents to do in Kenedy, other than attend school.

As far as Henry was concerned, it did not matter that Kenedy shut up shop when the sun went down. He worked long, though not particularly hard, hours at the telegraph machine during the week, and it suited him to have early nights. But the redeeming feature for Henry was that Kenedy was only an hour's drive from San Antonio, which had a lively and varied choice of entertainment. Almost every Saturday, Henry would head off to San Antonio as soon as he closed the Western Union Office at noon. Sometimes he made it back to Kenedy late on Saturday night, and sometimes he stayed in San Antonio, returning to the hotel on Sunday. Rarely, if he had a particularly enjoyable and successful weekend, he would drive back to Kenedy in the early hours of Monday, arriving in time to open the office at 7 a.m.

The ordinary, grinding routine of Henry's life was only partially mitigated by his weekend activities. However, he never lost sight of his long-term plan – his dream. He tolerated his time in Kenedy by constantly reminding himself that it was only short term. Once he reached the age of sixty-five, he could resume his life as a prospector in Mexico, where, he was sure, he would eventually strike it rich and return to a life of comfort and luxury.

40

PROSPECTOR, MARK II – OR III OR IV

Henry's time in Kenedy passed more quickly than he expected. He gave a month's notice to Western Union and resigned on his sixty-fifth birthday, 6 September, 1956, and immediately submitted his claim for a Social Security pension. After that, he made his way around all the work areas of the hotel and said goodbye to the staff.

After he said his farewells to the kitchen staff, he went out the back door of the kitchen into the open area at the rear of the hotel. If it had been properly landscaped it could have been a lovely Mexican garden, especially with the *conjunto* and *ranchero* music blaring from a radio in the hotel laundry. Unfortunately, though, it had been allowed to deteriorate into a dusty, rutted collection of red dirt and weeds.

Henry's send-off in the laundry was much more emotional and warmer than he expected – in a social sense. The hot, noisy and humid laundry room could not have been much warmer in temperature without endangering human health. Three of the four señoritas who worked there had, at one time or another in the previous few years, shared Henry's transient affections and his bed. A complaint by one of the hotel's paying guests had led to words between Rufus and Henry and a promise from Henry that he would no longer bring his lovers up to his room in the hotel. The end of his dalliances with the laundry women also probably came just in time to avoid jealous conflict in that section of the hotel workforce.

★ ★ ★

As Henry left the laundry, the loud and insistent Mexican polka music from the radio filled his ears. He was back on the dance floor of a seedy Mexican bar in San Antonio with a woman in his arms, twirling and dipping to the music. His memories also began to twirl and dip. Once again, his consciousness came back to him, in fits and starts. He became aware of bright lights and the usual noises of a hospital room.

A face. The woman in his arms? No. The face of a nurse.

"Hello, Mr Anderson. Can you hear me?"

Henry nodded, "Yes", and mumbled incoherently.

"My name is Carlotta and I'm here to take some blood for tests. I'll be as quick as I can, so you can get back to sleep."

She inserted the needle and drew out a couple of vials of blood. She patted Henry on the shoulder, made pleasant noises, then left.

Another nurse came to his bedside.

"Hello, Mr Anderson. My name is Jean. I'm your care nurse tonight. We'd like you to take a bit of water, if you can manage it." And, with that, she held a glass under Henry's chin with a straw that bent into his mouth.

He was able to raise himself slightly and suck a few sips of water before the effort overcame him. He dropped back onto his pillow and felt an overwhelming urge to go back to sleep. As his breathing became regular again and his slight snores rose from the pillow, the nurse straightened his bedding before leaving the room.

★ ★ ★

Where was he? Ah, back in Kenedy.

Where he'd left off last time. It began to come back to him. He was leaving again for Mexico.

Yet again, Henry had a substantial nest egg to fall back on. During his time in Kenedy, he had managed to contribute more than $18,000 to his savings account, leaving him with a balance of around $30,000. From now on, he would live on his Social Security income and hold onto his savings, just in case he ever needed quick money to pursue an opportunity.

By sheer accident, the timing of his retirement was perfect. Rufus and Lee had grown tired of the constant strain of trying to run a profitable hotel, when it was so old and needed so much constant repair. They had put the hotel on the market with a real estate agent in San Antonio, who specialized in hotel and restaurant properties. He found a potential purchaser for them almost immediately.

Mr Blanchard, the new owner, owned a rural property outside a small town called Crystal City, in south-west Texas near Eagle Pass, which is across the Rio Grande from the larger Mexican city of Piedras Negras. Crystal City was famous for its spinach crop, so much so that in 1937 the town council erected a larger than life, full-color statue of the cartoon character Popeye the Sailor Man in the town square. Of course, Popeye gained super-human strength whenever he ate spinach.

Mr Blanchard's property consisted of 1,300 acres, a little over half of which could be used for grazing or growing crops. The rest was a series of rocky gullies that were of no commercial value, although the flint stones that lay on the ground in those gullies had been prized by the nomadic Comanche Indians as a source of arrowheads and flint scraping tools from a time long before European settlement. The gullies were littered with flint arrowheads and tools of all shapes and sizes that had had flaws or had broken before they were finished.

The dwelling on the property was formerly a grand mansion. The drive from the road to the big house had once been lined with large palm trees, although most of them had died and the remaining few struggled to survive. Like the palm trees, the house, too, struggled to survive. There were nine bedrooms and five bathrooms on the second floor, although the plumbing in the bathrooms had long since ceased to work. Fortunately, the plumbing for the ground-floor bathrooms and kitchen worked, after a fashion.

On the ground floor was a large sitting room, a dining room, a kitchen, two bathrooms and two rooms, now used as bedrooms, but which had previously been used for other purposes. But the most impressive room in the house was a grand ballroom that took up at least half the floor space on the ground floor. The high ceiling was decorated with ornate plaster moldings, which were now in a state of disrepair. Half the floor had been carpeted with a fine, deep red carpet, now threadbare. Once-grand drapes hung from the high windows, faded and moldy. And, in the center of the main exterior wall was a massive fireplace, almost high enough for a grown man to stand upright inside.

The outbuildings, fencing and other ranching equipment were all in good condition, having been looked after by a kind of caretaker. He'd lived in the house for years, using only one downstairs bedroom, one bathroom and the kitchen. The rest of the rooms in the house were empty.

For many years, the property had been used to raise cattle. The cattle were managed by a Mexican farm manager, who lived with his family in a small house on the far side of the property.

After a few weeks' negotiation, Rufus and Mr Blanchard agreed to a straight exchange – Rufus would take ownership of the property in Crystal City and Mr Blanchard would take ownership of the Grand Hotel in Kenedy.

Henry's departure from Kenedy was timed to happen just before the properties changed hands. Mr Blanchard would have to find a new Western Union operator, if he decided to retain that business in his new hotel.

Henry decided to try his hand at prospecting again, this time in Coahuila State, the Mexican state that was separated from midwestern Texas by the Rio Grande. He had never tried his luck there, partly because he had no contacts in that vicinity, and partly because it was rumored to be even more lawless than Chihuahua or Sonora. On the other hand, he had made some friends in San Antonio on his weekends of carousing in the bars and dance halls who claimed to know about Coahuila and who had suggested that there might well be rich gold and silver deposits still in the hills and mountains.

Henry was also happy to stay a little closer to Rufus and Lee than he had previously. Now that they would be in Crystal City, he could easily afford the time to visit them more often than he had when he was living in Sonora or Chihuahua.

He spent a few weeks in San Antonio, purchasing the equipment he would need for camping and prospecting. This time he bought a more rugged car than he'd had before, an army surplus Jeep ambulance. It would stand up well to the rough mountain roads and tracks, and he could lock up his gear and provisions in the spacious area in the back. Once again, he was ready to pursue his dream.

41

A FEW TEETHING PROBLEMS

Henry decided to head for a small, isolated village north-west of Piedras Negras, called Moache. The name was obviously taken from the local Indian language and Henry had no idea what it meant. The landscape was different to that in the places where Henry had prospected before. Instead of high and steep mountains and hills, with small canyons and valleys scattered around, this country was much flatter, but far more broken and uneven. In the old cowboy movies, they would call it "The Badlands". There were, however, many flowing streams and even small rivers, which encouraged Henry in his initial search for alluvial gold.

Henry felt rather uncomfortable when he drove into the little village, which had perhaps 400 inhabitants. A few doors had opened as he drove past, and then immediately slammed shut. He headed for a building that looked like a cantina, parked the car and walked in. The interior was quite dark and there were only a few patrons, seated at tables, drinking beer.

He walked up to the bar and waited for someone to serve him. Finally, a relatively young man emerged from a doorway behind the bar. He walked up to Henry and looked him in the eye.

"*Si?*"

"My name is Enrique Anderson. I'm a prospector. For gold and silver. I'd like to look around this area for a few weeks, if possible. And I'd like to find a place to live for that time, a small house. Do you know of such a place available for rent here?"

"Señor, my advice to you is to turn around and go back where you came from. People do not like gringos here in Moache."

Henry weighed up his options. This situation was far from ideal. This man might be simply warning him off – or he might be testing Henry's mettle. To turn around and walk out would be a sign of weakness in this macho culture, and, in fact, might well be his most dangerous option. If there were really bad *hombres* in this place, they might attack him on his way to the car or ambush him down the track. Either way, his life would be in grave danger.

"I can understand, señor. There are many bad gringos around. I mean no one any harm. I'm a simple prospector looking for precious metals."

The young man behind the bar gave Henry a look that might have been indifferent, though it also might have been dismissive.

"If I find a good source of gold or silver, I will need workers to dig a mine. If any of your people want the work, I will give it to them at a fair wage. I will also need regular supplies of food and equipment, which I would procure here in this village."

Once again, the young man gave only a slight reaction; it was hard to interpret.

"I'm not from a large American company. I'm on my own and only work for myself. I'm not a greedy man, but, of course, my aim is to make money, in the end."

At that, the young man produced a definite smirk.

"I've worked in Chihuahua and Sonora, and I have always done my best to be an honorable guest in your country. I fully respect your laws and your culture. I'm only asking for a chance to examine this area for possible mine sites. There may be none

– that is often the case – but if I do find a viable source for gold and silver, not only I will benefit."

At last, the young man's interest seemed to awaken.

"This is your land, your country, not mine. If I am successful and I do find a possible mine site, I expect to share all profits with the people of this village. If you and your people agree to let me search this area for at least several weeks, perhaps a month or two, I wish to sit down and negotiate with your leaders and elders before I start. I wish to make a binding agreement to share any wealth I might discover."

The young man was now not so sure of himself. He was wary – there were too many stories about people who trusted gringos and ended up regretting it. On the other hand, this gringo was not a young man. He might be telling the truth, and it might be worthwhile to let him stay for a few weeks. His Uncle Pedro, the village leader, was sitting at a table in the cantina. He had heard the whole conversation. Perhaps it would be best to ask him to decide.

Using the local indigenous language, which he assumed the gringo would not understand, he spoke to his leader.

"Uncle Pedro, you've heard what this man says. Do you have any wise advice for me? Would you like me to question him further?"

"No, Felipe, that is not necessary. I've heard him, and I'll speak with him myself."

The young man turned to Henry.

"Señor, my Uncle Pedro is the leader of our village. He wishes to speak to you."

Henry looked back at the man sitting at the nearest small table, who gestured to him to sit down on one of the other chairs.

Henry sat. "Greetings, señor. Thank you for speaking with me. I assume you heard my conversation with your nephew. I'm seeking your permission to join your village for a short while. I need a place to stay while I search for possible gold and silver deposits in this area. I wish to make some money, as I told your nephew, but I'm aware that these lands are your ancestral home. It's only right and proper that I share with you any value I gain from your country."

The headman Pedro betrayed no emotion but signalled Henry to continue.

"As you can see, I'm not young, and I'm on my own. I'm a stranger here – I know none of your people and you do not know me. I can only ask you, respectfully, to give me the chance I request. If you don't wish me to remain here, I have no choice but to accept your decision and I'll leave immediately. However, if that is the case, I would ask you to grant me safe passage out of your lands. I have come in peace, and I wish to leave in peace."

At that, Pedro nodded slightly.

"On the other hand, if you're willing to allow me my request for a place to stay and permission to explore your land for a while, I'd be most grateful."

The man nodded, closed his eyes, and considered Henry's words. If he allowed the stranger to remain in his village, he would have to explain his decision carefully to his people. In particular, the Onelas and the Barquesas families would have to be convinced, given their hostility to gringos – a rightful hostility that stemmed from the killing of several of their ancestors by Yankee soldiers as they marched to take Mexico City many years ago.

His instincts prompted him to accept the words of this stranger and allow him to stay and search for gold and silver. However, he would have to be seen to demand a fair outcome for his people if the man's prospecting were successful. The man seemed to pose no threat to his village, and he was offering a chance, probably a slight chance, he had to admit, for his people to reap great benefits in the future.

He opened his eyes and looked directly at Henry.

"Señor, I have made my decision, which you can accept or not. I'm willing to let you stay for a few months here with my people and I'm willing to allow you to search our lands for the riches you seek. However, in return, I must demand that any precious metals that you find remain the property of my people. Nevertheless, I'm willing to share that property with you in a fair way that compensates you for your time and your work and rewards you for bringing this opportunity to the village of Moache."

Henry relaxed, smiled and nodded.

"Sir, I realize that there may be no gold and silver for you to find. I will ask of you a payment of one thousand Yankee dollars, up front, which you will forfeit, if, after ten weeks, you've found nothing, and I'll ask you to agree to leave our village immediately after the passing of ten weeks if you are unsuccessful. I will, in turn, guarantee your safe passage out of our country."

Henry pursed his lips and nodded slightly.

"In return, you will be allowed to stay without restriction in our village for exactly ten weeks. There is one unoccupied *casa* where you may live. It was used before by an elderly lady who has since moved on."

Henry knew that this meant she had died, but in many indigenous cultures it was taboo to speak directly of death or to name a dead person.

"If you're successful, and I wish you well because it will benefit my people, I'm prepared to allow you to take half the profits of any mine for one year. After that, my people will assume full control of such a mine, but we will continue to pay you twenty-five per cent of all future profits."

Henry realized that this man, whom most outsiders would have considered uneducated and naïve, was, in face, a very wise and competent negotiator.

"If you do succeed, we'll insist on this arrangement being confirmed in a contract which is legally binding under Mexican law. Normally, my people have as little to do with the state authorities as possible, but this venture has the potential to produce large profits and we must safeguard our rights."

Henry knew that he was dealing with a formidable man who knew how to conduct business deals.

"If you do find a viable mine, I will allow you to remain in our village for the first year of its operation, after which you must leave your temporary residence here. In such a case, you will be welcome to return for short visits at any time. This is my considered offer, señor. Do you wish to remain here on those conditions, or do you wish to leave immediately? If you do decide to leave, I will guarantee your safe departure."

Henry was somewhat taken aback by the stark language of the offer. He would have to relinquish control over any precious metal that he found. On the other hand, the leader's offer, if honored in the long run, could net him a nice income if he did find a decent source of gold. He had chosen this particular area because it looked most promising on the map. He would be relatively safe for the next ten weeks, so he stood to lose nothing by accepting the offer.

"Thank you, señor, for your carefully considered offer. You drive a hard bargain. I would have preferred a greater percentage of the future profits, but I believe your offer to be fair and I trust you to honor your word. I accept your proposition, Sir."

The two men shook hands and then sealed the deal with a bottle of beer and a shot of the best tequila in the house.

42

FORTUNE FAVORS THE BRAVE

Many people who have no experience of dealing with isolated groups of indigenous people often regard them as being, in some sense, unsophisticated. People like Henry, who had spent a lot of time working with such groups, know better. True, people like the inhabitants of Moache did not have access to, or knowledge of, the latest technological innovations. But they did have an intimate knowledge of their ancestral country and understood the intricacies and subtleties of their local environment as well as, or even better than, most academic scientists.

As well as that deep knowledge of their natural environment, many people in such isolated pockets of humanity often have a clear and sophisticated understanding of human nature. This knowledge may well be filtered through a complex cultural perspective, but that does not weaken its validity.

Henry understood well that his new neighbors were not child-like savages of limited intelligence. For centuries, colonizers, settlers, and those who wanted to exploit the indigenous people had underestimated their capabilities and often paid a price for that miscalculation. Despite his many character flaws and despite being largely a man of his time and place – a decidedly racist, white supremacist – Henry had progressively developed a respectful appreciation for the qualities of indigenous people, an attitude way before its time.

He spent his first week in the village settling in and trying to meet as many of the villagers as he could. He managed to curtail his womanizing instincts; making a mistake in that area could prove dangerous, even fatal.

One of the younger men of the village, Tomas Gutierrez, had learned a little English at boarding school. Most of the villagers had received little formal education, but he was an exception. A visiting padre had spotted Tomas's quick wit and ready intelligence and managed to secure a scholarship for him to attend a boarding school in Piedras Negras. He stayed for three years, but then his parents demanded he return to them to help with the farming duties. Tomas cultivated Henry's attention and constantly tried to practice his English on him. Henry humored the young man, who readily agreed to act as a guide for Henry until he got his bearings.

With the help of Tomas, Henry began to translate the abstract features of his map into a picture of the actual landscape. He worked out the most promising features and set out to assess them. At first, he didn't stray far from Moache, staying within a day's walk. Then, gradually, he expanded his search area so that he was away from the village for three or four days at a time.

Henry's plan of operation was simple. He would pan for alluvial gold in the many streams, and if he found a promising amount would then trek upstream looking for likely sources – veins of metal in gold-bearing rock. It was a pattern that had worked before, and he continued to use it.

In the middle of his fourth week in Moache, Henry made a promising find. He recovered not only quite a few grains of gold in the sand, but also found a small nugget on the stream bed weighing maybe a third of an ounce. In addition, the granular gold in that spot was in greater abundance than he had found elsewhere in the area and, in a sign that was very promising, there were many small pieces of quartz in the bed of the stream. Henry knew well that where you find white quartz, you often find yellow gold.

Henry returned to the village for two days to re-provision himself and to organize the use of a local burro to carry his tools. He then let it be known that he would be gone for a week or so. Henry suppressed any feelings of excitement to avoid unwarranted conclusions among the villagers. He had been in this position many times before and a couple of times had actually found a promising reef of quartz – but so far he had never discovered a valuable vein of gold. Would this finally be his time?

Henry found the spot where he had discovered the nugget and set up a campsite on a level patch of sandy soil with some grass cover. A more abundant grassy patch was not far away, and he could let the burro graze there. This burro, by the way, was an "ornery cuss" of an animal. He was headstrong, stubborn and tried Henry's patience to breaking point. Still, he was relying on the beast to carry his heavy tools, so he couldn't risk hurting him or stirring up even more resistance. Henry bit his tongue and refrained from yelling obscenities at the animal, despite being sorely tempted.

With camp set up and the burro safely tethered in the nearby patch of grass – "meadow" was too grand a word for it – Henry set about panning the sandy bottom of the fast-flowing, cold little stream. That afternoon he found two more nuggets, both slightly bigger than the first, and he had separated from the sand at least an ounce of granular and flaked gold.

Dusk fell and Henry built up a large fire. He brought the burro closer to the tent and tethered it to a nearby scrubby little tree. He didn't think mountain lions were much of a threat in this country, but the night-time air was filled with the howling of coyotes. They were, perhaps, not as great a threat as a mountain lion, but a large pack of coyotes could easily take down a burro – or a man. They, too, avoided fire, so Henry made sure that his campfire would burn brightly into the night.

He was encouraged and excited by his day's rewards. Tomorrow, he would head upstream, pan some more likely spots with good, sandy bottoms, and see where the stream led him.

43

EUREKA!

The next morning, the sun rose into a cloudless sky, the air warming quickly from its overnight chill. Henry ate a hearty breakfast, then washed out his pans and dishes in the stream – he had learned over the years never to leave any dirty dishes or scraps of food around his campsite, because they attracted all sorts of unwanted wildlife. He put the hobbled burro out to pasture, and then set about searching for gold.

As he made his way upstream, he found many small eddies or places where the little stream made a wide turn over a sandy bottom. As he panned and panned, the odd sock that he used to hold his gold dust began to fill up.

And then he saw it.

The sun was at a perfect angle to light up a bright yellow patch on the stream bed. Henry reached down and touched it. Then he tried to pull it away from the sand, but it refused to yield. Finally, he used his small pickaxe as a lever and prized up the nugget. It weighed at least a pound.

Henry was ecstatic. This was by far the largest lump of gold he'd ever found. He was sure that he was close to the real thing – a mother lode that would forever change his life again. The large nugget was worth thousands of dollars – but, more importantly, the vein of gold it came from was possibly worth millions.

He continued to move upstream, stopping to pan whenever he found a suitable place. He found many more small nuggets and had to tie off his sock and start filling another one. His excitement was intense. Henry had probably never felt like this before. Yes, he had been in raptures when he received news of the first successful oil well, but this was different. He was not removed from the source of his joy by hundreds or even thousands of miles. He was standing in it!

At last, Henry began to climb more steeply. The stream was tumbling down a rocky race and there were only a few large stones or small boulders that might hide bits of gold beneath their upstream sides.

And then he saw it.

The stream was, in fact, a spring. Its origin was at the base of a rock wall, which was at least 20 feet high. The wall gleamed white in the sun. It was solid quartz.

Henry's excitement increased until it was almost unbearable. This had to be it – the mother lode he'd been seeking since he started prospecting. He clambered up the hill over broken rocks until he could stand and examine the wall of quartz.

He thought he saw a gleam of gold within the wall's surface. A few blows of the hammer and he was staring at a vein of pure gold. It was only a small vein but, even so, it was a valuable find, worth thousands of dollars. What treasures lay deeper within the quartz? To answer that question Henry would have to open a proper mine and drill into the side of the hill where the quartz wall stood.

It was now time to return to Moache and discuss his good luck with Don Pedro, as he had taken to calling the village chief, much to Pedro's amusement.

Henry broke off a good-sized piece of gold-bearing quartz and carried it back to his campsite with the rest of the alluvial gold he'd found that day. He hurriedly packed up his things and fetched the burro. He carefully concealed and protected most of his heavy tools at the camp site, reasoning that the burro might be more co-operative with a lighter load. With any luck, he would make it back to Moache before sunset.

The burro was, indeed, less cantankerous with its smaller and lighter load. Henry walked into the "Main Street" of Moache – his name for the only dirt track in the village – just as the last rosy shades of the setting sun faded behind the western hills. He went to his little house to freshen up, shave and change his clothes. Then he walked over to the cantina, which was already doing a good evening's trade. He ordered a beer, a bowl of chili, and a couple of corn tortillas – which was that night's sole food offering, as indeed it was almost every other night.

When he had finished eating, Henry walked over to Don Pedro who, as usual, was sitting at his favorite table with a bottle of beer in front of him.

"Señor, we need to talk. Privately. If you can come to my small casa, it would be best. I will buy a bottle of good tequila to make it worth your while."

And with that Henry gave Pedro a cheeky wink. The village headman was immediately interested. Perhaps this gringo had some good news for him. If not, he would at least get to drink a few good shots of fine tequila. He had noticed that the gringo, Enrique, only ever bought *Don Julio Añejo*, the best tequila in the cantina.

44

TIME FOR A FIESTA!

Henry headed back to his little casa. He fired up his two oil lanterns and brought out two glasses, which he set on his table with the bottle of tequila. Then he went into the back room and retrieved his backpack, which he set down on the floor next to his chair.

He didn't have long to wait. Pedro knocked at his door and Henry called him in. He stood and they shook hands.

"Don Pedro, I have some wonderful news for you. I believe that I have found a valuable vein of gold on your people's land. It is at the wall of quartz rock where the stream your people call a*gua frio* ("cold water") emerges from the ground. This is my evidence."

And, with that, Henry produced the piece of quartz that contained part of the vein of gold. He then lifted the large nugget he had found from his backpack and put that, too, on the table. On a large dinner plate, he placed all the smaller gold nuggets he had found, and on a similar plate he emptied his socks of their gold dust.

"*Madre de Dios!*" ("Mother of God!").

Pedro was a Catholic, as were all the villagers, at least in name and according to baptismal records. Some of the villagers, mostly women and children, were very devout and practiced their religion fervently; although, no one would claim that many of the men in the village of Moache took their religion very seriously. It did, however, provide people like Pedro with some very useful phrases for swearing.

"Don Pedro, *mi amigo*, I wish to give to you this large nugget. It is worth more than half the value of the total amount of gold on the table. Please consider it a personal gift from me to you for allowing me access to your land. If you want to share it with the rest of your village that is your business. However, I want you to know that what is left on this table – the gold in the quartz, the nuggets, and the gold dust – is, as we have agreed, half for me and half for your village."

Then Henry poured out the first of quite a few shots of tequila drunk by the pair that night.

They discussed the situation at length and agreed that, for the moment, it was best to keep the knowledge of Henry's discovery a secret. They also agreed that Henry should return to the quartz deposit with two men from the village who could be trusted. They and Henry would begin to open a mine shaft and, with luck, they would find even more, larger deposits of gold. One of the men would be Tomas and the other would be Felipe, Pedro's nephew from the cantina. Neither was afraid of hard work, and both could be trusted implicitly.

Two days later, Henry, Tomas and Felipe, accompanied by two burros loaded with camping gear, tools and food, left the village and headed for the gold-bearing stream.

They soon reached the site of Henry's original camp where they pitched their tents and unloaded the burros. The burros were put to pasture on the only patch of decent grass while the men began to make their way upstream.

When they reached the wall they took a break, ate some food and slaked their thirst with water from the stream, before beginning to attack the dense quartz with picks. The work was hard and heavy, but they made steady progress. They followed the visible vein of gold to its end, collecting all the gold-bearing ore and chipping off as much quartz as possible. They loaded this gold ore into their backpacks. Then they took a break before continuing to carve a shaft into the wall.

Eventually, they found the yellow gleam of yet another vein of gold. This vein was larger than the first one and its existence suggested that more gold would be found the deeper they dug.

Henry was now satisfied that the site was a potential mother lode, a mine that could well make both him and the inhabitants of Moache very rich indeed. It would not make sense to continue digging by hand on a small scale. They knew enough about the deposit to know it was worth using explosives and machinery to extract the gold-bearing ore. Once it was definitively established that the mine contained sufficient gold to justify the expense, they would bring in stamping machinery to crush the rock and recover the gold on site.

They returned to the village and, once again, Henry met in private with Don Pedro. They agreed that the next step was to formally establish the claim over the site. For legal reasons, this would be most simply done in Henry's name. However, before the claim was settled, they would sign a legal contract to confirm the terms agreed verbally between Henry and Pedro.

The next morning, Henry and Pedro drove off in Henry's Jeep heading for Piedras Negras. When they got there, they went straight to the law office that Pedro's people had used in the past for legal matters. They explained to the lawyer what they wanted, and he agreed to draw up a contract for them. It would be ready the following afternoon.

Henry and Pedro checked into a good hotel and shared a wonderful meal that evening in a nearby restaurant. The pair finished off the night in the hotel bar, drinking tequila.

The next morning, the rather hung-over Henry and Pedro had a big breakfast in the hotel, then checked out and killed time sitting in the central plaza watching the pigeons until lunch time. They ate a light lunch of tacos in a small restaurant near the law office, then, at precisely 2 p.m., as arranged, they entered the law office and signed the contract.

With the help and advice of the lawyer, they drove to the Coahuila state government offices and registered Henry's claim on the site near Moache. Their mission complete, Pedro and Henry drove back to Moache, arriving shortly after sunset.

There was now no need for any further secrecy. The necessary legal screws had been turned and Henry's agreement with Pedro had been locked down by a legally binding contract.

It was announced that the following Sunday Moache would celebrate its good fortune with an all-day fiesta. It would begin with Mass at the local church. Then the priest would bless all the gold that had been recovered so far and ask God to provide them with even more.

That Sunday, they prepared a huge feast with several whole pigs and goats roasted on spits. The ladies of the village provided tortillas and beans, and the cantina sold its beer and tequila at cost. The local general store provided soft drinks, again at cost.

A mariachi band from Piedras Negras was hired to perform that evening. There was, quite literally, dancing in the street.

45

AFTER THE MUSIC STOPS

The fiesta must have been a great success because the citizens of Moache awoke on Monday morning with a collective headache. Everyone was now optimistic that they would be far better off in the future, all thanks to the old gringo, señor Enrique.

The night before, Henry had found himself paired up with a local widow, Marie-Clara Cano. How it had happened he wasn't quite sure. She was an attractive woman in her forties, rather slim by Moache standards – and she was obviously ready, willing and able to stick to Henry for the whole fiesta and then remain for the rest of the night in his bed. He suspected that Pedro had a hand in Marie-Clara's sudden appearance, but whatever the case he was quite happy with the results. Apparently, she had no other suitor, meaning she was available without the danger of a jealous male response.

The night was enjoyed by everyone. The next day, señora Cano moved into Henry's little house, for all intents and purposes, as his wife.

The next few weeks flashed past in a blur. The village elders, led by Pedro, took over management of the mine, although they wisely retained Henry as a consultant. After they had begun to carve out a reasonable mine shaft, explosives were brought in, and large areas of the quartz wall were blown out to expose what lay behind. Several weeks later, a new, much larger vein of gold was found about 80 yards underground. With the careful use of explosives, this gold was eventually recovered with its quartz sheath.

A small stamping machine, purchased from a defunct mine in Sonora at a very reasonable price, was transported to Moache. This allowed for the crushing of the ore and the extraction of the metallic gold.

Henry was content to sit back and enjoy watching the mine expand and move from strength to strength. And, of course, his bank balance had benefitted greatly as well. By global standards the Moache mine was small. Nevertheless, in its first year of operation, the mine made a profit of more than U.S.$500,000, half of which went into Henry's bank account. Nevertheless, in accordance with their contract, Henry was now required to leave Moache and from now on his share of the profits from the mine would be reduced to 25 per cent.

Henry's problem was Marie-Clara. Their time together had been lovely, but Henry had no intention of taking her with him when he left Moache. She, on the other hand, now considered herself to be his de facto wife. On the day before his scheduled departure from Moache, they had a screaming row. She demanded he take her with him. He refused. Then he told her that, as far as he knew, he was still legally married to his first wife, Cora. Marie-Clara could never be his legal wife.

When Henry left Moache the next morning he had no idea how much trouble he was in. He drove to Piedras Negras and crossed the Rio Grande into Eagle Pass, Texas. Rufus's new property was less than an hour away and Henry drove straight there.

46

THE CROWS COME HOME TO ROOST

Rufus and Lee welcomed Henry in the warmest way and assured him that he would always have a room in their house. He moved into a bedroom on the second floor and, finally, with the expensive assistance of several local plumbers, got his ensuite bathroom working properly.

Meanwhile, unbeknownst to Henry, Marie-Clara Cano was taking legal action that would ruin him. She sued him for false promises of marriage when he was already legally married, accusing him of breaking their binding agreement that she would become his wife and live with him in the U.S. She sought half of his property, and a sum of $300,000 for the mental strain and distress she had endured as damages. Her claim was lodged in the district court of Texas, in Eagle Pass.

Henry was blindsided. He hired a local lawyer who advised him to negotiate and to accept anything on offer that was less than the full $300,000 claim. He didn't think Henry had any chance of salvaging any more than half his property.

If the claim had been lodged in a Mexican court, Henry would probably have been able to ignore the suit. He would have had claims lodged against him in Mexico, but as long as he remained in the U.S., he would have been able to avoid paying them. But because she filed her claim in a U.S. court, Henry was fully liable.

Henry tried to negotiate, but Marie-Clara's lawyers, obviously aware of her strong legal position, refused. The case went to court in Eagle Pass and the result was full vindication for Marie-Clara and disaster for Henry. The judge ordered Henry to hand over $300,000 immediately to Marie-Clara and to make arrangements for her to receive half of his future income from the mine. Because Henry's personal possessions were not worth very much and would be difficult to split in half, and because his Social Security payments would also be hard to divide, the judge dismissed Marie-Clara's claim over that portion of Henry's property and income. Nevertheless, paying the court's judgment drained his bank account of almost everything. In addition, she had gained half of his 25 per cent in the Moache gold mine. His major source of income was now halved. It would take some time for Henry to recover, financially and emotionally.

Once again, Henry's roller-coaster life had lifted him to the heights, only to come hurtling down in a series of nauseating twists and turns.

He never quite accepted that this result was his own fault. But it was. His sense of entitlement with women had led him to the point where he never even bothered to consider how badly his actions affected his female partners. Now he was paying the price, a big price. At last, he began to realize that he needed to consider the impact his womanizing had had on the women he used.

Ideally, Henry would have loved to find Cora and re-build the genuine happiness that a family offered. But, even if he never found her again, from now on he was convinced that he had to be far more careful and considerate towards the women in his life.

Henry's once-assured future was now in doubt. All he had saved and worked for was gone. He had an income from the U.S. Social Security and 12.5 per cent of a Mexican gold mine that could be 12.5 per cent of nothing if there was no new vein of gold. He resolved to stay, once again, with Rufus and Lee until he could work out what to do next.

47

A BORING INTERLUDE FOR HENRY

Henry stayed in Crystal City for most of the rest of 1958. Yet again, he had been on the verge of realizing his dream, his bank account had grown to a healthy amount, and he had a genuine expectation of a worry-free financial future – only for everything to, once again, come crashing to the ground. His dream of owning a fine, big house in Mexico and of living the life of a wealthy grandee lay in tatters.

Henry was sixty-seven years old and living on his meagre pension supplemented by a monthly check from Mexico, which had already begun to shrink in size as the Moache gold mine slowly, but inevitably, exhausted its rich veins of high-grade ore.

One late autumn morning, Henry rose from his bed and went into the bathroom to shave. He looked at the aging version of who he used to be in the mirror. He was not cut out for the boring routine of life on a farm.

Henry did what he could to help Rufus, who was now buying up to 200 calves a year, just after they were weaned. He would feed them on grass and a crop of oats over the winter, supplemented by hand feeding with grain sorghum to fatten them for sale the following spring as yearlings.

Apart from an initial period of intense work, when the calves had to be branded, drenched and inoculated – and the bull calves castrated – followed by the work at the end of the cycle, loading the fattened calves for transport to the saleyards, there was never a lot to do. There was always the routine maintenance of farm equipment, planting the oats then, six months later, harvesting the sorghum and threshing the dried seed heads to fill sacks with the grain for storage – a repetitious cycle of work that Henry found incredibly tedious.

As he looked back at himself from the mirror, he made a quick decision. He would give mining one more go. He would return to Nogales and decide what to do with himself from there. His old friend and partner, J.J. Wagner, had died in the early 1950s, but there were still a few people in Nogales he could talk to. He would find out from them the most lucrative areas to explore.

After they ate breakfast and had a second cup of coffee, Henry told Rufus of his decision. He found the reply quite insightful.

"Well, Henry, I can't say that I'm surprised. You were never cut out for life on a farm, and I've noticed you getting more and more antsy during the last few months. All I can say is, I wish you well and you are always welcome back to stay with us when you need to."

Henry knew that, from now on, he would have to return to the U.S. regularly, even if he managed to establish himself again in Mexico. The Social Security regulations required all pensioners to spend at least sixty-one days out of every two-year period resident in the U.S., otherwise their pensions would be discontinued. Even if he never made another big discovery, he could still live comfortably in rural Mexico on his U.S. pension, and that was the life that he missed. He could still do some prospecting and, who knows, he might, yet again, strike it rich. But whether he did or not, he would be happier living in a Mexican village doing some prospecting now and then, rather than wasting away on his brother's farm.

By living with Rufus and Lee and helping around the farm in exchange for his room and board, Henry was able to save most of his Social Security money. He did drive to Eagle Pass once or twice a month for the weekend, doing the rounds of the bars – and, sometimes, the bordellos – but that was not an expensive form of entertainment. He would begin his new life in Nogales with a small nest egg to fall back on. Otherwise, he would live on his pension payments.

48

BACK TO THE BEGINNING

Henry still had his old army surplus Jeep ambulance. It was aging, like himself, but still reliable. He reckoned it would keep going for a long time yet, as long as it was not mistreated – and Henry always looked after his cars. He never pushed them beyond their limits.

Taking his time, he drove from Crystal City to El Paso and then on to Nogales. When he arrived, he checked into a cheap motel and contacted an old friend, Gilberto Morales. They met that evening in Consuela's Cantina, the same place where Henry used to meet J.J. and where he had begun his short career as a smuggler. After going over old times and lamenting the loss of so many friends, they finally began to discuss business opportunities in Mexico.

Gilberto told him that new mines had been opened in both northern Sonora and Chihuahua, several by speculative prospectors who had struck it rich. Henry listened intently. He knew these areas and had been there himself, but he had never been lucky enough to find a viable source of gold.

Now that the Yaqui Indians had reached an agreement with the central government in Mexico City and had regained some of their territory and some of their independence, their lands were, once again, relatively peaceful and available for prospecting. This was one area that Henry would consider. He would also have a look around other parts of Sonora again.

Henry and Gilberto had just finished eating a plate each of tacos and beans, washed down with a bottle of *Dos Equis* lager, when they were joined by Paco, a friend of Gilberto. Gilberto introduced Paco to Henry and explained that he'd asked Paco to join them because he was involved in cross-border business and might know about a few other opportunities.

The conversation began with a general discussion about business in the Arizona–Sonora border area. Paco pointed out that the U.S. was producing vast quantities of consumer goods at relatively low prices. As had been the case in the past, high import duties and local taxes made these goods expensive in Mexico. Find the right items to buy in Arizona and sell in Sonora, avoiding the Mexican customs duties, of course, and a man could make considerable profits in a short time.

Having engaged in smuggling many years ago, Henry was aware of the risks and the potential rewards. And, he thought, he wouldn't mind building up his capital before he embarked on more prospecting.

More beer and a few shots of tequila later, Henry was well on his way to re-entering the world of smuggling. This time, however, he would not trade in fine wines and gourmet foods, which required too much preparation and were awkward to handle. No, he would now turn to the medium-sized luxury goods that were readily available in the U.S., and which could be transported in his ambulance.

The obvious items were televisions. Used TVs could be picked up in Arizona for next to nothing and sold for a good price in Mexico where the taxes on TVs were prohibitive. He could carry at least a dozen in his Jeep. If he only made three or four successful trips to Hermosillo, he would make enough money to nearly double his bank account. The only problem he could see was how to off-load the TVs safely in Mexico.

Paco had a suggestion. He had a business associate who lived near Hermosillo. Several times this man had offered to buy all Paco's goods as a single package. Paco sold them to him at a discount, of course, but it was still worth his while. One deal and it was done, and Paco had avoided the hassle of finding reliable customers for each individual item and the need to hang around in Hermosillo until all his goods were sold.

Henry took the man's name: señor Ernesto Balboa, who lived in the small city of Ures, just east of Hermosillo. Paco offered to contact him and alert him to Henry's plan.

Two days later, Paco rang Henry's motel room. Señor Balboa was most interested in acquiring used television sets. He was willing to pay top dollar for up-market TVs in good condition.

The next day, Henry drove north to the larger city of Tucson. He had spotted numerous TVs for private sale advertised in the local paper. After a day of driving around Tucson and haggling with people over the value of their old TVs – they always thought they were worth more than they were – Henry had fourteen televisions loaded into the back of his Jeep ambulance, carefully packed and separated by sheets of corrugated cardboard to avoid any damage on the road trip. Henry had chosen only the best quality TVs, most of which were being sold by people who had upgraded to a larger screen or a newer model. He had managed to convince most of the sellers that a used TV was worth very little. He told them that he planned to refurbish the old sets and sell them with new-set guarantees. He pointed out that his price, never more than $25, was probably as much as they could get from anyone, and that he was there, cash in hand, ready to buy their used TV on the spot. Most of them caved in and took Henry's offer.

Henry left before sunrise the next morning, crossing the border at an unsupervised point on a minor dirt road. But he didn't follow that road directly to the main highway, which the Mexican customs officers sometimes patrolled. Instead, Henry took a series of tracks and small unpaved roads until he made it to the back streets of the Mexican city of Nogales. He found his way through the residential areas and finally connected with the highway to Hermosillo.

He arrived in Hermosillo without incident a little over three hours later. He then turned east, and half an hour later was in the small city of Ures. Following the directions he had been given, he arrived at a warehouse owned by señor Balboa just before noon.

Henry had spent his time on the road calculating the price he might ask for the fourteen TVs. His outlay was less than $300: $240 for the TVs and $60 for fuel. He decided to ask for around $100 each, or $1,400 for the lot. He expected to get rather less than that in the end. Such negotiations take time and follow certain clearly defined rules. The vendor always asks for more than he expects to get, and the buyer always offers less than he expects to pay. Eventually, they reach a mutually satisfactory agreement.

And so it was with señor Balboa. He carefully examined the TVs, one by one, noting any slight flaws or scratches. There weren't many – Henry had chosen his purchases carefully. He then asked Henry how much he wanted for the lot, and Henry replied, "Fourteen hundred U.S. dollars."

Señor Balboa looked pained. Shaking his head, "*Mi amigo*, these TVs are not made of gold. I couldn't possibly give you more than six hundred and fifty dollars."

The haggling went on for another ten minutes or so. The agreed price was $975.

One of señor Balboa's men unloaded the TV sets, while Henry and his new customer sealed their deal with a shot of tequila and a handshake. Balboa made it clear that he could take a shipment like this one about once a week, although he asked Henry to telephone him and confirm dates and times for all deliveries in advance.

Henry had a late lunch in Hermosillo and then drove back to Nogales that afternoon. He had hoped to make a bit more on the TVs, but, in the end, he was satisfied with a profit of almost $700. Not bad for two days' work.

Over the next four weeks, Henry made three more trips to sell used TVs to señor Balboa. He had to drive three hours to Phoenix for the last two weeks because there were no more suitable used TVs at the right price in Tucson.

After his fourth trip, Henry had cleared $2,500, enough of an increase to his nest egg for him to start prospecting once more.

Henry telephoned señor Balboa and told him that he would be returning to prospecting and that he would make no more deliveries of TVs in the near future. He assured him that he had enjoyed doing business and if he ever returned to Nogales to live, he would contact him about resuming their business. Señor Balboa made equally polite noises before they ended the call.

49

HENRY ENCOUNTERS THE POLICE

Henry chose his site carefully. It was in the far north-east of Sonora state, not more than 200 miles south of the U.S. border and just northwest of the state border with Chihuahua. The land was rugged, rough and barren. There were only a few isolated villages in the area, and they were mostly quite small.

Henry finally settled on a village with about 700 inhabitants called San Alonso. He packed his Jeep with camping gear and mining tools and, once again, set out to find his fortune – or, at least, to enjoy some isolation.

He drove for miles along a dusty, washboard track until he crested a hill and saw the village spread out in the valley below. The bright green fields testified to a reliable water supply, but their small size indicated a lack of fertile land.

He wound his way down a steep, switch-back track to the village. He was surprised to encounter a rather large Federale, dressed in the brown uniform of the Federal Police, which was straining somewhat along the button line to hold in the man's belly. He raised his hand, palm out, fingers pointing up, in the universal signal:

"*Alto!*" ("Stop!")

Surprised, Henry rolled down his window as the Federale strutted over.

"Who are you, señor? Do you have your papers? Please show them to me and explain what business you have in San Alonso."

"My name is Henry Anderson. I am a U.S. citizen. I'm hoping to find a place to stay while I prospect for gold and silver in this area. I think you'll find my passport and visa are in order."

"My name is *Capitan* Morales. I must warn you, sir, there has been some trouble here in the past few weeks. A group of unhappy Indians has joined forces with a small number of left-wing activists from the university in Mexico City. They have been disrupting the peace. We heard that they might be sheltering here, so I was dispatched with ten good men to round them up. Unfortunately, they disappeared into the mountains before we could contain them. My *comandante* has decided to pull us out again and we are leaving this afternoon to return to our compound in Nuevas Casas Grandes Municipality, just across the state border in Chihuahua. As a *Capitan* in the Federal Police of Mexico, my advice to you, sir, is to find somewhere else to stay, although I cannot forbid you from staying here, if you insist."

"Thank you for your advice, *Capitan*, I will consider it carefully. I am a simple prospector looking for precious metals. I carry a licensed pistol to protect myself from snakes and wild animals in the mountains, but I am a man of peace, and I obey and respect, totally, the laws of your country. Is there a cantina of some sort in this village where I might have a cold beer and something to eat?"

"*Si*. You cannot miss it, sir. As we speak, my men are sitting in the plaza out front, having a beer themselves before we set off."

With that, the Federale stood aside and allowed Henry to continue into the heart of the little village. Sure enough, an unruly group of young men in brown uniforms sat drinking at tables in a small plaza. Behind them was the entrance to the local cantina.

Henry parked his Jeep and walked through the open door. There was one patron, an elderly gentleman, seated at a table drinking a beer. A beaded curtain parted to the right of the bar and a young woman emerged.

"What do you want?" Her tone was not particularly friendly.

What a shame, thought Henry. *She's rather attractive.*

"I'm Henry Anderson and I'm prospecting for gold and silver. I'm hoping to be here for a few months searching for deposits in the surrounding hills. May I have a beer, a *Dos Equis* lager, if you have it, and something to eat, if that is possible? I'd also like to arrange to stay somewhere in the village for the next three or four months, maybe longer. Can you help?"

"*Si,* señor, I can serve you a beer. We have chili with beans and tortillas, if that suits you. As far as a place to stay, you will have to talk to our headman. He is away this afternoon but will be back this evening."

"Thank you, señorita, I'll have a beer and a bowl of your chili, beans and tortillas."

Henry sat down at a table with his back to a wall, facing the front door. This was his usual practice in a strange place. He was unarmed, but at least he could see who was entering, and he might be able to take evasive action if it looked like there were going to be any hostilities.

The young woman brought him his beer and, shortly after that, a steaming bowl of chili accompanied by a covered basket of warm corn tortillas. The chili was surprisingly good, well-seasoned with chilies, just as Henry liked it.

He finished his meal and ordered another beer. He could hear a large vehicle, a truck, as it turned out, pull up outside the cantina. Then he heard shouted commands in Spanish. He could see through the open front door that the members of the police detachment were all climbing into the back of a truck with their backpacks and equipment. It was a flatbed truck with raised sides and a tailgate, which was slammed shut after the last policeman climbed in. Over the back of the truck, a tightly fitted canvas cover arched from one side to the other, providing some shade from the sun. Along the sides of the truck's bed there were wooden benches for the men to sit on.

The police captain stuck his head through the doorway.

"*Adios, muchachos.* (Goodbye, guys.) We'll return if we hear that those mad bastards have the balls to re-appear in San Alonzo. And a special *adios* to you, my sweet Lucia," as he blew a kiss in the barmaid's direction.

He turned on his heel and walked out of the cantina.

Out of the corner of his eye, Henry saw Lucia expertly dispatch a large gob of spittle, which arched high in the direction of the door, landing on the floor just behind the retreating boots of the captain, who climbed into the front seat of the truck and drove away.

Henry decided that he'd better not laugh out loud, but he did catch her eye and, smiling broadly, give her the thumbs up. Of course, Henry fancied her. But he was aware that he would have to know a lot more about the social arrangements in this village before he attempted any romantic advances with the local womenfolk.

50

HENRY ENCOUNTERS A REVOLUTION

That evening, the headman, known as Esteban, returned. After an appropriate delay, Henry approached him and explained his intentions. For a village leader, Esteban was surprisingly young, perhaps just into his forties. He listened attentively to Henry's request, but he did not show much emotion, and he certainly didn't crack a smile.

"Señor, we have very few outside visitors to our small village. We are a close-knit, independent and reasonably contented extended family. We are wary of strangers and always have been. Equally, we are not happy when the federal or state authorities visit us and try to assert their control."

Henry nodded to indicate that he understood.

"We are a proud people and we have fought in the past and paid a price in blood to safeguard our independence. Nowadays, the authorities generally leave us to our own devices, but every now and then, as you saw today, they attempt to assert their power and control. And, as you also saw today, they rarely succeed."

Once again, Henry nodded his agreement.

"Señor Anderson, I have no reason to doubt your words. Equally, I have no reason to trust you. I am inclined to ask you to leave tomorrow at your earliest convenience; however, Lucia has put in a good word for you. She admired the way you reacted to that *bastardo Federale Capitan*. Lucia is usually a good judge of character, so I am prepared to let you stay a week, after which I will discuss with my advisors how to proceed."

"Thank you, señor. I'm honored by your trust, and I'll do nothing to make you regret it. I'm sure that by the end of the week you will have every reason to allow me to stay in your village for a while longer."

"There are three unoccupied *casas* in the village at the moment. They've been used by those bastards for the last three days, so they probably all stink. You are welcome to choose one for yourself for the next week. If we decide to let you stay among us for a longer time, we can negotiate the terms of payment. Your first week will cost you fifty American dollars, payable to me now."

Henry thanked him again for the chance to stay and paid him the $50. He asked if he might buy Esteban a drink. Esteban accepted his offer, and they downed two shots of good tequila and shook hands to seal the arrangement.

Henry examined the three small houses that were available. One was far better furnished and more recently refurbished than the other two, so he chose it straight away.

He brought in his clothing and some equipment. The rest he left in the ambulance. The beds all looked comfortable but the bed linen was dirty and stained. He stripped one bed and resolved to wash the sheets and pillowcases in the morning. That night, after refreshing himself at the water pump outside the back door, Henry climbed into his sleeping bag and quickly fell into a sound, deep sleep.

The next morning, as his bedroom began to brighten, Henry emerged from his slumber. Suddenly, he was alert in an instant. Someone was in the house. He had left his pistol in the car, so he couldn't defend himself if he was attacked. There were, in fact, two voices, both young and male. They stopped talking. He didn't know it, but they had just seen his pile of gear in the main room and realized that someone was using the house.

"*Hola*, who is there?" Henry called out.

He saw a young man, perhaps twenty years old, dressed in blue jeans and a T-shirt imprinted with the face of Che Guevara on the front, peer around the door frame.

"Pardon, señor, we thought this *casa* was unoccupied."

A second head appeared above the first. He was dressed in a similar fashion.

Henry quickly sized up the situation. These must be the "revolutionary" university students – or two of them, anyway – that the Federale mentioned yesterday. They looked harmless and Henry decided a bit of sugar was better than vinegar at catching flies.

"*Si,* comrade, this house is occupied by me since last night. I'm staying for a week and then I'll either move on or remain here for a few months to prospect for gold and silver in this area. I'm Henry. Enrique if you prefer. I met a *bastardo Federale* yesterday who told me he was looking for a group of, as he put it, unhappy Indians and left-wing university students. He's well gone, thank god. Would I be wrong to presume that you're two of the 'left-wing university students'?"

The two young men looked at one another, then back at Henry.

"If we were, what would it matter to you, 'comrade'?"

"It wouldn't matter at all. Your revolution is none of my business and I'm in no position to judge you or your activities. I suspect you're hungry, though, if you've been on the run for a few days. If you let me get dressed, I'll be happy to share my breakfast with you."

The two lads nodded, looked at each other and withdrew.

Henry rose and dressed. He walked out into the main room. As with most of the cottages in such villages, there was one big room for living and eating and one or more bedrooms for sleeping – this house had two bedrooms. He opened one of his ice chests and removed some eggs and bacon. He set up his gas-fired cooktop, which had two rings, and placed a frying pan over the heat on one side. On the other burner, he put a saucepan into which he emptied two cans of beans, and then he turned down the heat.

"*Mi amigos*, it would be easier if I knew what to call you. Then I could ask one of you to fill my coffee pot with water so we can have coffee with our breakfast."

"I'm Fidel – I chose the name myself after the great leader of the Cuban revolution."

"And I am called Karl. My parents named me Carlos, but my comrades prefer the name of the great founder of Marxism."

"Alright, Fidel or Karl, I don't care which of you, will one of you please fill this coffee pot outside at the pump?"

Fidel took the pot and quickly filled it. Henry set aside the beans and turned up the heat under the coffee pot until it was boiling, then he added coffee to the percolator basket. Within minutes they were sitting down to a meal of bacon, fried eggs, beans and coffee. The young fellows ate like starving wolves.

They can't have had much to eat on the run, thought Henry.

When they had finished, Henry turned to Karl.

"Since Fidel got the coffee water, it's your turn to do the washing up. I think I've done enough by providing the food and doing the cooking, don't you? If Fidel wants to help with the drying, that's fine."

After a certain period of hesitation, the two young men picked up the dishes and the pans and took them to the sink out the back to wash. *They're probably more interested in the theory of a collective society of workers than in the practicalities*, thought Henry.

After the breakfast dishes were washed and dried, Henry and the boys sat down for a chat. He explained to them that he was a prospector. Yes, he was a gringo, a Yankee imperialist, but, in fact, while he intended to make money from his prospecting, he was also conscious of the rights of the indigenous people whose land he was using. He intended to share any wealth he might uncover with his hosts, or, rather, he intended to ask them to share their wealth with him.

He continued telling them that he was no longer a young man, and he only required enough money to end his days in some comfort. He wasn't sure how all this might fit into Marxist–Leninist political theory, but that was not his problem, was it?

He explained that he needed only one bedroom in the house, so if they needed a place to stay and if it was approved by Esteban, he was happy to let them use the second bedroom. They immediately accepted his offer.

After their chat, Henry wandered over to the cantina, where he encountered Esteban sitting at a table drinking a coffee.

"*Hola*, señor Esteban, I trust you had a good night."

"*Si*, Meester Anderson, I slept well. And you?"

"Oh, I slept very well, thank you. However, I was woken up by two strangers in the house, two of the naughty revolutionary students the Federales were after, I believe. I gave them breakfast – they were starving, poor boys – and offered them the second bedroom in the *casa* I'm using for at least this week, subject, of course, to your approval."

Esteban smiled broadly.

"*Gracias*, señor. One of those 'naughty students' is my little brother. My parents named him Bernardo, but he has chosen to call himself Fidel. I would have thought that Bernardo, as in

Bernardo O'Higgins, the Liberator of so much of South America, would have been sufficiently revolutionary for him, but, no, he says he requires a much more modern and Marxist name – so now he is Fidel. In any case, I appreciate your kindness to them. If you wish, I'm happy for them to stay in your *casa* – but I warn you, sir, they eat like horses and do not often contribute any payment or any food for the larder."

"Thank you for the warning, señor, but I am sure I will be able to come to some kind of amicable arrangement with my house guests. If I am not being too presumptuous, I'd like to know what kind of trouble they're in. The fat police *Capitan* yesterday seemed quite serious about capturing them."

Esteban thought for a minute, then decided to trust the gringo. If he turned out to be some kind of spy or informer, his people would deal with him – but he was more inclined to think of him as a genuine man who was what he appeared to be.

"Altogether, there are five students from the university in Mexico City who have come here to support our *compadres* in their struggle. They want their stolen lands returned or, at least, fair compensation for the land taken from them over the years by the greedy owner of the *Rancho de Rosario*, a fat toad of a man who calls himself 'Don Vincente Vasquez'. He claims to own almost half the land in the district, which he treats as his own personal kingdom and which he rules from his grand hacienda about 50 miles east of here.

"San Alonzo lies just west of his holdings. He's never dared to threaten my little village, but the same is not true for my *compadres*. Don Vincente and his well-armed thugs have forced the people of the villages that they seized to either work for him at very poor wages or get out. We are now giving shelter and support to nine of my relatives here. Of course, he has the politicians of the district in his pocket, and they use the Federal Police and even the army to support him."

Henry thanked Esteban for being so forthright and walked back to his *casa*. He had every sympathy for the dispossessed local people. He even admired the students for coming to their support – though he wasn't sure how much use they would be in the long run. They seemed to him to be full of idealism without a lot of practical experience to back up their political theories. Still, they were willing to risk incarceration, or worse, and he admired them for that.

On the other hand, Henry was wary of becoming involved in their fight. He might have to re-think his decision to base himself in San Alonzo and find another, less dangerous, village.

51

WHEN THE RED REVOLUTION COMES

Henry spent the rest of the day pondering his situation. He decided to make a few forays into the surrounding hills, day trips not far from the village. If he came across any promising signs of gold or silver, he might re-evaluate; otherwise, he decided, he would leave San Alonzo at the end of the week.

He also decided to have his evening meals in the cantina. The fare rarely varied, but it was tasty and wholesome. Apart from the spicy chili, which Henry was particularly fond of, once or twice a week and usually at the weekend the cantina served a milder, but still tasty, stew. The meat was usually rabbit, though when someone was lucky enough to kill a wild turkey, then that was used, and it was full of vegetables, always corn, beans and the local yams, or whatever else was in season. The thick reddish-brown sauce had a hint of *mole* about it – the classical Mexican dish that uses unsweetened chocolate as an ingredient.

By eating in the cantina, Henry avoided stocking up on food. At the end of the week he could leave without having to pack a lot of perishable items or leave them behind.

He prepared his backpack for an early start the next morning and wandered over to the cantina.

For some reason that evening the cantina was particularly busy. Henry ordered his beer and chili, found a table and sat down. He now knew a few of the villagers so he nodded greetings to several people at adjacent tables. However, most of the people in the cantina were strangers to him and a few of them, he could tell, were surreptitiously watching him.

He was just finishing his second beer and preparing to leave, when Esteban strode into the cantina, accompanied by two other men Henry did not know.

"Ah, señor Enrique, I am pleased you are here. This is my cousin, Miguel, and his friend, José."

Henry rose, shook their hands, and invited them to sit with him and have a drink. The three men sat down, and Henry brought four glasses of tequila to the table. As the men reached for their glasses, the man named José took his glass and raised it. "*A la revolución!*" ("To the Revolution!"), he declared in a strong voice, but not so loud as to be easily heard at the other tables.

The other two raised their glasses and repeated the toast. Henry joined in after only the slightest hesitation.

José spoke. "We need to talk in private, señor. If you agree, we will meet you in your *casa* in about ten minutes. Is that suitable?"

Henry felt he had little choice.

"I'll get a bottle of decent tequila from the bar and bring it home for our meeting. In ten minutes, then."

Henry rose, bought the tequila, then walked back to his little house. The man José, whom he'd just met, had an air of superiority about him. He was obviously some kind of leader of the disaffected people. Henry was worried about what might follow. He would have to very carefully avoid offending either of his recent acquaintances, or Esteban, for that matter. He'd do his best to control his emotions until he knew what they had in mind.

Henry entered his *casa*, put the bottle on the table and fetched four glasses from the cupboard. He had no sooner put them down than the men knocked at his door and entered.

They all sat at the table while Henry poured out the tequila. They each took a drink, then put down their glasses. Again, José did the talking.

"Señor, we have a great favor to ask of you. Esteban has assured us that you're a good man and that you have sympathy for our cause. I understand that you are not a young man and that you are a guest in our country, therefore, I would not expect you to join us when we fight the *bastardos* who have taken our land. However, you can help us greatly without taking any grave risk."

Henry nodded his assent briefly, though he could see that any kind of help he gave these men would be far more dangerous for him than they implied.

"I have received information this afternoon that the Federales are delivering new automatic weapons and ammunition to all their police posts in this district, starting tomorrow. They will supply the station in Aguas Calientes late in the afternoon, then they will return to Hermosillo. They must slow down to cross the old bridge near the village of San Miguel on their return journey."

Henry could see what was coming and he didn't like it. However, he repressed his fears while maintaining an outward appearance of interest and support.

"Our plan is twofold. First, we will plant explosives under the bridge and detonate them as the munitions truck passes over. With luck, no Federales will survive the fall into the canyon below. A group of our men will see if there are any weapons, ammunition, or other things of value that we can recover from the damaged truck.

"Second, we will attack the police post in Aguas Calientes at approximately the same time as we destroy the bridge. We estimate there are no more than six men at the garrison, and at that hour they will probably be having their evening meal. We will have the element of surprise on our side and should quickly overcome any resistance. Then we will seize all the new automatic weapons and the ammunition.

"We have many supporters, señor, but few decent weapons. This operation, if successful, will give us all the weapons we will need for some time, weapons that will match the best the Federales themselves have.

"Now, señor, this is how you can help us. We will need an escape vehicle that is sturdy enough for the mountain tracks and large enough to carry the weapons we seize. Your old ambulance is perfect."

Henry's heart sank. His worst fears were realized. Obviously, he could not refuse this request. If he tried, they'd probably take it anyway and shoot him as well, because he'd know too much. He'd have to go along with the plan as enthusiastically as he could and face the consequences later – and he was certain there would be consequences.

"*Mi amigos*, I am happy to do anything I can to support your cause. Of course, you may have my old Jeep with my blessings and good wishes for your success.

"I will remove all my belongings first thing in the morning and ensure that the fuel tank is full, and everything is in order. You may take it whenever you want and use it for as long as you need."

Then Henry raised his glass and proposed the toast, with questionable sincerity.

"*Viva, la revolución!*"

To which, the other three raised their glasses and repeated Henry's words.

52

NOTHING IS SIMPLE

The next morning, Henry did as he promised; he emptied the Jeep, topped up the fuel from his supply, checked the oil and the tire pressure, and left the keys in the ignition. He then had breakfast with his housemates, who were quite excited to be involved in José's bold plan.

Henry slung on his backpack and headed off to explore the hills near San Alonzo. There were several likely streams within five miles or so of the village, all across extremely rugged terrain. One stream proved promising. He panned quite a few grains of gold and found one very small nugget, the size of a pebble, which he almost missed because a cloud moved across the sun. When he happened to look at the same spot again, this time in full sunlight, he easily spotted the shining yellow pebble.

He moved upstream and found more grains and flakes in his pan before the weather changed. A wild thunderstorm formed by heat convection over the desert blew across, soaking him in a few minutes. The stream rose around him rapidly, so Henry retreated.

Henry had several hours to kill before it would be time to go to the cantina for his evening meal. After he had dried off and changed into clean, dry clothes, he sat down at his table to think.

He was not at all happy with his situation. If José's military raid went to plan, he and his men wouldn't be back in San Alonzo before about 10 p.m. They had planned their escape using mountain tracks that had to be driven with great care at any time, let alone in the dark. If the plan was successful, Henry reckoned the Federales would be in the village within a day, two at most. Someone would have seen his very distinctive-looking Jeep ambulance and reported it to the Federales, who would be searching for it.

Of course, if disaster struck and the plan failed, the Federales would still show up in the village and demand an explanation from Henry. All these scenarios made him sick with worry.

There was a discernible tension in the cantina that night – everyone seemed on edge. Henry had his dinner, this time a very good rabbit stew, accompanied by a few beers. Then he wandered back to his house. Unusually for him, Henry downed a few glasses of tequila on his own, trying to calm his nerves. Finally, at about 10.30 p.m. he heard the noise of his Jeep driving into the village.

Overall, the raid had been a success but it had not gone perfectly. In the attack on the police post at Aguas Calientes, a police guard had spotted the attackers and raised the alarm. José's men still managed to overwhelm the Federales and drove away with the old ambulance loaded to the gills with weapons and ammo. Unfortunately, it was also loaded with three bodies of men who hadn't survived the attack. Two others had some serious wounds, and the other eleven men escaped with only minor injuries.

They would not meet up with the group who had carried out the detonation of the bridge, but on the police radios that they captured, it sounded like that part of the plan had worked perfectly.

Sadly for Esteban, one of the fatalities was his brother Fidel, or Bernardo. The other lad, Karl, had escaped with a few minor wounds.

Henry walked out of his *casa* and over to the cantina, which was open late for the returned warriors. The mood was both triumphant and sombre. They had succeeded in their plan, reached their goal, but the cost had been greater than expected. Henry's ambulance was, once again, parked outside his house.

The booty of weapons and ammunition had been stashed in several pre-arranged, prepared sites along the mountain track back to San Alonzo. The dead bodies had been buried in temporary graves and the badly wounded men had been left at the camp headquarters for the revolutionaries deep in the bush. One of the men with experience as a nurse was tending to the wounded men there. They had some medical supplies, and adequate food and water to last for the time it would take the men to recover.

Henry approached José, who was struggling to reconcile his mixed emotions – elation at their tactical success, but despair at losing three of his good comrades.

"Greetings, comrade. Congratulations on your success today – and commiserations over the loss of your men. I have decided that it would be best for me to leave early tomorrow morning and return to Nogales. I'm sure someone would have described my ambulance to the Federales, and they will know to come here. I'm hoping to make it back across the border before they find my car. Otherwise, they will undoubtedly seize it and, if they catch me, they will arrest me."

To be honest, José did not particularly care what happened to Henry. The vehicle had been useful for their operation, but now he had other concerns. He would have to lead his men out of the village that night and melt back into the bush, where they would hide until the Federales once again withdrew, as they certainly would, eventually. The old gringo would have to look after himself.

"Do as you please, señor. On behalf of the revolution, I thank you for your assistance."

53

AND NOW, THE CONSEQUENCES

The next morning, Henry rose at dawn and quickly packed his Jeep. He had a cold tortilla for his breakfast, topped up the fuel tank and made a quick visual inspection of the tires. What he saw made him slightly dizzy with worry.

In the dead center of the passenger side door and farther back on the same side of the Jeep, just above the wheel well, were two bullet holes.

If he were stopped by the Federales, he would have no way to explain them. Even if he weren't stopped, anyone he encountered, whether they were passing in a car or standing on the side of the road, would see the bullet holes clearly.

Henry poured a cup of water into a bowl of soil and stirred it with his hands. Then he did his best to pack the sandy mud into the bullet holes and smear lots more mud all around the two spots. He was sure that the mud would eventually dry and fall out of the holes, but his attempt at camouflage was the best he could come up with.

He wiped his hands clean, jumped into the driver's seat and drove out of San Alonzo as fast as he could. He figured that the faster he left the area, the less chance he stood of being caught by the Federales. He soon came across a track that headed into the scrub to the north-east after branching off from the main track from the village. Henry turned onto it and headed cross-country. The little track was hard to follow over rocky ground; Henry had to drive slowly and with great care, but, in his mind, it was a better option than following the normal route north from the village.

He was pretty sure that the track he was on would eventually lead him to the main Mexican Federal Highway 2, which ran east–west, just south of and parallel to the U.S. border between New Mexico and Arizona. It would be too risky for Henry to use the main highway for very long, but he was pretty sure that he would find an intersection only a few miles along that would take him to the border town of Naco. He was familiar with the many tracks and trails that crossed the border between Naco and Nogales, having used them often in his smuggling ventures. If he could make it that far, he had a reasonable chance of getting safely back to Arizona.

The sun was high in the sky when he drove up over the crest of a hill and saw the highway in the valley below. A few cars and trucks were using the road, but the traffic was quite light. Henry thought he had a good chance of driving the nearly twelve miles to the next unpaved track that headed north without being spotted. Alternatively, he could turn east, which the authorities wouldn't expect if they were looking for him, and, eventually, find a safe crossing point into New Mexico. The down sides of such a manoeuvre were that the Federales would probably be coming from that direction, and Henry was not at all familiar with the tracks and trails along the border with New Mexico. No, he would head towards Naco and take his chances in that area.

Henry approached the main highway with great care. He waited for a lull in the traffic and then turned west onto the paved road. Twenty minutes later, he passed the turn-off for Naco and, after another fifteen minutes, he spotted the dirt track heading north that he was looking for. He turned onto the dusty track and immediately slowed down. The easiest way to be spotted was to race down a dirt track at high speed, raising a huge, tell-tale cloud of dust in your wake.

For that reason, he drove slowly, but he was also wary of the dangerous rocks and deep sand patches all along this particular track. He drove for about an hour and knew that the border was not that far away now. He began to relax a bit. He stopped for a short break to take in a few gulps of water and to let out about the same amount. He got back into his Jeep and, once again, slowly and carefully, headed for the U.S. border.

He followed the track around a scrub-covered hill and climbed up a low ridge. When he looked to the west, he could now see the faint track of the border road less than a mile distant. He descended the low ridge and rounded yet another scrubby hill. Henry's heart sank. Directly in front of him, not 80 yards away, the road was blocked by a Mexican Federal Police car. Three Federales were standing on either side of it, pointing their semi-automatic weapons at Henry's Jeep.

54

AND YOU THOUGHT HELL WAS BAD?

They didn't treat Henry gently. He was ordered out of his Jeep with his hands in the air, pushed against the side of the old vehicle and thoroughly searched. He decided that a certain amount of co-operation on his part might help his cause.

"Señor, I have only one firearm, an old .45 caliber pistol. It's in a small compartment below the driver's seat. Please be careful, it is loaded. I also have a box of spare ammunition in the glove compartment. I have no other weapons. I am a peaceful man. I have come to your country in peace, and I wish to leave in peace."

With that, the senior Federale in charge of the other two in this squad slapped Henry with force on the right side of his face.

"You pig! Do not try to lie to us. We know who you are. This vehicle was used yesterday in a cowardly attack on the police station in Aguas Calientes. Six of my fellow officers died there – murdered by you scum!"

And, with that he hit Henry again, this time punching him in the right kidney. The pain was intense. Henry sagged to the ground.

"Please, señor, I beg you to stop. I was nowhere near Aguas Calientes yesterday, or for many weeks, in fact. My vehicle was stolen the day before yesterday and returned to me late last night in the village of San Alonzo where I was prospecting. I have no idea what it was used for or where it was driven. I suspect my Jeep must have been used in some illegal activity because it has some damage. I left San Alonzo this morning. I am driving to Nogales. I'm never coming back to San Alonzo again."

The Federale gave Henry a heavy kick to the ribs and then another to his right leg. He cried out in terrible pain. He was sure that both kicks had broken bones.

"Save your lies for my *comandante*. He will interrogate you in Agua Prieta. He is not a nice man when he deals with murderous gringo scum like you. After two days, you pig, if you are still alive you will beg to have me back again. Compared to my *comandante*, I am a gentle angel. Now get up."

Henry struggled to get to his feet, but each breath was a knife wound in his right side and he couldn't put any weight on his right foot. One of the Federales grabbed him by the right arm and roughly jerked him to his feet. Henry wobbled, almost passing out with pain.

Handcuffed, he was rudely shoved into the back seat of the police car. Two of the men got into the front seat of the police car, the other into the Jeep. They headed for the large town of Agua Prieta less than two hours away.

Henry remembered little about the next two days. He was thrown into a filthy, airless cell and dragged out every few hours to be interrogated. Sat in a chair with his arms handcuffed behind him, he was asked incessantly about his "terrorist scum friends" – what were their names, what did they look like, where were they hiding, where had they come from, who was funding them, what their further plans were. Henry gave them what he knew – first names and vague descriptions – but he could not answer the bulk of their questions because he did not know the answers. Each time his responses failed to satisfy the interrogator, he was beaten again.

Finally, after two days of unbearable suffering, only bits of which he could later recall, Henry was moved from the small police station in Agua Prieta to the much larger Federal Police compound in Nuevo Casas Grandes in Chihuahua state.

Once again, he was taken to a foul-smelling, airless cell. But at least he was allowed to wash himself and was given a clean prison uniform to wear.

Henry's injuries were serious. He had at least one broken rib, his right leg was swollen badly and he could not put any weight on it, the skin on his face and arms displayed most of the darker colors of the rainbow, and both eyes were blackened and only opened as small slits.

He was seen by a prison doctor, who gave him some aspirin and told him that he would have to get his broken leg attended to soon, or he might lose it.

They brought him into an interrogation room and seated him in a chair, but this time he was not shackled. His interrogator took the "good cop" approach, sympathizing with him about his "unfortunate" injuries and promising to see that his jail conditions improved – as long as Henry co-operated fully with the authorities.

He asked Henry the same questions that his former torturer had asked. Again, Henry could only supply the information that he knew and that was very little.

"Señor, I would help you more, if I could. I'm an American citizen. I've come to your country to search for gold and silver. I respect your customs and your laws, and I'm a man of peace. A few years ago, I found a valuable deposit of gold near the village of Moache in Coahuila state. I wasn't greedy. I didn't try to steal the gold. Instead, I acknowledged that it was the property of the people of Moache and we agreed that I was entitled to a fair share of the profits. The headman of that village, a man named Pedro, can vouch for my honesty."

His interrogator betrayed little emotion.

"I do not support any revolution against your government. I met two university students from Mexico City when I was in the village of San Alonzo. They claimed to be Marxist revolutionaries. One called himself Fidel and the other called himself Karl. Frankly, I didn't take them seriously. What I mean is, I thought they were all talk – talk about some wild left-wing theory. When I heard that the boy who called himself Fidel had died in a raid on a police station in Aguas Calientes, I couldn't believe it. He was only a silly boy who got himself into a situation he couldn't control."

The Mexican policeman allowed himself a slight smile.

"I'm sorry he died. But I'm also sorry that several of your men died. They were only doing their duty."

The Federale nodded slightly.

"If I could tell you more about the only man I met who was a truly dangerous terrorist, I would. However, I only met him twice. Once, when he demanded the use of my vehicle, and second, when my vehicle was returned. His name is José and I have provided as full a description of him as I can. It is vague and general, because I saw and spoke with him only briefly. I was in no position to deny his request for the use of my Jeep. If I had refused, I'm sure I would have been shot and the vehicle taken anyway."

Once again, the interrogator adopted an inscrutable face.

"Señor, I can tell you no more. I am sixty-eight years old and I need medical treatment badly. I beg of you to allow me to contact my relatives in the U.S. I also beg of you to allow me to hire a lawyer."

Henry was returned to his cell without being beaten.

55

HENRY RISES FROM THE DEAD

That evening, Henry got the first decent meal since he had been arrested. It was difficult to chew with his injured mouth and hard to breathe or move because of his broken rib. He was running a fever, and his right leg throbbed painfully. Nevertheless, he managed to finish his bowl of stew and a tortilla.

The next morning, he was not dragged from his cell at the crack of dawn as had been the usual custom. Instead, he was taken to the interrogation room later, maybe around ten or eleven o'clock. Henry had no real way of knowing.

After a wait of maybe ten minutes, the "good cop" interrogator entered the room carrying several sheets of paper.

"Good morning, señor Anderson. I hope you had a restful night. I have been doing a little research on you, señor. On the one hand I found a strange record of a court proceeding in Hermosillo from quite a few years ago, when you were required to pay an enormous fine for illegally modifying a motor vehicle, which you had to forfeit to the state. Yet, no other offense was recorded. This is very strange. The magistrate actually acted illegally. The fine he levied is far more than is allowed for that relatively minor offense – which, by the way, is normally used to fine young men who remove their mufflers to obtain a much louder, publicly offensive, engine noise. And he certainly had no grounds that I can see to confiscate your car. Do you have any explanation for this puzzle?"

Despite his pain and grogginess, Henry realized immediately that he was being tested. He opted to tell the truth — well, most of the truth — and hope for the best.

"Señor, you are very wise. I was suspected of smuggling wine and spirits into Mexico, but the authorities had no proof, so they threw the book at me on a minor charge. I must confess that from time to time I did bring bottles of good wine and whisky to several of my friends in Hermosillo that I let them buy from me at cost — which, of course, was much cheaper than the cost here in Mexico. At the time, I believed the magistrate had been unfair, but I thought it best to cut my losses and return to the U.S."

"Ah, I see. Now, señor, I have also uncovered a few more facts about you. An inspector from Piedras Negras visited the village of Moache yesterday. He interviewed the headman, Pedro, who remembers you warmly. He confirmed that you had been most honest in your dealings with him and his people. He did say that you had a little problem at the end of your time there with a lady who was not happy with you, but he said that you are a good man, and he is happy to vouch for you. Our inspector has noted that Moache is well-known for its hostility to gringos, so, when the headman spoke so positively about you, he must have been genuine."

Henry breathed a sigh that was almost relief.

"I have carefully considered this information, señor Anderson — and your reaction to it. I am inclined to believe that you have, indeed, told us the truth about your involvement in the terrorist activities a few days ago. I can see no likelihood that you have ever been involved in such terrorist activities yourself. I have consulted with the public prosecutor, who is willing to drop the serious charges against you if you plead guilty to the minor offense of attempting to cross the international border with the U.S. at an illegal crossing point. The fine for such an offense, the first time, is two hundred U.S. dollars. I will return your possessions to you and release you from custody immediately, if you can hand over the amount of the fine."

"Señor, I cannot tell you how grateful I am for your most welcome decision. Among my possessions in my Jeep, there is a canvas hold-all bag. I have documents and currency in that bag."

"Really, señor Anderson? My report on your possessions says nothing about any currency. Documents, yes, currency, no. You must be mistaken."

His money had obviously been taken by the Federales – and probably already distributed among them. He wouldn't have been surprised to learn that his "good cop" interrogator was perfectly aware of this – and had probably received his own cut.

"*Si*, señor, I must have been mistaken. However, if you allow me access to my vehicle, I will have a look for my missing currency. It must be somewhere, no?"

The man was a bit puzzled by both Henry's reaction and his request. But he called a policeman in and asked him to accompany Henry to his Jeep, which was being held in the police vehicle storage compound. Henry made his way, painfully, to his Jeep. It was not locked, and the keys were in the ignition. He leaned in and put his hand under the dashboard. There, where he always kept a stash of money – which up to now he had jokingly referred to as his "get out of jail money" – he found the little metal box with $2,000 in it, along with 30,000 Mexican pesos. The Federales obviously hadn't searched his car that well.

56

HENRY GETS SOME HELP

Henry limped back into the police station, carrying his precious money box. The interrogator took him to a desk on the ground floor, where Henry signed papers admitting his guilt for attempting to exit Mexico illegally and paid the fine. He then pulled out 20,000 pesos, which he left on the desk.

"This is my contribution to your police retirement fund," he told the interrogator, who smiled and seemed quite pleased. Henry was certain that the cash would go straight into the man's pocket as soon as he left.

With that, Henry was told he was free to go.

He had been given a form releasing his Jeep from the storage lot. It started immediately. He drove to the gate and handed his release papers to the guard. The guard pushed open the gate and stood aside for Henry to leave. He was free at last. It was only four days since his arrest, but it seemed like four weeks, at least.

Henry's broken leg, on which he had been walking for the whole time of his incarceration, was so badly swollen and painful that he knew he couldn't drive very far. The leg was hot to the touch and looked like it might be infected. He was going to need medical treatment before he could consider driving back to Texas.

As the crow flies, Henry was about 500 miles from Piedras Negras, but the Mexican roads do not go as the crow flies. His best route was to head north to El Paso and then drive back south to Eagle Pass and then to Crystal City, where he knew Rufus and Lee would offer him a place to stay. He estimated that the road journey would be at least 700 miles, probably slightly more, but there was no way he could undertake such a journey in his present condition.

Because he was a foreign national, Henry had received a list of the consular offices in the town when he was released. It was not a big enough city to have proper consular offices, but there were honorary consuls for several European and South and Central American countries and, of course, for the U.S.

The honorary consul for the U.S. was a Mexican lawyer named Benito Sanchez. He had extensive business dealings with American companies, and it suited him to exercise the limited powers of an honorary consul. Henry drove to his office, which was in the town plaza. He parked his Jeep and painfully limped into señor Sanchez's office.

"Can I help you, señor?" asked a pleasant, and very attractive, young woman seated behind a desk.

"My name is Henry Anderson. I am an American citizen. There was a misunderstanding with the police, and I was held for several days in custody before the matter was resolved. I was released this morning. As you can no doubt see, I had a bad accident while I was in jail. I require consular assistance to contact my relatives in Texas."

He was, of course, referring to his physical appearance – the bruises and the black eyes, as well as to his obvious difficulty walking on his right leg.

"Please take a seat, sir. Señor Sanchez is on the telephone right now, but when he finishes I will tell him you are here."

Henry sat down slowly and carefully in the only chair that looked high enough, and had arms, to allow him to get up again with the least pain. Ten minutes later, he was ushered into the consul's office.

"Good day, sir. How can I help? Conchita has told me that you need to contact relatives in the U.S. I can assist you with that. It is part of my duties as an honorary consul of the U.S.A."

Henry decided to telephone his niece, Katie Lee, who was married to a prominent businessman in Odessa, Texas. Odessa was a city several hundred miles east of El Paso. He figured that they were the closest relatives he could contact quickly and easily. He could phone Rufus in Crystal City, but the telephone line to the old mansion where he lived was not very reliable. Ideally, he would like to contact his youngest nephew, Clarence Anderson, who had recently finished law school at the University of Texas and was working in the office of the Austin City District Attorney, but Henry did not have his nephew's new address or telephone number.

Señor Sanchez arranged for Henry's call to be put through. When Katie Lee answered, Conchita handed him the telephone. Henry explained his situation, asking her to contact Clarence. He would need help to drive back to Texas and he would need to find medical care for his injuries after he made it over the border. He told Katie Lee to contact señor Sanchez, or to get Clarence to do it, when they had come up with a plan to help him. With concern in her voice, she promised to contact Clarence as soon as possible and to get back to Henry later in the day. She had never heard her Uncle Henry sound so weak and vulnerable, and she knew that she needed to act quickly. She urged him to find a local doctor immediately and, promising her love and support, she hung up.

57

IT'S ALL ABOUT WHO YOU KNOW

Señor Sanchez recommended a reputable clinic on the north side of town. It was only a few blocks away from the Hotel Hacienda, which he also recommended as a suitable place for Henry to stay until he could find a way to leave Nuevo Casas Grandes.

Despite the great pain in his leg, Henry drove the short distance to the hotel. How ironic, he thought, that the closest to a grand hacienda he might ever get was a mid-market hotel in a small Mexican town. He checked into an airy and comfortable ground-floor room, as a hotel porter brought in his two pieces of luggage – a battered old leather suitcase and a canvas zippered bag.

Henry carefully managed a quick shave and a shower, his first chance for a proper wash in almost a week, before dressing in clean clothes. With broken ribs as well as a broken leg, any movement at all hurt Henry considerably.

Nevertheless, he managed to drive the few blocks to the clinic where he was immediately seen by a local doctor. He confirmed that Henry had two broken ribs and a spiral fracture to his leg, although the bone had not separated. As Henry would be receiving treatment soon in Texas, the doctor recommended stabilizing the leg with an inflatable cast. He injected Henry with penicillin to combat any possible infection and prescribed a course of antibiotic tablets and some strong painkillers. Finally, he was given a pair of crutches. To Henry, the charges seemed very reasonable. He paid cash.

When he returned to the hotel, there was a message from señor Sanchez. Clarence had phoned and was making arrangements to evacuate Henry. Señor Sanchez gave him Clarence's contact number and assured him that he was there to help if he needed any more assistance. Oh, and by the way, a bill for his services had been delivered to the hotel desk and he would appreciate Henry's payment before he left Nuevo Casas Grandes.

"What would you expect from a lawyer?" Henry asked himself, as he phoned his nephew Clarence – another lawyer.

Concerned, Clarence asked him how he was doing. Obviously, Katie Lee had emphasized the poor state Henry was in. Henry explained that he'd had medical treatment, and while he was very sore, the strong painkillers were already beginning to dull the pain. A decent night's sleep in a decent bed would help immensely, he was sure. Clarence said that he had arranged for an old friend to get Henry out of Mexico as quickly as possible. Things were not yet finalized, but he would contact Henry in the morning on his hotel phone with all the details.

Exhausted, Henry ordered a room service meal, which proved to be surprisingly good, washed down with a bottle of beer from his bar fridge, took another painkiller and fell into a deep sleep.

The dawn was just beginning to reveal itself when Henry was woken up by a loud knock on his door.

★ ★ ★

The knocking increased in volume and intensity, until Henry truly woke up.

"I am so sorry to disturb you, Mr Anderson. There seems to be an anomaly between your passport, which calls you Henry Rawson Anderson, and your Arizona Driving License, which calls you R.H. Anderson. Can you explain this please? Our medical insurance consultants need to sort out this problem before they approve payment for your stay with us here in Victoria County Memorial."

Henry was nonplussed. He was groggy and unsure of himself, but he tried to raise his head from the hospital bed to speak:

"I ... I am ... Henry ... Anderson. T-Talk to my ... my nephew ... Judge Anderson. I can't help ... help you anymore."

The woman made a note on his insurance file and passed it on. Henry, blissfully, went back to sleep.

★ ★ ★

"*Momento*," he called out, as he struggled to his feet. He hobbled to the door and was quite taken aback when he opened it to be confronted by the face of the police interrogator who had released him only yesterday. His heart sank. He had thought he was perfectly safe now, and he was eagerly looking forward to his return to Texas. Now this. What could it mean?

"Señor, you must have friends in very high places. I have just received an order, direct from Federal Police Headquarters in Mexico City, that I am to offer you every support, including transportation to the local airport at two p.m. this afternoon. A Mexican military helicopter will take you from Nuevo Casas Grandes to Piedras Negras, where you will be met by American consular officials who will see to your transportation back to Texas."

Henry was stunned. This was obviously Clarence's work, but he couldn't imagine how his young nephew could pull such strings.

"Thank you, señor. I'll rest here this morning and will be packed and ready to leave for the airport well before two this afternoon. I am worried, however, about my vehicle. I cannot leave it parked here in the hotel car park. I have no idea when I might be able to return for it."

"That, too, has been taken care of, señor. The local U.S. consular representative here in Nuevo Casas Grandes, señor Sanchez, whom I believe you contacted yesterday, has been instructed by your State Department to hire a driver to take the vehicle to Piedras Negras. It will be there for you, or your representative, to collect from the central police compound in a few days. Señor Sanchez has also been told to waive any fees he might have charged you. You are now considered a special honored guest of the Mexican government and they will pay your hotel bill as well as any charges señor Sanchez wishes to present. Enjoy your morning's rest, señor. We will pick you up at approximately one-thirty p.m. *Adios.*"

"*Adios.* And *gracias!*"

Henry couldn't believe what he'd just heard. He was trying to work out what might have happened when his room phone rang.

"Call for señor Anderson, I will connect you now."

"Hello. Oh, hello, Clarence. Yes, I'm feeling much better, thank you. Yes, the local Federal Police have contacted me and told me to be ready to fly to Piedras Negras this afternoon on a military helicopter. Yes, they have decided to drive my old Jeep ambulance to Piedras Negras later in the week. Suddenly I find myself an honored guest of the Mexican government. The day before yesterday, they were beating the shit out of me. How the hell did you manage all that?"

Clarence explained everything. When he was still in law school at the University of Texas he got a job in the political office of The Honorable Sam Rayburn, Speaker of the U.S. House of

Representatives in his home congressional district in north-east Texas. He got to know the great man quite well, so he had contacted him as soon as he heard of Henry's problems.

Sam Rayburn was a man of great power and influence in Washington. He had been a member of the U.S. Congress since 1913 and had been the leader of the Democrats in the House of Representatives since 1940. He had already served as Speaker of the House for three separate terms when the Democrats controlled it. When he died a couple of years later, in 1961, he had been Speaker for more than seventeen years in all. In 1959 he was at the peak of his powers. He had mentored Lyndon B. Johnson, a powerful U.S. senator in his own right, who was elected as vice-president to John F. Kennedy the following year and who became president himself when Kennedy was assassinated in November 1963.

It had probably taken Mr Rayburn only a phone call or two to organize Henry's retrieval, with the full support of the Mexican government. He knew exactly who to contact; furthermore, nobody ever said "No" to Sam Rayburn.

Well, thank God for that, thought Henry.

The "cherry on top" for Henry arrived as he was leaving the hotel lobby. The manager walked over to him and handed him an envelope with his name printed on it. Inside was a full refund of his medical charges from the previous day. In cash. Obviously, the Mexican government looked after its "special guests" very well. It was just a pity that he didn't have that status a few days earlier.

58

REST AND RECOVERY

Everything went according to plan. Henry was flown by Mexican military helicopter to Piedras Negras, where an ambulance met the plane. He was quickly examined by an American doctor and then driven across the border to Eagle Pass. He was examined in more detail at the small hospital in Eagle Pass before being admitted for the night. The next morning, the ambulance drove him all the way to Victoria, Texas, where he would be close to his nephew, Al, who was a doctor there. He was admitted to the large public hospital, Victoria County Memorial, and over the next few days, Henry was X-rayed, given various tests, and his broken leg was properly plastered. He was also treated for a bad skin infection he had picked up, most likely in one of his Mexican jail cells.

Henry recovered quite quickly. The doctors all agreed that he had amazing fitness and resilience for a man his age. As he recovered, he also managed to flirt with the nurses who attended him, so that his nephew Al had to urge Henry to behave on one of his daily visits. He decided he'd better conform to the rules and consciously restrained himself when the nurses were present.

After twelve days, Henry was finally released from hospital. He still had to practice his daily rehabilitation exercises and was quite restricted by his cast, but he was happy to leave hospital after his first ever extended stay in one.

Henry continued his recovery at Al's house, even though Al's wife, Betty, was unhappy with this arrangement. She was a strait-laced, conservative Catholic and regarded Henry's lifestyle as abhorrent. She certainly didn't welcome his presence in her home, where he expected her to wait on him hand and foot. Nor did she appreciate Henry regaling her young boys with tales of his sexual exploits, which he thought was a great joke.

Eventually, Betty had enough and told Al that, as far as she was concerned, while she didn't want to undermine his standing in his family, it was time for Henry to go. Luckily, the cast on his leg was due to come off in the middle of the following week. Al promised that as soon as Henry was free of his cast, he would strongly suggest that it was time for him to move on.

Henry's cast was duly removed the following Wednesday, allowing him to walk on his own, gingerly, with the help of a cane. After dinner that night, and after the children had gone to bed, Al was preparing to confront Henry when the phone rang. It was his cousin, Rawson Cleaver, telling him in tears that his mother, Emma, Henry's twin sister, had suffered a massive heart attack and died on the way to hospital.

Of course, this terrible news changed everything. The funeral was arranged for the following Monday afternoon in Sutherland Springs, where the entire Anderson family would assemble on the day.

The next day, Al phoned back his cousin Rawson to commiserate with him. They had been close since boyhood, when they spent every summer together. Al asked who would be living in the old Cleaver homestead now that Emma was gone. Rawson replied that it was a bit of a problem for them because they didn't have anyone to live there, and they didn't want to leave it unoccupied for any length of time. Criminals from San Antonio kept a lookout for empty rural properties, and often arrived with a large truck ready to strip them clean. Al suggested that Rawson ask Henry to live there for a while, as a way of solving several problems at once.

Rawson rang Henry that evening and offered the Cleaver house in Sutherland Springs to him to live in for as long as he liked, in return for keeping an eye on the place and looking after basic maintenance. He would be helped by most of the Cleaver family who all lived nearby on other rural properties. Henry jumped at the chance. When they drove up for the funeral, Henry took all his belongings with him and moved into the house that very day.

59

HENRY BIDES HIS TIME

Henry spent the rest of 1959 and the next two years living alone on the Cleaver farm in Sutherland Springs. He was no farmer and was not prepared to plough the fields for the corn and watermelon crops that had been grown there for decades. Instead, a Mexican–American farm hand was hired to look after the commercial side of the farm. Henry was happy tending the kitchen garden and a small flock of chickens. He fed and protected them from predators, and in return he benefitted from fresh eggs and the occasional meal of chicken and dumplings made using old boilers that had stopped laying.

It took longer than he expected, but Henry gradually regained his strength, returning to his old regime of lifting weights each morning and eating only healthy meals, which was easy to do on the farm. Most Sundays, he'd be invited to Rawson's house or to one of the other Cleaver family homes for his dinner. During the week he never drank anything stronger than coffee or iced tea.

He also resumed his old lifestyle of visiting the bars and nightclubs in San Antonio on Friday or Saturday nights, returning to the farm in the early hours of the next morning – sometimes on his own, sometimes with a new lady friend.

Henry was slipping into a mindless routine, so to counter that he began reading voraciously. He tackled all the books on the list of "Great Books of the World" which he had found in a Sunday newspaper magazine. The small local library in Sutherland Springs, only open on Tuesdays and Thursdays, could barely keep up with his demand for books, all of which had to be ordered in from the Central Bexar County Library in San Antonio.

He also read books and magazines about the mining business. He had never lost his dream of finding the mother lode that would give him status, that big, beautiful hacienda that signified his success and would provide comfort for the rest of his life.

Sometimes his mind wandered back to happy times spent with Cora and Maddy, and to their madcap days of living the A-list life in Hollywood. He also recalled the bad times when he had lost almost everything: his money; his marriage; his beautiful daughter. Secretly, he still hoped that one day he would hear from Cora and would be able to see her and Maddy. As the years passed, that yearning faded but it never completely died.

Since the Civil War, the Texan conservative voters had always voted for the Democrat party. In the 1952 and 1956 elections that tradition began to change. Many politically active people sported bumper-stickers and campaign pins with the phrase "Democrats for Ike". The Democrat candidate, Adlai Stevenson, was too left-wing for their liking. Eisenhower, a Republican, carried Texas in both elections.

For Henry, 1960 came and went – dominated by the presidential election. Henry voted for the Democratic ticket of John F. Kennedy and Lyndon B. Johnson. Texas was a state divided by that election. Richard Nixon, the Republican candidate and a "good, solid conservative" was against the liberal, left-wing Democrat, Jack Kennedy. Kennedy's vice-presidential running mate, Lyndon B. Johnson, was a "good ol' boy" from Texas. In the end, it was close, but the Democratic ticket won the state by 2 per cent of the vote.

Henry noted a quirky anomaly in that election. The town of Nixon, on the road from San Antonio to Victoria, voted heavily for Kennedy. The town of Kenedy, only 30 miles or so to the south-west of that little town, voted for Nixon.

Sometime around the middle of 1961, Henry began to pine for his old life of living in a small village in Mexico and prospecting. Despite everything, especially the terrible events of a few years ago, he remembered the happy and contented times he had spent in northern Mexico the best. He yearned again for the freedom to do whatever he pleased, to roam the wild hills and canyons whenever he wanted, or to have pleasant days at home with his "housekeeper", if the mood took him.

And then there was always that dream of finding gold – enough gold to keep him in luxury and comfort for the rest of his life. The intensity of that dream might wax and wane, but it was always there in his mind. In truth, he could see no satisfactory future for himself in the U.S. For Henry, despite the risks and dangers, Mexico offered him his only real chance to make a lasting success of his life.

It was a hot summer night in 1961. Henry was sitting on the front porch of the Cleaver home in Sutherland Springs. As he watched the bright yellow sun setting behind a grove of oak trees, spreading a brief golden hue over the whole landscape, he made up his mind. He was going to go back to Mexico, and he wouldn't let anyone stop him.

He was washing up the dishes from his light dinner a bit later, when the phone rang. It was his daughter, Maddy.

60

SHOCK, SADNESS AND ANGER

"Hello."

"Hello. Is that Mr Henry Anderson?"

"Yes, speaking."

"My name is Laia Lopez. Many years ago, in a very different world, you knew me as Maddy Anderson, your daughter. I've agonized about this phone call for several days."

Henry couldn't believe his ears. After all these years, his Maddy was on the other end of the phone. Before he could speak, she continued:

"Before I go any further, I wish to make one thing clear. I want no reconciliation with you. I can never forget nor forgive what you did to my mother and me. I never wish to see you again and I ask you to repay my decision to contact you this way, by never trying to find me. I'm sure you could, if you tried. But please don't. You will not be welcome."

Henry fingered the telephone line and moved it back and forth in his hand.

"Cora died three weeks ago in California. She fought a long battle with cancer, and she finally lost. Before she died, she asked me to contact you and tell you about our life since we last met, and as much as I didn't want to, I had to agree."

Henry suddenly felt a great wave of sadness rush over him. He would never see his beloved Cora again.

"I won't go into details, but for the last twenty-five years or so, my husband and I have been touring as classical Spanish dancers. It's been a great success for us – 'Laia and Louis'. We've danced around the world, in Hollywood movies and on Broadway, and we've won great acclaim. But most of our time has been on the road."

Henry started to ask a question but realized that she might end the phone call if he did.

"Cora came with us as our manager – both financial and artistic – and made our lives so much easier for many years. Thanks to her help and planning, Luis and I now have enough put by in savings and investments to retire."

Henry only then became acutely conscious of his age – his only daughter was now old enough to retire.

"In a final tour, billed as our farewell to the world of dance, we have so far performed across Europe, South and Central America. Now, on our last lap, we are touring North America. We have one show tomorrow night in San Antonio. Since we are both connected to this city, it seemed appropriate that this would be our very last performance. However, because of Cora's death and her funeral, we had to re-schedule several performances in and around Los Angeles. We're traveling to California immediately after we finish here."

Henry ached to see Maddy at least one more time but decided not to risk interrupting her.

"I feel that I have now completed my obligation to my mother. I will only reiterate – please, please, do not try to find me. Luis and I are looking forward to a long and happy retirement. Please do not ruin that for me.

"Oh, I nearly forgot. Cora said I must tell you that I've never had a child. Luis and I chose our love of dance over the love of children.

"Goodbye, Mr Anderson. I wish you well, but I no longer regard you as my father."

With that, Maddy abruptly hung up.

Never before in his life had Henry felt such waves of emotion. He was shocked and deeply saddened. His only child had rejected him totally. His wife, whom he once dearly loved, was dead and gone forever.

Henry wept like a child.

He faced a storm of conflicting emotions. On the one hand, his sadness at losing forever his beloved Cora was overwhelming, but his rejection by Maddy cut him to the quick.

If Henry had been more self-aware, he might have grasped some insights from his swirling emotions. He might have been able to face his guilt and accept that he had made grave mistakes that caused those he loved most to reject and abandon him. He might also have learned a truth about himself that was difficult to accept, but was very, very real: Henry was an incredibly selfish man.

Unfortunately, Henry's basic selfishness usually blocked out the acceptance of any responsibility for his own misfortunes. On the other hand, from time to time, he was able to entertain the notion that he had some role in his own sad losses, even if he always found a way to shift at least some of the blame to others. It always had been and always would be that way for Henry Rawson Anderson.

The phone call from Maddy prompted Henry to understand that it was his actions that had caused his family breakdown. And with that acknowledgment came deep feelings of overwhelming sadness. He desperately desired to see her once again, but he also understood that it would be counterproductive to violate Maddy's plea for him to respect her right to a permanent and final separation.

61

FROM THE PAST TO THE FUTURE

First thing on the morning after Maddy's phone call, Henry drove down to the filling station in Sutherland Springs and bought a newspaper.

On page three the headline jumped out at him:

LAIA AND LUIS
ONE LAST PERFORMANCE ON THEIR FAREWELL TOUR

Tonight, for the last time, the acclaimed Spanish dance team of Laia and Luis will perform for their many fans in San Antonio. Their final program will start at 8.00 p.m. in the Municipal Auditorium. There are very few tickets left, so be quick if you want to see this outstanding dance team perform for the last time in San Antonio.

Laia and Luis have spent the last 25 years entertaining audiences around the world with their interpretation of Classical Spanish dance, including Flamenco and Folk Dances. The high energy of their performances and the breathtaking beauty of their costumes still enthrall their fans, after all these years.

Laia and Luis (Mr. and Mrs. Luis Lopez in real life) have announced their retirement from the stage immediately following the end of this tour. They plan to settle in California after their final performance.

Laia was born in San Antonio and Luis, who was born in Mexico City, attended High School here in San Antonio. They have always acknowledged their links to our city and have frequently honored us with their performances over the years.

It is only fitting that we, the citizens of San Antonio, turn out tonight to farewell our own internationally famous dancers, Laia and Luis.

Henry drove straight into the city and bought one of the last tickets for that evening's performance.

With what was, perhaps, a fleeting moment of insight, Henry decided that he would honor his daughter's request. He would never try to find her again and would give up all hope of meeting her in the future. Nevertheless, his curiosity and desire to see her at least one last time drove him to attend the performance that evening.

Henry's seat was high up in the back row, as far away from the stage as it was possible to be. It was the only ticket he could get. He brought with him his battered old binoculars and kept them trained for the whole night on his beautiful daughter. She was now in her late forties, but she wore her age well and looked and danced like she was twenty years younger. He was enthralled by her performance. She twirled and stamped her feet, and at times she moved across the stage with her heels hitting the floor with such speed that her legs were a blur. The rhythmical cacophony of sound was loud enough to reach Henry's ears, over two hundred feet away.

The noise, the movement and the color of her costumes made for a great spectacle; Henry loved every minute. As they danced their final number, raucous applause brought forth two encores. Then, finally, holding hands in the center of the stage, Laia, his Maddy, and her dance partner and husband, Luis, bowed time and time again to their fans. The director brought Laia a magnificent bouquet of flowers and then they left the stage for the last time.

All at once, Henry felt both elated and deflated. He marvelled at the skills and the professionalism of his daughter – at the creativity and the sheer hard work that had obviously gone into her life as a dancer and made her an international celebrity in her field. However, he was also depressed, because he had missed out on her life and would never see her again, never give her a hug, never offer her a father's love.

Now, he had to turn his attention to re-constructing his own life. More than ever, he longed to be back in Mexico. He would leave as soon as it was practical to do so.

"Are you alright, sir?" the lady sitting next to him asked.

Henry could only nod, as the tears rolled down his face.

62

A TIME FOR DEEP REFLECTION

Henry drove home that night in a kind of trance. His emotions ranged from elation at Maddy's success, to despair at the thought that he would never see her again.

He parked his car and wandered into the farmhouse. Uncharacteristically, he poured himself a stiff drink of tequila and knocked it back in one gulp. Then he went to his bedroom and took a metal box out of the closet. He went back to the kitchen, placed the box on the table and opened it.

Inside were several of his important personal documents, such as his passport, his Social Security Card, and various deeds and other official papers from his past life. What he was looking for, however, was far more important to him at that time – the small number of photos of his late wife, Cora, and their daughter, Maddy.

Henry eagerly examined each of the photos, recalling the times and places when they were taken and remembering the happiness of his long-lost family life.

Two were taken at the very farm where he was now living, when it had belonged to his twin sister, Emma, and her husband, Clarence Cleaver. In one, Maddy, aged about four, was standing in front of a fence, smiling wistfully. In the other, she was seated on the back of a horse, bareback and near his neck, with no fewer than five of her cousins lined up behind her. Henry remembered the day clearly. It was just before he, Cora and Maddy left Texas and moved to Arizona.

Another two photos were taken no more than a year later in Nogales. In one, Maddy stood on a flight of steps that led to the front door of their rented house, squinting slightly in the bright sunlight. In the other, his darling Cora was holding Maddy by the hand in front of the Stevenson Stationery Company. They were both dressed up for a fine lunch in a restaurant to celebrate Cora's birthday.

In the final photo of his meagre collection, Henry saw Maddy, aged about fifteen, standing on the back patio of their grand Hollywood mansion, her arms above her head and her back arched in the pose of a flamenco dancer. Little did he know when that photo was taken that she would later become a world-famous Spanish dancer.

Henry poured himself another shot of tequila; he sipped slowly as he picked up each of his precious photos in turn and remembered the wonderful, happy times he had known with his little family. He regretted bitterly the loss of that happiness and, as he continued to sip the tequila, he knew he had no one to blame but himself for the breakup of his once happy family.

It was a rare time of introspection and honest analysis of his past behavior, and Henry spent another few hours studying the photos and drinking tequila to ease his sorrow. Eventually, he fell asleep on the chair at the kitchen table.

The next morning, after a big breakfast and many cups of black coffee, Henry made several decisions.

First, he took out his typewriter, rolled in a piece of paper, and wrote a letter to Maddy. He had no way of knowing where to send it, but that didn't deter him. He was determined to leave behind him a letter of apology to his darling daughter, even if she might not ever see it. At the very least, she might read it after his death.

The letter wasn't particularly long, but it was Henry's best effort at saying he was sorry to Maddy for the hurt he had caused her and Cora, re-stating his love for her, despite all that had happened between them, and hoping that she might find a way to forgive him someday. He signed the letter, sealed it in an envelope on which he wrote her name, and put it with his papers in his metal box.[3]

Henry also made a second major decision that morning – he would go back to Mexico as soon as possible and resume his life as a prospector.

---

[3] Author's note: Unfortunately, Henry's letter was never seen again. It was not found with his other papers after his death, and no one knows what became of it.

63

ONCE AGAIN, THE PROSPECTOR

Henry sold his old Jeep ambulance to Rawson's eldest son. It was probably worth a bit more, but he was happy to leave it in the family for the grand sum of $250. The boy was now old enough to move into the old Cleaver farm on his own. He would appreciate having the use of the old, reliable Jeep around the place.

Henry then bought a nearly new Ford pick-up truck with a canvas cover for the back. Two weeks later, re-stocked yet again with camping and mining gear, he set out for Arizona.

When he reached Nogales, Henry contacted his friend, Gilberto. As before, they met in Consuela's Cantina and spent a long afternoon drinking and reminiscing. Gilberto was no longer active in any kind of cross-border business. For Henry, it was really a social call. He knew where he wanted to go and what he wanted to do, and he needed no advice.

This time, he would find a village in Sonora a bit farther south than the areas he had visited before. About 100 miles northwest of the town of Moctezuma, there was an isolated village called Pedernales. It had the basic requirements for Henry: a small population; a cantina; a general store; and an available *casa*. He could arrange for a housekeeper later.

The area around Pedernales was extremely rough and barren, but there were several swift-flowing streams that offered the possibility of alluvial gold.

Henry could prospect whenever he felt the need. He was still driven by the dream of striking it rich, but he had mellowed now and knew that he had plenty of time to search for the elusive gold. In a sense, now that Henry had reached the age of seventy, he could regard himself as semi-retired. Prospecting for the right señorita to be his "housekeeper" was almost as important to him as looking for gold.

He embraced the lifestyle he had established for himself, becoming quite content with life in small Mexican mountain villages that he visited on his solo treks into the hills.

For almost twenty more years, he continued to live this way. It was not always an easy life, but he loved it. Most men his age would not have been able to keep up the pace that Henry set himself, but Henry was fitter and more driven than most.

Every two years, he returned to the U.S. for at least two months in order to retain his Social Security pension. For most of the 1960s and '70s, he used his enforced breaks as times to reconnect with his family in Texas. In fact, he found the free room and board handy – not having to spend his pension left him with more money in the bank when he returned to Mexico. But, more importantly, he was able to re-establish his loving relationships with his brother and nephews. In his old age, Henry had come to appreciate the power and the satisfaction of familial love, a love he had squandered with his own family.

Every other year, Henry used the break as an excuse to change his location in Mexico and find a new place to live. Two years in one place was usually enough time to exhaust the possible sites for a gold mine in that area. He found that the need to re-establish himself regularly kept him interested and enthusiastic about his life, and kept him fresh and alert.

And so it was that Henry found himself in the village of Santa Áurea in 1981, where this story began.

64

THE END OF THE DREAM

Henry woke with a start. Where was he? It gradually came back to him. He was in the hospital in Victoria. Al and Clarence had brought him here. The bed was cool, and the sheets were freshly laundered. All around him, electronic machines buzzed and beeped and hummed. An intravenous drip was attached to his right wrist, where a needle fed into one of his veins. On the middle finger of his left hand, a blood-oxygen monitor was clipped over the nail. Another tube was fixed to his nose, gently releasing oxygen into his lungs.

Suddenly, Henry was aware of the presence of another person, the doctor.

"Hello, Mr Anderson. Remember me? I am Dr Garcia, and I am looking after you. If you can hear me, please nod your head. There is no need to speak."

Henry nodded his head slightly. He was groggy, but he could clearly hear every word the doctor spoke.

"There is no easy way to tell you this, sir, but I am afraid you've sustained major damage to your kidneys and liver. If you are in pain, you must tell us immediately. There is no need for you to be uncomfortable. Would you like to see a minister of religion?"

Henry shook his head, no.

"Your nephews should be here shortly." Dr Garcia patted him on the shoulder gently, then left.

So, this is it, thought Henry. *The end of my life?*

He was groggy and had great trouble concentrating. Nevertheless, he realized that he would never achieve his goal. There would be no more gold and there would be no luxurious lifestyle in a grand hacienda.

He smiled slightly.

Who knows, he thought, *maybe I'm going to the big hacienda in the sky.*

With that, he laughed out loud, just once, closed his eyes and left the world of the living with a gentle sigh.

65

AN IRONIC CONCLUSION

Al and Clarence, Henry's nephews, arrived just after his last breath.

The funeral arrangements were made and Henry was buried, without a full religious service, in the cemetery at Sutherland Springs. Despite Henry's avowed atheism, the local Baptist minister made a few perfunctory remarks. As funerals go, it was ordinary. All the Anderson family were there, as were the members of the Cleaver family. A few people who knew Henry from his time living in the Cleaver homestead also showed up. But that was it.

As they trudged back to their cars to start the two-hour drive back to Victoria, Al and Clarence had a brief conversation. Clarence, who was now a district judge, told Al that he and another officer of the court had looked through Henry's possessions. They had found a sheaf of documents, which included an apparently valid will leaving everything to the two of them and to their late sister, Katie Lee. Because she had died childless, the estate would be shared evenly between Al and Clarence.

Of course, Uncle Henry's estate wouldn't amount to much, or so they thought. His possessions included a sum of just less than

$2,500 in cash and a book for a savings account in a San Antonio bank that had nearly $7,000 in it. Apart from his old car, which was still in Mexico, he owned very little of value. He had spoken warmly of the man who drove him to the hospital in Chihuahua, and they decided to contact him and give him the car. But there was one other item in Henry's things that had to be investigated. With his bank book was a key to a safe-deposit box located at the same bank. It was clear from the book that an annual payment for the box had been deducted for many years.

Clarence had been named as Henry's executor in his will. He told Al that he had to be in San Antonio for a meeting the following week and would visit the bank and see what was in the safe-deposit box, as well as collecting the funds in the deposit account.

Clarence duly collected the cash and the contents of Henry's safe-deposit box. He brought the whole lot back to Victoria and went over to Al's place to go through the surprisingly large number of documents that he had found.

It immediately became clear to them that most of the documents were old shares in various mining and oil companies. All of Henry's old Three Sisters documents were there, as well as several documents from various other deals and investments he had made over the years. There were a few deeds of ownership among the documents, including the deed for his 20 per cent of the Pleasanton Oil Field property. In addition to that, there were seven more deeds to part-ownership of various properties around Texas. Clarence undertook to have a colleague of his examine the deeds to see if any of them had any value. It looked to them like everything in the safe-deposit box was worthless paper, but they would check it out.

The next afternoon, Clarence rang Al.

"Al, you're not going to believe this, but there is a deed in Uncle Henry's stuff for his share in a property in West Texas, near

Odessa, which is, apparently, a valuable piece of land with a working oil well on it. I have handed the matter over to an old classmate of mine who is a lawyer in Midland, near Odessa. He specializes in oil field law."

Three days later, Clarence again rang Al.

"Al, this just gets better and better. My old classmate has discovered that the oil company that drilled the well on the property that Uncle Henry owned 25 per cent of never contacted him to get his permission. The other three owners assumed that Henry was dead. They tried various ways to track him down but couldn't find him. On the deed, he styles himself as 'R.H. Anderson', when his name was really 'H.R. – Henry Rawson – Anderson'. I have no idea why he did that, but it explains why they couldn't track him down.

"The oil company decided to go ahead and drill on the land anyway. That well is one of the best producing wells in Texas. The other owners have averaged – averaged, mind you – ten thousand dollars a month in royalties. The well has been pumping for twenty-five years. In other words, each of them has received approximately three million dollars over that time.

"My classmate assures me that we have the oil company over a barrel, so to speak. He thinks they will settle with us for a back payment of three million dollars and future royalties worth twice the value of the others. We could go for an enhanced back payment, but he doesn't recommend that based on his experience of what courts are prepared to allow in such situations. What do you think?"

Al said that he would be more than happy with $1,500,000 and another $10,000 a month, or thereabouts, as his half of the value of the doubled royalties. On the other hand, he wondered if they might be able to do something with all that money to honor the life of their Uncle Henry. Neither of them needed the extra cash – they were both well set for retirement and their families had been looked after.

Eventually, Clarence and Al settled on the purchase of a property just outside San Antonio, not far from the old Cleaver farm. While the rather grand house needed repairs and maintenance, it would provide accommodation for at least twenty-five underprivileged children of Mexican heritage and a chance for them to learn basic ranch skills. A small, but dedicated, team of carers and teachers was assembled, and they did their best to help the children, many of whom had appeared before the courts for acts of violence and vandalism, to find a meaningful life and useful skills working on the ranch.

The claim was filed in a court in Midland and two months later, Al and Clarence each received $1,500,000. In addition, they were both set to receive an average of $10,000 a month for the foreseeable future. They immediately donated and signed over the full amount for the purchase and upkeep of the small working ranch that offered troubled children the chance for rehabilitation.

Even though he kept paying the annual fee for his safe-deposit box, Henry must have thought that nothing in it could be worth much. How wrong he was!

With a cash sum of $3,000,000 and a steady income of $20,000 a month, Henry could have bought and maintained a beautiful Mexican hacienda. His fondest dream could have been a reality.

But that didn't happen. He died blissfully unaware that he could have been living a life of luxury for his last twenty-five years – or more.

In the end, his life was not the disappointment it might have seemed. Henry's unusual life, with all its highs and lows, finally ended on a high. He might not have thought about such an outcome, but, in the end, it seemed a fitting tribute to his flawed, but always positive and hopeful life.

The ranch was opened in 1984 by the Governor of Texas, who praised the foresight of the original donors and promised that the concept would be supported in the future by state grants as well as public donations.

It was named "Uncle Henry's Hacienda".

Henry had spent his whole life pursuing his dreams. He had both successes and failures along the path that his life followed and, while he never achieved his goals perfectly, at least his life had purpose and direction and he never stopped trying to get there. In the end, he lived a more meaningful – if, inevitably, flawed – life than many people do.

AUTHOR'S NOTE

This work of fiction is based, rather loosely, on the life of a real person — my paternal grandfather's brother, Henry Remson Stevenson.

My first encounter with Uncle Henry, that I can remember, happened when I was six or seven years of age. I clearly recall seeing him sitting at the Western Union telegraph machine in my grandparents' hotel in Kenedy, Texas.

After that, my memories of him all happened when he was temporarily living in Texas for brief periods, usually with my grandparents. He mostly lived in Mexico but had to return to the U.S. for at least two months every two years to retain his Social Security pension benefits. I would have met up with him no more than four or five times when I was an adolescent or a bit older. He told me stories about prospecting for gold in Mexico, and did his best to scandalize me by bragging about his many sexual conquests.

Uncle Henry was always a man of mystery to my family. His unconventional lifestyle and his often outrageous attitudes made him the family's black sheep. He had declared himself an atheist, which did not go down well with most of the family, who were quite religious — Roman Catholics on the one side and Southern Baptists on the other. He was a tall, straight-backed, reasonably handsome man. He spoke with an accent that was quite artificial, as if he were always in a stage play. He was, almost certainly, extremely intelligent. He was also, without doubt, a very vain man and a serial womanizer.

Most of his life was spent away from his family in Texas. He kept in touch but did not often appear in person. Therefore, a folklore grew up about him – amazing stories that fascinated impressionable young members of the family.

I decided to try to write a biography of Henry. I did many hours of research during the COVID lockdowns here in Australia. What I found largely debunked the family folklore. On the other hand, I discovered aspects of his life that were at least as incredible as the false stories had been. When I seemed to have exhausted the online sources of information about Uncle Henry, I realized that I would never have enough reliable details to write a legitimate biography. There were simply too many gaps that could not be filled in with verifiable facts.

It was then that I decided to write a novel, creating a central character named Henry, who, in many ways, is reminiscent of the historical Uncle Henry, but who is also, in many other ways, very different to him. In the end, the Henry Rawson Anderson of my novel is NOT my Uncle Henry Remson Stevenson.

None of the other characters in this novel are historical people either – apart from a few public figures who have no role in the narrative. I have retained the given names – or at least parts of the given names – of people in my family: Uncle Henry's parents, siblings, nieces, nephews, and so on. The surnames have been changed, however, in all cases. These characters, while having links to historical people, are my fictional creations.

I have also followed the historical timeline of Uncle Henry's life, as far as it suits me. Some of the dates are historically accurate for the real Henry, some are not. The same goes for places. Many of them are linked to my Uncle Henry, but others are invented. The names of the towns and cities in Texas, Arizona and Mexico are real, but I have invented all the names of the Mexican villages mentioned in the novel.

I have been especially careful not to use even the given names of his wife and his daughter, whom I never met. Again, there are certain aspects of their lives, as they appear in my novel, that are, most certainly, historically accurate for the two real women. However, there are many more aspects of their lives presented in my novel that are completely fictionalized.

My Uncle Henry's only child, a daughter, is called "Maddy", for Madeleine, in this novel, where she becomes a famous dancer using the name Laia and marries her dance partner, Luis Lopez. In real life, Uncle Henry's daughter danced under the name Carla and married her dance partner, Fernando Ramos. They became an internationally famous dance team, specializing in Spanish and Mexican dances.

I have undertaken research on the times and places in this novel, and have attempted to make them as believable as possible. If I have made some technical or historical errors along the way, I appeal to the reader not to judge the book only by those flaws.

Finally, I must say a word about my main character. In a sense, this novel is about a deeply flawed man. Henry Anderson, my character, was born in 1891 – as was my Uncle Henry. While some of his attitudes are surprisingly modern and ahead of his time, many are not. He was sexist, displaying a sense of male entitlement that was probably more common and certainly more acceptable in those days than it is now. Of course, that doesn't excuse him.

I have tried to create a complex character in Henry Anderson. Like every other human being, unless you believe in saints, he has good qualities and bad qualities. Without descending into moral crudities, I hope I have indicated clearly enough that most of Henry Anderson's failures are, in some sense, linked to his character flaws – a fact which he seems to finally grasp by the end of his life.

On the other hand, his life, like that of my real Uncle Henry, was long, characterized by a repeated pattern of extreme highs and extreme lows, always interesting and never dull.

I hope you enjoyed reading this story as much as I enjoyed writing it.

Holloways Beach, Queensland, Australia
April 2024

ABOUT THE AUTHOR

Charlie Stevenson was born and raised in Victoria, a small city in south-central Texas, USA. He studied at the University of Notre Dame in Indiana and then served in the U.S. Army in Germany. He continued his studies at University College, Dublin, Ireland, and embarked on a career as a university academic. For the next ten years, he lectured in several universities in Ireland and the north of England, specialising in Medieval English literature, the history of the English language, and Old Norse language and literature. In 1983 he and his Irish wife, Aideen, moved to Australia, where he was appointed to a lectureship in the English Department at Monash University in Melbourne. In 2004, he and Aideen both took early retirement and moved to Holloways Beach, a suburb of Cairns in Far North Queensland.

During the long COVID shutdown, he wrote and privately published a memoir of his time in the U.S. Army. After that, he wrote *Uncle Henry's Hacienda*, his first novel. Apart from enjoying a relaxed lifestyle in the tropics, he spends his time reading, writing, working on family history and sorting and identifying family photographs.